FROZEN HELL

Eli Bonnet walked uphill to search the wilderness ahead, leaving Jesse Peacock behind to watch the dogs and sled. He scanned the unbroken snow with his field glasses for any signs of life until he could no longer bear his freezing hands and feet. Finally, he jogged in place to warm himself.

Then he heard noises—clicking and thumping sounds. He twisted his head back and forth, wondering what the racket could be. Suddenly, he saw the danger. Caribou! Hundreds thundered across the hillside toward him. Eli whipped around and yelled at Peacock, screaming to stop the dogs. But he saw Jesse had moved away from the sled. Then to his horror he watched the dogs bolt after the stampeding herd.

When he reached Peacock, his companion lay sobbing on the snow.

"Eli, I didn't mean to let the dogs loose," Peacock said. "I didn't know the caribou were coming."

Eli looked at the distant mountain where the dogs and sled had vanished. At last he said, "I think you've just killed us, Jesse."

WHISPERS
OF THE
MOUNTAIN

The great mountain called Denali forever waits
for men who make mistakes. . . .

WHISPERS OF THE RIVER
BY TOM HRON

They came from an Old West no longer wild and free—lured by
tales of a fabulous gold strike in Alaska. They found a land of
majestic beauty, but one more brutal than hell. Some found
wealth beyond their wildest dreams, but most suffered death and
despair. With this rush of brawling, lusting, striving humanity,
walked Eli Bonnet, a legendary lawman who dealt out justice
with his gun . . . and Hannah Twigg, a woman who dared death
for love and everything for freedom. A magnificent saga filled
with all the pain and glory of the Yukon's golden days. . . .

from SIGNET

Prices slightly higher in Canada.   (0-451-18780-6—$5.99)

WHISPERS OF THE MOUNTAIN

Tom Hron

A SIGNET BOOK

SIGNET
Published by the Penguin Group
Penguin Books USA Inc., 375 Hudson Street,
New York, New York 10014, U.S.A.
Penguin Books Ltd, 27 Wrights Lane,
London W8 5TZ, England
Penguin Books Australia Ltd, Ringwood,
Victoria, Australia
Penguin Books Canada Ltd, 10 Alcorn Avenue,
Toronto, Ontario, Canada M4V 3B2
Penguin Books (N.Z.) Ltd, 182–190 Wairau Road,
Auckland 10, New Zealand

Penguin Books Ltd, Registered Offices:
Harmondsworth, Middlesex, England

First published by Signet, an imprint of Dutton Signet,
a division of Penguin Books USA Inc.

First Printing, October, 1996
10 9 8 7 6 5 4 3 2 1

To Gwen Frary and Clare Wesley
Their spirits soar above. . . .

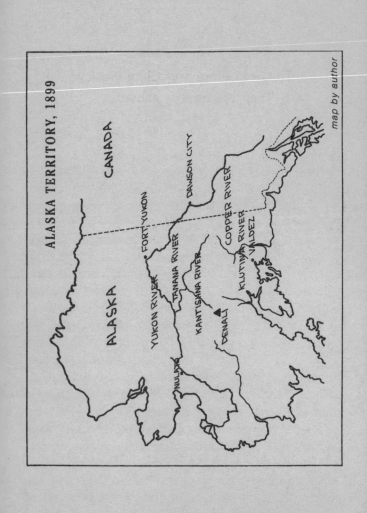

ALASKA TERRITORY, 1899

CANADA

ALASKA

YUKON RIVER
FORT YUKON
DAWSON CITY
TANANA RIVER
KANTISHNA RIVER
COPPER RIVER
KLUTINA RIVER
VALDEZ
DENALI
NULATO

map by author

PREFACE

Denali

Athabaskan Indians in Alaska believe that man can never hide from Denali, the great sacred mountain watching over their ancestral land. They say its spirits beckoned in the very beginning—more than a thousand dead shamans back in their past. Coming up from Canada, they describe finding a mother country filled with caribou and salmon and other wild things to eat, and an uninhabited place where they could live forever.

Settling along the mighty rivers flowing around their god, they soon found copper and obsidian, birch bark, and warm furs beyond their dreams. They grew and prospered in their new homeland, calling themselves, D'en'e, the earth's only true people. Inhabitants of the seacoasts, the Aleuts and Eskimos, learned to stay away—the followers of the Great One would kill every unbeliever daring to walk under the mountain's shadow.

Russian explorers were the first to challenge the spirits of the mountain. In 1848 an expedition of eleven men crossed Prince William Sound and paddled up the Copper River toward Mount

Drum of the Wrangell Mountains. Many years later, the natives of that region, called Midnooskies by the Czar's men, confessed to slaughtering them all, handing over a few remnant journal pages as eulogies for the missing adventurers. Two more fearless parties followed, only to have their heads hacked off with axes at a village named Taral near the mouth of the Chitina River.

The first white men able to pass safely through the forbidden land were led by Lieutenant Henry Allen of the Second United States Cavalry. In 1885, he and two companions crossed almost twenty-five hundred miles of the interior of Alaska, much of it on foot, one of the most difficult journeys ever made by man.

They fought across stormy seas in Eyak Indian canoes; they poled up coffee-and-cream torrents rushing down the Copper River through deep canyons and past calving glaciers; they hiked on thin ice and waded in deep snow in search of the fabled copper mine of the Chitina and Chitistone rivers; they backtracked, then roped up the Upper Copper River, rounding Mount Sanford for the first time; and they packed over the Alaskan Mountain range to the Tanana River, starving all the way. Then, desperate, they launched downriver in a moose-hide boat, running thunderous white water for days until reaching the Yukon River, finally finding enough food to save themselves from hunger.

After a week's rest, they marched farther north

until they sighted the Koyukuk River. Bartering at an Indian camp for two birch-bark canoes, they ran that winding flow down to the Yukon River again. Pushing downstream on the father of Alaska's waters, they learned from natives of a primitive crossing to Norton Sound and the Bering Sea. At last reaching saltwater again after five months of wilderness wanderings, they hired Eskimos to paddle them across to Saint Michaels and a ship waiting to return them to San Francisco.

But Denali avenged that brave trespass in 1898 during the Klondike gold stampede. Hundreds of men bought passage to the port of Valdez to join the rush northward to Dawson City. They began by climbing several thousand feet with their grubstakes to the top of the Valdez Glacier—then by dropping down the Klutina Glacier to the frozen lake and river below. All the way across the surface of the ancient ice, those foolhardy stampeders, one by one, dropped from sight forever in crevices hidden beneath the snow. Then, when springtime came, more cruel disasters took place.

First the stampeders drowned by the dozens while shooting the murderous rapids of the Klutina River as it roared toward the Copper River. Next, coursing along the foot of the smoking, mysterious Mount Wrangell, dozens more drowned trying to ascend the silty flood pouring from the north. Forced back, yielding and dying by the hundreds, the survivors turned away from the misadventure, the scurvy, and the heartbreak. Lastly the battered remains staggered back into Valdez, only to be crippled further by sickness, some turning crazy for the rest of their lives from fear of ever wishing for gold again.

This story is dedicated to those stouthearted men who lost their lives to the giant mountain one hundred years ago—and tells of their courage in searching for every man's dream.

PART I

Despair

CHAPTER ONE

Trapped

The instant the Newhouse trap snapped on his right hand's fingers, Red Shirt Moses sensed he had killed himself—he was just not yet dead. He heard the chain slide down, chinking below on the drowning wire, locking its catch forever. He pulled as hard as he could, now feeling how the beaver struggled, dying slowly, a leg clamped by steel teeth. Despite pulling again with all his strength, the trap stake stayed stuck in the bottom of the pond and froze on top by ice, telling him to sing his last song. Denali, he cursed, why have you punished me so—the deeds of my past were done to please you.

He rolled off his belly to his right side, fumbled awkwardly with his free left hand, and gripped his prized skinning knife, laying it next to the hole he had chopped into the frozen beaver pond. Staring, thinking, he judged the thickness of the ice, next the thickness of his arm. Was it possible, he thought, to chip away enough to reach his fingers and cut them off? Was it possible to reach and cut his arm off at the elbow—or the shoulder? How long does it take to bleed to death, how much pain could he endure?

Hearing old Wahnie whine, he looked across to his sled dogs anchored nearby. He called sadly to his leader in Athabaskan dialect, "Ah-eeh, old one—I have trapped myself! I will die soon unless you have a miracle. Chew from your harness and save yourself. Those stupid ones behind will kill and eat you tomorrow—then they will eat my body afterward. Run away, old one, run from here. My foolishness today will make this an evil place."

An icy blow fanned snow onto his face, moistening, then freezing his skin; he could see the same winter dust frosting the wolverine hair around his parka hood, sinister against the deep brown. What was it? he wondered—five below, ten below—no one could expect to live for long in such cold. The wind hurried again from Denali, north off the Alaskan mountains, those immortals standing overhead.

He looked back down into the boggy water, colored like coffee, puddling around his arm. Why had he been so thoughtless to reach down and feel for his trap. Why had he believed he had caught another beaver to skin? He could see the crinkles of ice freezing from the edges of the hole, soon to lock around his sleeve, then to his arm inside, finally to the very marrow of his bones. He angrily splashed with his free hand, breaking back the wicked grip, but feeling numbness already creeping into his shoulder, sensing once more the death that would surely come. Leastways it would be peaceful, he thought, like when he had placed the ancient one to die in the sacred shaman's cave to join the thousand skeletons heaped there before. He would soon sleep, dream of the eagle soaring, dream of the land always.

No—not yet, he decided, his middle shivering with the cold. My daughter will never find my bones to take them to the secret place if I die here. Hearing a raven squawk above, he twisted to see six of the black prophets perched above him on a cottonwood branch—waiting to peck his eyes first, then other soft parts bared to their hungry gray beaks. He knew they would call the magpies and whiskey jacks to join in; next would come the lean fox to tear away his clothing, to bare his belly to ease every creature's winter fast. Wolves would scatter his bones then, hiding everything forever from human eyes. His people would wonder what had happened to the last shaman to visit those who had passed on before to the giant mountain.

Clutching his skinning knife, he picked into the ice, enlarging the hole circling his arm. Chipping wildly, the struggle warmed him; his heart pumped with the effort from his pounding of the blade's point into the glassy surface. November's covering is thin and soft, he thought, and soon there will be room to reach through and cut free. My wrist will be the best choice, severed and pulled off like the skinning of paws of pine martins trapped in the spruce trees. Then Denali's breath will freeze the gush of blood from my arm.

Wahnie will dash away, leading the other dogs on a mad chase to my cabin, to my woman and daughter. They will cauterize and bandage the stub. I'll not be crippled much from the loss of just one hand.

Then, suddenly, his mittened hand slipped and lost its grip on the caribou antler handle. Flashing once, the silvery blade disappeared below into the beaver's murky, winter home. He stared after his last hope, his spirit sinking like his knife. Why, Denali, why . . . ? What have I done to deserve a death like this, trapped like the beaver, otter, and mink I've caught in the past?

Breaking into a mad struggle for his life, he yanked, kicked, and twisted about, trying to tear off his fingers, trying to break the trap or chain. His shrieks echoed between the valley walls, manically answering his own angry curses against the pain and suffering, against the injustice of dying before he wished to pass away.

Then Wahnie and the other dogs joined their howls to his, filling the mountains with a chorus of calls chilling enough to spook the ravens waiting in the branches overhead, sending them flapping fast for roosts farther off.

At last he tired, unable to thrash any longer. He lay panting, weeping—not cold now, yet feeling the sweat changing into icy drops falling along his ribs. The sickness of exhaustion, of resignation crept into his soul, leaving him jealous of those he had shot, of those he'd beheaded with one swing of his ax. That was a much better way to die, he judged, much better than seeing oneself freeze.

His mind drifted to memories of a lifetime spent in the Alaskan wilderness. Born along the Yukon River in the village of Nulato, he had learned early of fishing and hunting, packing, and camping, the essence of an Athabaskan's life. Only later had he sampled the ease of the white man's ways. During boyhood, he had been taught by his elders to use the bow and arrow, the spear, nets, snares, and deadfalls, any useful means to harvest the salmon, moose, and caribou living upon the land. And the shaman and leader before him had taught the healing, the sorcery, the calling for spirits of the ancestors and of the great mountain to comfort his soul and the souls of others around him. Life had been good for so long. . . .

Just as he had become skillful as a young man in the lessons of the D'en'e chiefs and medicine men, the black robes had come along the river to school his people with other teachings. And those same white preachers had mockingly named him for his favorite color and manner of leadership. Then they had wrested much of his power from him, harming him forever in the eyes of his own people. But they had paid in blood—he had seen to that. The slaughter in 1851 of the English Naval Lieutenant Barnard and his men near the mouth of the Koyukuk River had been the first punishment for the insults; the death of every unwary trader and prospector afterward had added to his revenge. But now it seemed the spirits were angry with his hateful ways, and they would soon end his life by his own spiteful hand.

He wasn't sure of the time that had passed in his remembering. Stiffness, numbness, dullness were inside him; death was creeping closer. He had seen this in others before. The cold gripped you motionless after the shivers, wrapping around, squashing your heartbeat and stealing your breathing away. Then your eyes glazed, partly from unconsciousness, partly from sad tears freezing in place. Lastly your body hardened like ice, like the butchered meat of animals exposed to winter winds. Only your spirits could flee, to fly above, dancing here and there upon the land.

Slowly . . . he began to hear Wahnie whine, then yip shrilly, excitedly. The other dogs joined in, starting a chorus of yelps bouncing about the hills. He rolled to his side and stared; he saw a lone figure shuffling fast on snowshoes toward him from down the creek leading into the pond. Hot breath puffed behind the jogging stranger like steam from a bubbling tea kettle on a frosty morning. Bundled like a bear, the man looked clumpy in his black beard, gray furs, and earflaps tied under his chin. He is strong, heavy, though not skilled on the snow paws he wears, Red Shirt observed. But, Wahnie, he is the miracle I begged for. You have saved me!

The stranger neared and crouched just above, panting, "What you doin' with your arm stuck down there, Injun? It's colder'n hell!" His forehead wrinkled, perplexed.

Red Shirt endeavored to answer in English. "I caught hand in beaver trap. Take my ax from sled—cut wood pole out—over there!" He pointed with his left arm to the spruce stake poking above the snow-covered ice.

"You gotta cabin someplace round here?" The bundled man stayed hanging overhead.

"Down trail—after dark-time we get there. Hurry—chop me free!" Red Shirt shifted his arm to point out a packed path through the spruce woods circling the pond.

"Who's there? You got friends waitin'?" The steam continued to puff, frosting the man's bearded face.

"My woman—daughter girl. They will cook moose and beaver tail to eat—I have whiskey. Hurry, must get out or arm will rot with black sickness!"

"Any more Injuns or white people round here close?"

A stab of dread beyond the horror of dying on the ice stuck into Red Shirt's belly. He paused, then decided truth, lies, words, who would know the difference. He must tell enough to gain freedom.

"No one lives here close ... Whites are south by water that never freezes. My people live across land like spirits." He pointed for a third time to the six ravens sitting and watching, overhead again. "Me chief, medicine man. I know many secrets ... of things white man want as much as life."

Swiping his runny nose with his right mitt, the stranger sneered through the freezing mucus on his mustache, "What've you got more than that sled an' dogs—what've you got I need more than that?"

"I show you gold eagle on mountain—more gold than sled can carry—more gold than hundred sleds can carry!"

The wrinkled forehead creased more on the hairy face. "If you know where gold is, why are you trappin' out here in the middle of nowhere? If you got gold—you can be sittin' in Seattle rich an' warm!"

"What I do in city? Die on white man foods cooked in white man ways. I only need gold for new Winchester, maybe new shirt or more bullets. I never leave my land!"

The stranger stood slowly and stared down for some time. Abruptly, he turned, snowshoed to the dog sled, then came back with the ax clenched in his mitts, crouching once more. He purred, "We gotta make a deal, Injun. How do I know you're goin' to show me nothin' but your backside once I chop you out? You're goin' to have to tell me more about the gold—or else I'll leave you here!"

"There is cave where all my people's medicine men go to die. The gold is there . . . But you can't see till hummingbird comes. This place not far . . . but you can't find without me. Me the last medicine man. Chop out—I show you."

"Injun, that's a mighty fancy story—but I ain't believin' it. If there's really gold, why you need hummingbirds to find it. That's the strangest tale I've ever heard!"

"It is true—I can't lie now. The place is there—above river of ice coming down Great One." Red Shirt pointed his free arm by lying it on the snowy beaver pond straight toward Denali, his mittened hand aiming toward a hollow leading up to the towering summit. Gray cliff walls and inklings of indigo glinted through sagging snow fields at the end of the valley as it pitched up into the mountain itself.

The stranger turned his head and gazed along Red Shirt's outstretched parka sleeve. After pausing, he grunted skeptically, "How can a man get up there? It don't look possible. You're lyin' to me, Injun, I know you are!"

"I show way. Chop me free—there is gold for you!"

"You better tell me more. Whereabouts in that hellhole do I go?"

"See where mountain is like steeples on many white men's churches. That where cave is. Gold other side of river of ice—but only me know how to find. Chop me out—"

"Show me some gold from there. I still think you're lying to me!"

"Don't have gold now. Trapping beavers and martins—woman sew clothes for me. See—beaver mitt—very warm!"

The stranger picked up Red Shirt's fur mitten lying by his side, pulled off and placed there just before he had dipped his arm down into the water earlier. Turning it about, peering, the big man removed his own winter mitt and shoved his hand inside. Then, grinning, he approved, "Injun—this is nice—better than my leather choppers. You Injuns sure know how to live in this godforsaken country. I bet your squaw knows where the gold is, too, don't she?"

"No—woman never see spirit place. I know secret. No other—"

The stranger reached out and pulled Red Shirt's other mitten from his outstretched left arm, snatching it off in a blink. He then stood, sneering. "Injun, if there's gold, I'll find it without you. And I think your squaw knows right where to look if you're tellin' the truth. You can stay here and feed the varmints I see gatherin' in the trees. If I chopped you loose, you'd run away or kill me the first chance you got. You don't look to be the trustworthy sort."

Red Shirt lay staring, his black eyes fixed on the dark bearded face above him. Why had he been so unwise as to think Denali would free him after his betrayal—and after he had jeopardized his woman and daughter? He began to chant his death song, calling softly for his end, the just penalty.

"What's that mumble-jumble you're singin', Injun? You tryin' to spook me?"

Stopping his song, Red Shirt paused, then spoke in broken English for the last time, "White man, you will die worse than me. You will be killed forever while I dance above. Remember my words always as you count your days." Then, rolling onto his stomach and hiding his head, he sang again, weeping his anger, his sadness.

The stranger shuffled back to the dog sled and removed his snowshoes, glancing warily at Red Shirt lying on the snow. After storing the ax, he pulled the snake whip free and snapped it high above Wahnie's head. The lead dog yelped, jumped, then tumbled headlong as the eight other frightened dogs hit him from behind. The whip cracked again, this time spanking his hindquarters, drawing blood from his grayness. He righted himself and pulled, running ahead, leading down the trail through the darkening forest.

Shadows stalked across the beaver pond as brassy sunlight dipped below the tree branches where the ravens waited. Watchful, a hunting fox slipped from an alder tangle and sat still, ears pricked against Red Shirt's song as it lingered above the ice. A wolf howled far back in the wintertime. As nightfall settled, the lean fox stepped once, twice . . .

CHAPTER TWO

Courage

Doll Girl listened through the cabin's logs as Wahnie and the other dogs, yipping cantankerously, trotted off the ice of Sleepy Lake and swung around in the front yard. Running to the low door cut above the earth floor of her home, she pulled her wolverine parka off a wooden peg. She darted through the bottom of its rabbit fur lining as fast as the winter weasel, which trimmed the parka's dark brown covering.

Before opening the door to run outside, she called, "Mother, I want to help feed Wahnie. Father will be tired. He is so late tonight."

She watched her mother turn from the hot cookstove, hurrying with a pan of sputtering bannock, now that her man had finally come home. "Stay away from the young dogs. They jump around so crazy, you might get knocked down!"

"They are so silly. My friend Wahnie needs to bite them so they behave. They pull the whitefish away from me before I can throw them down." Doll Girl spun on her feet to leave the cabin.

As she reached for the wooden slide latching

the door, she heard her father open the outside door and step into the woodshed entry. Startled that he would leave the dogs so soon, she stepped back nearer her mother, clearing the way for him to come in.

Suddenly she screamed, rhyming her mother's cry, as a wolf-clothed stranger shoved in, blinking his eyes to adapt to the lamplit interior. The man paused just inside the door, clutching her father's ax. His hand were covered by the beaver mittens she had helped decorate, with blue porcupine quills and red beads.

Her mother reached out and hugged her close, wailing, "Where is my husband? What man are you?"

The stranger stopped blinking, and carefully looking left and right, answered, "I found your man froze to death. He got caught in his own beaver trap. I come here to tell you. The old leader dog knew the way."

"Why are wearing my husband's mittens? Why are you carrying his ax?"

Doll Girl thought her mother's voice sounded more horror-stricken than ever before. And they had faced, gripping hands, side by side, grizzlies and angry moose mothers in the past.

"Sorry . . . took some of his stuff. Didn't think I should leave everything behind. Needed them . . . those sled handles are so cold. Brought the ax in to protect myself. Didn't know who would be in here." The bundled-up man leaned the ax against the wall near the door.

Doll Girl thought her mother sounded even more dreadful when she cried, "You have brought him home to me?"

"No ... didn't know to. Didn't know here or where. I just let the old dog lead the way." The man began to pull off his furs.

Doll Girl felt her mother slip to the floor, falling, sitting down with both arms wrapped around her hair and face, smothering her noisy sobs. Doll Girl slipped down as well, not yet believing, but bawling just as loud.

The stranger finished removing his outer coat, a heavy wool liner, and a fox-skin cap. After throwing all three on the floor, he shuffled over and sat on the bench attached to the whipsawed lumber table centered in the room. He picked at dried salmon placed there earlier, his eyes still shifting back and forth.

After what felt like an hour, Doll Girl felt her mother stand and pull her up alongside. She watched as her mother sighed and dried her eyes with a rag lying nearby. Her mother then pulled the smoking pan of bannock off the stove top and knocked the charred cakes into the waste pail. Gray fumes snaked up.

Her mother spoke again to the white man. "I will fry new bannock and moose steaks for you. Do you drink tea? I am sorry. I forgot to be polite in front of a guest in my home. My daughter will tie and feed the dogs now. You sit and tell me more about my poor husband."

Doll Girl saw the stranger's hasty black eyes

focus on her own. She sensed danger—from him—from her mother's diligent use of the English words.

"Ain't right to let a little girl do it. I'll bed the dogs . . . when I get done eatin'." The man's dark gleaming eyes remained fixed and unfriendly.

"No—sit and rest. You must be tired and cold. My daughter can do it. She is strong. I will tell her to work fast. She can tie each and feed them their fish. You stay and help me feel better."

My mother is not the same. She has never given me permission to tie the young ones. They would pull me down and run away, Doll Girl thought. She is warning me.

Then she heard her mother's throaty syllables in Athabaskan . . measured and resolute. "Daughter, go from here quickly and cut Wahnie free. Walk with him across your father's traplines to the Yukon River. Find men to come back and help me. Do it now. Don't look back—be brave and hurry!"

She glanced at her mother's eyes, knowing disobedience was unpardonable. Their lives had always depended on her following guidance exactly, without delay, when she saw danger. And she had been taught not to cry when awful threats appeared. She needed to act wisely. Tears only weakened one's mind and blinded one's eyes, just when you needed to see distant trails. She turned away, ran to the door, opened it, and dived through without looking back.

The darkness outside made her feel a little safer.

She saw Wahnie standing by himself at the front of the other dogs, lying rowed across the snowy ground. He whined and pranced as she fished her jackknife from her parka and opened it, with its sharp blade folded out. She had been taught to carry a knife, a bottle of matches, her beaver mittens always. Her father had yelled many times, pretending their cabin had caught fire. He had trained her to escape fully prepared to live outside in unsettled weather.

She ran to Wahnie and cut off his leather harness with two swipes of her knife. Whispering, "Wahnie, come," she shut the blade, shoved the knife back into her pocket, and jumped over to her snowshoes, standing nearby in a snowbank. Tucking both under her arm, she ran down onto the frozen lake, heading toward its middle. She ran along the packed path as fast as she could make her feet fly in moose-leather moccasins.

When she reached the place on the lake where her father's trapline trails branched in four different directions, she stopped and studied the sky. Yes, there! She pointed to the Big Dipper and the North Star, both sitting above the Yukon River far away. So far off she didn't want to think of all the days that waited ahead.

Kneeling down, she watched Wahnie prance and pant, happy to be free of the sled and disorderly dogs, forever fighting behind. She motioned him close, circled his soft neck with one arm, and pointed to the North Star again. In her mother's tongue, she commanded, "Wahnie, help me, go!"

Suddenly, just as she stood up to run north with her dog, she heard human outcries break into the night—an outburst of her mother's screams and the stranger's English cursing. Then the young dogs yelped and howled. She looked back and listened to Wahnie's whimpers and the other fearful sounds echoing in the blackness. No—no, she thought. I did not hear and will not cry. Wahnie has protected me since my mother first wrapped me in moss and caribou skin diapers. I'll go now and save her. Wahnie and I will walk together until we reach the place my mother sent us to. He will be my father and mother till the day I return.

Carrying her snowshoes over her shoulders, she set a quick pace behind Wahnie's steady trot, as he followed the path running north across the lake. Curling a bitter smile on her lips, she thought about the stranger trying to catch her with eight sled dogs without a leader. The young dogs would jump up and down, tangle harness lines, and knot them altogether. Then they would fight wildly, trying to pull away. When the stranger tried to straighten out the mess, they would attack him. It would be days before he would learn how to handle the team ... by then her footprints would be drifted over. She would be hidden away forever in the secret land.

She walked until the middle of night, judged by the Big Dipper's handle pointing down. Then she stopped, feeling exhausted, with her hands and feet numbed by the cold. She called Wahnie back, pushed him down, and sat next to his belly. Then she pulled off her mitts and boots and laid them on the snow like a cushion. Lastly she shoved her hands and feet against his warm underbelly, leaned on the side of him, and curled up in her parka. The old dog groaned. She knew how much he hated her iciness, but he would lie motionless for as long as she wanted to sleep.

In the morning she woke up in a winter storm and found Wahnie's and her legs drifted over with little heaps of snow. Rising winds moaned through the trees and shook white veils from the branches and boughs overhead, whenever the hard gales blew powerfully enough to throw the deep accumulations down. Frosted beads slanted back and forth and turned the surrounding forest into a gray mist. Now and then sooty shadows ghosted through, when the icy bursts blew by sheltered places. And high up, flying scud hid the sky from her view.

Sitting straight and pulling her mittens and moccasins back on, she watched as Wahnie stood up and shook, dusting himself clean. Her front glowed from his damp warmth—but her back shivered in the cold wind, reminding her of being held by her mother, and of the many times they had snuggled together in the past winters. A pang of sentiment then shot through her breast, but she shook it away, like Wahnie had shaken off the snow. Her father had taught her to stay strong, that an aching heart meant weakness, and dark cloudiness over her courage.

She believed she stood midway to her father's

first trapline hut, north of their home. And she knew Wahnie would lead her there, even though the trail remained only a scattered trace because of the windstorm. Her dog could use his nose to see. She wouldn't have to worry about getting lost until they reached the second hut, the place where she would have to strike out across the burn, the forest of skeletal trees killed by wildfire in the past.

Following Wahnie up the trail through birch thickets, she marched along on her snowshoes, swinging her hands high, eager to reach the camp ahead. She had traveled along the trapline trail several times with her father; she knew the hut ahead would be stocked and ready for her visit. Her father had always readied his rest stops for his next trip through, lessening the work required to start a fire, boil tea, or fix a meal. Her stomach growled with hunger. She sucked harder on a bit of icicle she had picked up, teasing her need for a full cup of water to slack her thirst in the dry frosty air.

She tramped into her father's first camp as the sun broke through the thick cloudiness and reached its midday height, just above the distant mountains and trees standing behind. Wahnie bounced around, tongue lolling out, proud to have led her so quickly into the first stop, and sensing he would get to eat and drink, too. She pulled the caribou hide door aside and stepped in, staring, letting her eyes repair to the darkness of the eight-foot square built from logs and moss. Yes, the can-

dle set waiting, a wooden match lying alongside.
Yes, the little tin stove stood in the corner, its door
open, kindling and firewood stuffed inside and
matches sitting on top. And just as she had pictured, the teapot sat ready to be thawed, boiled,
and poured over tea and beans. She stepped over,
scratched the first match, and lit the candle.

She worked through the late afternoon, rushing
to find an old frozen skinned beaver carcass for
Wahnie to eat. And she chopped off a hind ham
for herself, happy that a wolverine hadn't dug it
out first and spoiled it with foul scent and urine.
She thawed ice and snow, then chilled the water
for Wahnie and her to drink, filling them for the
first time in a day. Then, as darkness settled, she
boiled beans and fried fat beaver slices for supper,
stuffing herself for the night to come. Finally she
filled the teapot once more for the bowl of oatmeal
she intended to cook in the morning. And she
carried each thing inside she thought important
for the trek ahead, choosing for the backpack she
planned to carry.

That night, before sleep in her father's caribou
hide bed, she smelled him close by: his tobacco
and strong human odor. Again she felt her heart
hurt. Then she recalled his whispers, nearness,
and wish for her to stay strong forever, to stay
Indian and smile and see his spirit dancing above,
guarding against unhappiness and tears of sorrow. She would never cry again. He had taught
her well. She was warm, well fed, and unafraid
to go on.

The next morning she jumped out into a clear, frosty day, one of the impermanent sunny moments she loved so much, uncommon for late November near the Alaskan Mountain Range. Everything around the camp glittered with hoarfrost shining uneven light back and forth. It was the kind of dawn she and her mother had cheered about in the past. The kind that had blinded them till they had squinted their eyes and laughed about their queer faces, while hugging and playing in the snow.

She turned north once more and followed Wahnie, watching his gray tail flip back and forth while he snuffled for the proper path. She then sensed he knew exactly where the next stop lay.

Even lazy beams of sunshine lift spirits during a day like this, she thought. And this day lies etched in fine light, with turquoise skies, white shadowy mountains, and stately, barren trees waving from here and there.

Soon she saw disturbed squirrels jump across drowsy evergreens in front of her. She listened to them chatter, scolding Wahnie and her for coming close and spoiling their noisy play in the branches. Later she saw dark brown moose, with their horselike heads thrust out like odd spirit masks, peering from the bushy bottoms choked with little willows and birches. Then quick weasels darted back and forth, their beady, obsidian eyes and tipped tails barely visible on the snow as they hissed their fright from seeing two uncommon creatures tramping along. She shut her mind to her worries and gazed through Wahnie's breath, misting the air ahead. His foggy puffs seemed to flash away like little ghosts caught out in the sunlight.

They reached the second trapline camp under stars dimmed by snaking yellow, red, and blue brilliance high up in the sky. Northern lights glowed everywhere, pulsing brighter and brighter, leaving her staring up, glancing only now and then at Wahnie's tail flagging the way.

But the dancing light above reminded her to get inside. She realized the temperature had fallen too far for her to stay outside any longer. She would have to plan carefully for the crossing over to the Kantishna River on the following day. The weather would be clear again—but twenty below or more.

She woke early and sorted through her father's things. Her father had always kept a small, narrow toboggan for carrying firewood and running muskrat traps across nearby frozen marshes. Finding the curled-board sled leaning against a tree, she slid it to the hut's door and started loading.

First she set eight old beaver carcasses on its bed in a row, food for her and her dog. Then she folded two caribou hides on top. She packed an ax, hand saw, cooking gear, rolled blankets, beans, and flour. She added her father's ice pick: a stout pole with a sharp iron point; she stowed a butcher knife so she could cut snow blocks and babiche for snowshoe repairs. She found some of her father's spare clothing, bundled up dry tinder and kindling, and loaded those items on top. Then she stood back and wondered if she had forgotten anything she had ever seen her father and mother carry on a midwinter journey in the past. Finally she lashed the entire load down with leather thongs.

After harnessing Wahnie, she yelled, "This way!" Then she led out across the burns—remembering her father's rules: keep the sun and wind fixed on the same part of your body, find landmarks ahead and behind to steer by, and watch out for walking in circles. She knew that once Wahnie had traveled far enough for him to sense the destination, he would find the Kantishna River for her. The remaining distances then lay along winding, ice-covered rivers, where she couldn't possibly get lost.

Black trunks of burnt spruce stood in her way, with twisted, barren limbs for as far as she could see. An awful place, she thought, empty of animal tracks and birdsongs. Snowdrifts lay unbroken out to the horizon in every direction, sullied by long thin shadows cast out by the cowering copper sun.

"Wahnie, this is a bad place . . . talk to me. It is so lonely here!" Doll Girl heard her dog groan, heaving against the heavy toboggan, dutifully following her snowshoe tracks as she broke trail. Smiling, she called again, "You talk to me more! Come on, we'll get halfway across today!"

Old Wahnie answered again.

She rested often . . . for herself and her dog. Deep snow fluffed the crossing, forcing her to lift up and sink down her snowshoes again and again. At twilight she stopped and built a snapping orange fire from the abundance of dried wood leaning into the snow. She thawed snow for water, roasted a leg of beaver, and threw down her caribou hides for sleeping. Then unequal winds brushed back and forth on her face and neck. Seeing high clouds, she judged it would grow warmer through the night. But she fretted about getting lost. Snowy weather might hide the correct direction in the morning. She pulled her sled around and pointed it for daybreak. Then she crawled under her blankets and caribou hides, with Wahnie beside her to help keep her warm. Tomorrow, she dreamed, we will find the Kantishna.

Before nightfall of the next day, she yelled, "Wahnie, we've found the river!" She grinned at her dog, hunkering on the frozen surface. His tongue flopped around as he sat at the front of the load he had hauled for so long.

"You always know the way. I can never get lost when I'm with you." Then she rested also and searched for a place to camp on the darkening shores on each side.

Waking in the morning, she felt ashamed of having slept for so long after daylight, never stirring once. She supposed it was because she and Wahnie had struggled so mightily through miles and miles of deep snow for two days—and the temperature had warmed so much. Now, she thought, we can go faster. We are on open trails

and weatherbeaten snows. Our only difficulty will
be walking so much farther because the rivers
bend back and forth, winding all the way to the
Yukon River.

She loaded the toboggan, hooked up Wahnie,
and started downriver. The gray sky hung low
with just a little brightness to read north and
south by. Scattered snowflakes floated down, fluttering around without hard breezes to push them
one way or another. She found she could catch a
ride on top of her load, sitting astride on some
stretches of the river. The surface lay packed and
smooth, letting Wahnie scoot ahead at a fast trot,
not slowed a bit by her extra weight. Catching
unlucky snow particles on her parka sleeves, she
broke her boredom by peering at each one, trying
to see if one was the same as any other. Then
she watched to see how fast her breath melted
them away.

Tiring of snowflakes, she eyed the river's surface. Suddenly she yelled, "Wahnie! Look, otter
slides! See how they sled like us. See over there—
blood—a mink killed a muskrat. Look here at the
moose tracks. A big one! He bellied the willows
over and ate them all. The fox passed here, too.
Look at his tracks ahead. Follow him, maybe he's
still close!" Then she smiled, recalling her father's
stories about all the animals they lived with every
day. And she heard her old dog answer back as
well.

She jumped from the top of the toboggan and
cut corners, wandering the river, reading signs left

behind by her animals friends. But her dog stopped ahead and moaned, waiting restlessly.

Suddenly crashing down, she screamed and stopped herself with both arms thrust out. She lunged forward, thrashing, clawing for a grip, trying to hold on to the broken ice. She then felt the river's current sucking on her moccasins and parka.

Terrified, she screamed over and over, "Wahnie, help! Wahnie, help!" Then, bawling helplessly, she cried. "Please help me get out, Wahnie! Please get me out!"

Wahnie leaped sideways and whipped the sled around, tipping it over in his hurry. He plowed the spilled load, jump after jump, yelping as he hit his harness with all his strength. He slowed . . . crept forward. At last he snapped her left sleeve in his teeth and yanked back with a flip of his head and shoulders, flashing his grayness.

Doll Girl felt herself fly up, head-over-heels, stunned by the fury and quickness and muscle of her dog's rescue. Then instantly she sensed another danger—and Wahnie couldn't save her now. Scrambling out of her somersault, she jumped up onto the shoreline, calling for her dog to follow. When she saw him safe from the dangerous ice, she ran back to her sled and ripped into the side for her father's clothes and its store of tinder and kindling. She had only a few minutes to start a fire, gather firewood, and build a blaze to warm and dry her. She had to light the fire with one or two matches—or else she would be too chilled to save herself. Of all the awful jeopardies her father and mother had warned of, the most dangerous one now faced her.

She found her bundle of fire-starter, raced to a clearing, kicked the snow away, and threw her armload down. Yanking off her mittens, she quickly stacked her tinder and kindling and pulled out her little jar of matches. The lid was already frozen shut! She ran again, grabbed her ax, dropped that beside her bottle. Kneeling, whispering to her sacred spirits, she busted the glass and scratched one of the redheaded matches on the steel of the ax blade. It flashed white hot. She cupped the flame with her hands, shielding it. She touched the wood shavings below the kindling. The match instantly smoked out! Grimacing, she pinched another between her frozen fingers and scratched once more. At last the yellow fire licked up. She didn't mind when it burned her fingers.

Keep moving, don't stop, she thought! Her parents' warnings haunted her. She jumped up again, with her ax gripped halfway up the handle. She swung repeatedly, cutting deadwood as fast as she discovered short lengths to chop off. Thanking her spirits, she wondered about their secret kindness: the warmer air and all the firewood lying nearby. It must be her father flitting back and forth overhead, not the tiny black-and-white chickadee.

Once orange flames fanned skyward, she freed Wahnie and carried her caribou hides and blankets to the fire's edge. She changed into her father's clothing, squealing about her brief nakedness, while she ripped and knotted to keep the oversized garments covering her body. Then, squatting and draping herself in a blanket, she began the long, hard task of thawing, squeezing, and drying clothing, sopped by her misbehavior. She had been scolded many times not to act childish in the wilds. But she had forgotten and ignored Wahnie's warning as well, playing like a baby. It seemed time for her to grow up. Her life depended on it.

Two days later she stepped onto the river again. She followed her dog cautiously, spearing the snowy surface with her father's ice pick, testing it for thickness. She now knew Wahnie could smell danger and would whine warnings. But she would check the ice anyway.

They marched day after day for as many hours as Wahnie could pull. She rode as often as she could, watching her dog's tail and trot and worrying about his load being too heavy. Whenever deep snow and drifts slowed their way, she walked behind. And when Wahnie's tail lost its steady wag and drooped low, she knew it was time to camp and let him curl up in the snow and eat his share of the food.

Each day slipped by in a gathering maze: some cold, some snowy, some warmer. Her old gray dog pulled on and on, hardly ever stopping to rest. He even seemed happier when she rode on top of the heavy load. He grinned his steady persistence, lolled out his pink tongue, flipped his tail, and trotted with his paws pounding down.

Then one afternoon she cried, "Wahnie, we are on the Tanana River now!" They ran out onto a wide channel, filled with long wooded islands, scattered westward, toward where she knew the Yukon River waited.

"Two suns, three suns from today, we'll find old Father River. Then we can ask someone to save Mother. It is so good to be off the crooked one behind. We can go fast now!" She smiled as her dog sped away, sensing as well the end of their journey just ahead.

The next day she saw the telltale signs—caribou tracks stretched out, moose tracks loping across, all mixed with paw prints. Wolves! She and Wahnie were passing through their hunting grounds!

Her father had pointed out their fatal ways in the past. Hunting wolves first wounded their prey with their sharp fangs—then they ripped out their victim's guts from its slashed belly from behind. Finally they pulled the poor creature down, while it screamed for its life, and tore pieces from the rear end, even before its death. She had seen the carcasses and bloody snow for herself.

She shuddered in silent horror. Wahnie understood, too. He stood soundlessly, his tongue pulled in, his nose held high, sniffing the chilly wind.

"Wahnie, we need to go fast. If the pack finds us, they will try to kill us. It is winter and they are hungry now." She gripped her father's ice pick hard, wishing Denali's holy land didn't include the black killers, the cunning robbers forever stealing food from her people. All animal life belonged to the D'en'e, not to the dark shadows that haunted their lives.

Then she heard the wolves strike her and Wahnie's trail. Their long howls echoed down alongside the river banks, frightening her and her dog into peering backward with white rounding eyes. She jumped from the toboggan's top and yelled, "Wahnie, come on, we must hide ourselves!"

Running, pumping her legs through the snow covering the river, she led the way to a tangle of driftwood, heaped and frozen ashore against a steep bank. Her father's lessons had been clear—always face dangerous animals! If you tried to run from them, they would just pull you down!

When she reached the jumble of dead trees, she saw she had chosen well. The wolves would have to come through a narrow opening. And Wahnie would fight them when they tried.

"Wahnie, in here!" She yanked off his harness the instant he reached her barrier. Then they both backed against the high wall behind.

Six lean wolves padded downriver, their long noses down low, scenting the trail beaten flat by the passing sled and human feet. They stopped when they spied the two strange figures standing huddled close together. One shape appeared larger than any one of them. The other shape seemed odd and stood covered with brown fur, smelling like the dreaded wolverine. Running forward, they peered and pranced, trying to comprehend what they were hunting. Then their yellow eyes narrowed—beaming wildly. The two-legged creature had moaned just like all the animals they had killed many times before.

The black leader feigned an attack. But Wahnie ripped his rear before he could dart away. Doll Girl shuddered. She had never seen her friend behave so savagely. He looked more dangerous than the wolves themselves. Then she thought she had better help—their lives depended on it. She stuck out her father's ice pick, ready to spear the first wolf that jumped too close.

She could see the wolves communicating, scheming the best way to pull them down. She then watched as the black one and his white mate turned to attack Wahnie. Another old gray female crouched to come behind, intending to strike as well. The remaining three wolves acted younger and hung back, but looked ready to leap the moment their parents had crippled the strange prey. Then they would pile in and help tear the corpses apart, too!

In a single instant she glimpsed both lead wolves charge Wahnie. Then she saw the gray bitch leap for her. Screaming, she jabbed her spear at the flash of white fangs, black nose, and seething eyes. She pushed as hard as she had ever pushed before. Feeling herself knocked backward and hearing a sudden howl, she saw Wahnie and the first two wolves roll in a wild tumble. The animal sound wailed again. Then she saw the gray female slip off her father's ice pick, pulling away from its sharp point.

Straightening back up with her spear, she watched Wahnie win his advantage. Her own wild shriek and the female's wails had bewildered the two wolves attacking her dog.

Wahnie ripped open the black leader's neck, splashing bright red on the snow. Then, before the white one could recover fully from a knockdown, he charged and drove her back. At last he tore at both wolves' hindquarters as they turned and ran out of the gap, which now had become a trap.

Doll Girl yelled, stopping her dog from following them. All six wolves then trotted back up the river, three of them limping and dripping blood. Wahnie stood in front of her, growling his fury, as the pack faded away. She knelt and hugged her dog's neck, pulling him close. The wolves wouldn't come back. She and Wahnie had beaten them.

"Wahnie, are you hurt? Let me look. Quiet! The wolves are gone now. You are scaring me with your growls. We're safe." She searched her dog's body for injuries. Finding none more serious than the bites that she had seen him get during fights with other dogs, she patted him until he quit his loud rumbles.

They camped overnight inside the driftwood, using the natural protection of the high bank and the abundance of firewood that lay around. After building a fire in the narrowness that had let them defend themselves so well, they slept until the early gray light began to sneak downriver from the east.

Getting underway again, Doll Girl saw that Wahnie seemed weakened by his fight with the wolves. The old dog's stride looked measured, and his long tail had lost its bounce. Instead it swung along with his body as he strained against the toboggan's weight.

They had eaten all the beaver; she had only a little flour and beans. If they didn't reach the Yukon River by the end of the next day, she knew they would face another fight. And this battle would be against the greatest enemy of the land she called home. She and her parents had been hungry before. When there had been no game to kill, no fur to trap, and each meal had been either watery soup, moldy bannock, or old beans. She had watched her father sort through their sled dogs and wonder out loud whether one should be killed for the pot, instead of being kept for the sled.

At dark she found an abandoned fish camp. She stared at its cache, high up in four dead trees. Dried salmon and other good things to eat sat above. She had seen Wahnie sniffing, but there was no way to climb. The cache's ladder lay frozen in the snow nearby. And it looked too long and heavy for her to handle alone as well. Ah-eeh! she thought, so much food and we can't get to it. She heard Wahnie's belly grumble, then her stomach murmured, too. Finally she led her dog away, trudged to the birch bark, spruce bough, and pole shack across the clearing to spend the night.

"Wahnie, tomorrow we will walk to the Yukon and find men to help us. They will have food to eat." She huddled with her dog and slept on the floor of the shack, using her mittens like a pillow.

They reached the Yukon River the next day before dark, as she had promised her dog. For the first time in countless days, she saw human tracks from recent times. A well-used sled trail ran by the end of the Tanana River. She knew from travels with her parents in the past this was the common highway of Alaska. Within hours someone would come along.

She sat up that night near a small fire, hugging close to her dog. Occasionally she nodded off, but mostly she waited for black dots to appear in the distance, when it grew light again. She knew Wahnie would see them also and bark at her. Then the stranger would brake his sled to a stop, hollering at his dog team while he tossed out the anchor to hold them.

"Wahnie, here someone comes! Look—a long team. They are going fast. This man will be good to us!" She watched in the early-morning light as twelve dogs came headlong upriver, snow rolling up behind. Hard yells echoed across the ice from a tall musher riding on his runners.

"Little girl, what in tarnation are you doin' by yourself out here in the middle of this big river?" The musher wrinkled his face around his eyes and nose, after he had dragged his dogs to a stop.

Doll Girl struggled to speak the English language she knew. "I got Wahnie with—"

"I mean where's your parents? What the hell you waitin' for? You look half froze and starved to death!"

Her mind raced to remember again. "Father dead. Bad man got mother . . . cabin by Denali. You help!"

The wrinkled musher peered off his right side, toward the far-distant white mountains, hardly visible above the tree line. Then he stared at Doll Girl. "Ain't possible! I ain't even fit to make that trip, little girl!"

"Need help mother. You help!" Doll Girl clutched her dog's neck, wondering what she had to say to get the man with the fast dogs to turn up the Tanana.

"I can't help—I ain't brave enough. Get up here an' ride upriver with me. I'll drop you when we see some of your people."

"No! You help!" Doll Girl recalled she had promised herself to not cry. But she felt so weak.

"Little girl—listen. I can't stand here and argue. I got government mail to run, and I can't wait no more. You get on. Ain't no excuse for slowin' the mail. I ain't tellin' some darn bureaucrat that I went off to rescue some Injun. He'd fire me in a city boy's second, that's for sure. You get on. I'll find you help upriver, I promise."

She felt too tired to resist any longer. What was government? What were bureaucrats and mail? She realized her fate always rested in Denali's hands, but why hadn't the spirits let her turn back at once? She climbed on the wide sled piled high with soft bundles and wriggled to a sitting position. Then she watched Wahnie sprint to keep up, faithfully staying close by her side.

CHAPTER THREE

Riddles

The knock rapped halfway up the height of the door, interrupting Eli Bonnet from his *Klondike Nugget* newspaper article about milk costing thirty dollars a gallon. A small woman or child, he thought ... but why would either person walk around Dawson City at night when it's twenty below? He stood up from his chair alongside the potbellied stove and stepped into the hallway. When he opened the door, cold air stirred in, fogging the entrance, ghosting the Indian boy and girl standing outside.

"Mr. Bonnet, do you remember me?" The boy stood still, clutching a leather bundle in his mittens.

"Son, I can't see you out in the dark. Step in here with your friend and come out of the cold." Eli stepped backward and swung his right arm, waving his visitors inside.

The two children scampered in, their black eyes blinking at the bright light of the living room. Eli stared hard, trying to recall the faces. Then he remembered the boy, even though his tawny human features lay hidden behind the wolverine hair around his winter parka hood.

After closing the door, Eli waved his arm again toward the hot stove across the room. "Remove those parkas and warm yourselves. Get over by that fire and thaw out. Your faces look frozen from all the cold."

He watched both children pull off their long winter parkas. Then he saw their dark eyes dart around, peering at each piece of furniture, the stove, even the walls. True Indians, he mused, taught by their elders to examine their surroundings from the first instant. Both youngsters reminded him of the Sioux and Blackfeet children he had seen many times while serving as a Deputy U.S. Marshal in the Dakota and Montana territories. He suddenly felt homesick as he recalled his past, bright-eyed days in the Old West after the Civil War. He still missed the boundless wilderness he had seen ruined by breaking plows, barbed wire fences, statehood, and civilization on its willful march.

"Who's come to visit?" High cheeks, brunet face, and pink mouth—Hannah Twigg peeked around the kitchen corner. Then she cried, "Eli, those children look awful. What's wrong?"

"I'm not sure. This boy is the one I've talked to before . . . downriver at Fort Yukon. His great granddaddy is the medicine man that gave me my wolf dog." Eli smiled at the woman who had journeyed north with him during the Klondike gold stampede of the past year.

The two of them had struggled to reach the gold fields around Dawson City in the last months of 1897 and through the following summer. Now they planned to be married on Christmas Day. Although the children's visit seemed disastrous for the solemn celebration just ahead.

The boy spoke again. "I have brought your spirit coat. My father's grandfather asks that you wear it once more. He wishes for you to find the white man that has taken Hnay't'aeni's mother." Pausing to point at his small companion, the dark-eyed boy added, "In English you call her Doll Girl. She has no father or mother now!"

Eli looked at Hannah across the room. They had shared their lives for nearly a year. Their secret bonds spoke feelings without words having to pass between them. He had hoped their marriage of the hearts would soon be one of ceremony. But now he wondered if the two youngsters had suddenly spoiled their happy plans.

Taking his old Sioux spirit coat from the boy, he unfolded the leather jacket and uncovered the sacred symbols stitched all over the outside. Lakota women had sewn on blue beads, red beads, long fringes, and eagle feathers long ago, all spiritually gathered from the Dakota prairie those native people loved so much.

He had helped drive the Sioux off their ancestral lands and onto their wretched reservations, seizing the famous coat for himself during a dangerous battle. Wearing the ancient garment, he had continued riding the Old West as a lawman.

Then he had followed the Klondike gold stampede to the North. Now the Gwich'in Indian boy to whom he had given the sacred coat in the past autumn had returned with its storied charms.

The coat brought back many deep memories. He and Hannah, a prospector named Noodles, and another U.S. Marshal named Jesse Peacock had all joined the gold rush in the past year from San Francisco, California. They had climbed the Chilkoot Pass and White Pass of Alaska and had challenged the wildest rapids of the Yukon River in wooden boats. They had lost old friends to fatal accidents and had suffered awful privation for months while tramping the Yukon Territory, each fighting on for specific purposes.

He and Jesse Peacock dated back many years. They had fought each other in the Civil War—Eli a Confederate soldier, Peacock a Union officer. They had become U.S. Marshals afterward, forever quarreling about Jesse's silly compassion for wrongdoers. At last they had chased a brutal murderer all the way north to Dawson City, only to have the man disappear into the Alaskan wilds because of Peacock's senseless ways.

Noodles, for his part, had come north to carry on his lifelong hunt for gold. A small, whiskered old fellow in his seventies, he had wandered all over as a younger man. Finally he had run out of places to prospect.

"Providence, by Jeez!" the spry prospector would shout when he was asked about his luck through the years. "Providence pulls me!" he would cry when he was told to slow down. Then he would whisper devilishly, "Providence, by Jeez, Providence!" after he had heard the gossip of another new frontier to explore. Eli had always laughed about the gossip that Noodles' forgetfulness of the places he had just come from only seemed to be exceeded by the riddle over where the old man planned to go next.

"Have you two children eaten?" Hannah's question jolted him from his quiet reminiscences. He watched as the little girl eyed the boy. She looked skinny, worn out, and unwilling to speak on her own.

After exchanging a few Athabaskan words with the girl, the boy said, "Doll Girl is always hungry now. We've come far to see you."

"Son, did you two just come up from Fort Yukon?" Then Eli thought he already knew the answer. And he supposed they had completed the long journey without any help.

"We used my father's dogs and sled. We put Doll Girl's friend Wahnie up front. You should see him run, Mr. Bonnet. We came fast!" The boy's eyes beamed.

Glimpsing Hannah's astonished face, Eli also couldn't help wondering about children capable of crossing such distances in the middle of the Yukon winter. He also wanted to drive a dog team that far himself, something he had yet to do.

"Where are your dogs and sled?" He hadn't heard anyone mush up to the house.

"We tied them at the edge of the river. Where

the riverboats are pulled up on the shore. Wahnie is watching."

"Why have you brought back my old lucky coat? I meant for you to keep it. Come sit in the kitchen and tell me why you've traveled so far to find me."

After seating the children at the kitchen table, Eli watched as the boy and girl gobbled down the bread, meat, and pie Hannah had dutifully carried in from the pantry. Waiting for them to fill their stomachs before asking further questions, he smiled and winked at Hannah to let her know they were just two hungry kids.

He judged Doll Girl to be nine or ten years old. Lean, dusky face, sharp obsidian eyes—she looked like an odd wild creature. She wore Indian things: fur, leather, very little cloth, and that single piece of fabric looked woolen. All her clothing appeared stitched with gut and sinew, in knots using ancient patterns. As close to a true Indian, he thought, as anyone could find nowadays. Plainly one who had been living a long ways from the white people who were pouring into the North on the last great stampede for gold.

At last the boy said through the food in his mouth, "A man came to Doll Girl's cabin by great sacred mountain named Denali. He told her that he'd found her father dead, but he wore her father's mittens and carried his ax." Pausing for breath, he added, "Doll Girl's mother warned her to run away and find help. She and Wahnie came to find someone to go back. She has found no one yet." The boy stretched his arm over the table for the last piece of pie.

Listening to Hannah's long, noisy sigh, Eli asked, "How did Doll Girl's mother know to warn her? Perhaps the stranger was innocent."

"No—Doll Girl's father was Red Shirt Moses. He was chief of all Koyukon Indians and a medicine man like my father's grandfather. Her mother is also very wise. If she said to run away, it was good to do. She would not send Doll Girl to the Yukon River without reason. It is very far."

Suddenly, Hannah cried, "This girl walked across Alaska in the middle of winter?" Then, with her voice pitching higher, she asked, "How could she have done that all alone?"

"Wahnie help. You help now!" Doll Girl sat erect on her chair, like a wild bird, and stared back at Hannah. Then she looked at Eli with the same round, black eyes.

"I didn't think she knew English—" Hannah sighed again.

"She knows a few words. I am teaching her more." The boy picked up the last few crumbs scattered on the table.

Hannah looked at the boy. "Where did you learn to speak English so well?"

"The preachers taught me . . . but I learned the Holy Bible is wrong. Last fall when Mr. Bonnet paddled to Fort Yukon to give me his spirit coat and help his sick friend, he told me to listen instead to the old shaman chief. I have learned the truth from him!" The boy, still searching for crumbs, missed Hannah's frowning eyes darting to Eli.

Eli supposed Hannah would scold him later about the advice he had given the boy several months earlier. Then he wondered about the shaman chief's inaction. "Why hasn't your great chief sent his men back to help Doll Girl's mother?"

"The mail sled carried Doll Girl to us. Her tribe is gone from the river, hunting and trapping for the winter. The white men in Fort Yukon will not help. My people are Gwich'in Indians and cannot walk on Koyukon land. It is forbidden by the spirits. Great-grandfather told me to come find you. He says you will go."

"Why are the Gwich'in people forbidden to walk on Koyukon land?" Then the boy's solemn gaze made him feel foolish.

He had seen scores of men and women killed all across the West. Ancestral lands were taboo, he thought, and trespassing meant blood. Indians behaved just like white pioneers in that way.

He added quickly, "Son, I guess you needn't answer. I have an idea it's the same as when I rode the Dakota and Montana territories . . . if you know about the places I mean." Then he dropped his head. He hated growing older; he hated his rocking chair, and wintering in town.

The boy's face stayed expressionless. "I learned after you gave me the magic coat. The preachers told me. You have always hunted men. Now you can hunt again!"

Then both children looked like wild birds, like

winged hunters perched on tree branches. Eli began to squirm. They had Indian eyes, sharp, un-blinking orbs that seemed to spear straight through, or make you squirm in the belly, shuffle your feet, and look away when you couldn't bear their judgment any longer.

He realized they knew he would go. Hannah appeared to be the only one who didn't know, and it would break her heart. He stood up, calling, "Put your parkas back on. Let's go get your dogs. You and Doll Girl can sleep tonight in the storage room. We'll talk more in the morning."

They walked to the frozen Yukon River, listening to their winter boots crunch cold, dry snow. As they passed homes with shining yellow windows and bright barrooms and gambling halls, they heard joyful cries and drunken revelry floating in the night.

Dawson City held thirty thousand people, all intent on taking everything from any person who had struck it rich. Winter, summer, day, and dark—time made no difference—the human madness would last until the gold gave out. Then, Eli mused, everyone would drift away, abandoning the settlement, trading it for some other boom-town. He had seen it that way from Deadwood to Virginia City, from Bannack to Helena. Dawson City would end the same someday.

He heard the dogs on the hard snow of the river a little while before seeing them. Whining and yip-ping, the team bounced around when they marched up. Then he listened as the children spoke low words to the dogs, calming them. Finally the boy jumped onto the sled's runners, yelled out in odd dialect, and swung the team back toward the house. Doll Girl ran ahead, alongside the tall gray dog at the front of the team.

His own dog barked when they returned to the home he and Hannah had rented for the wintertime. He had spent most of the previous year chasing a killer from San Francisco, California, at last catching him at Lake Bennett on the headwaters of the Yukon River. After sending the man down to Dawson City to be turned over to the U.S. Marshals, he had learned later that Jesse Peacock had lost the prisoner during the riverboat passage out of Alaska. Paddling downriver in a small canoe, he then had journeyed to Fort Yukon to rescue Peacock from the desolation of the old trading town.

When he had first stepped onshore at Fort Yukon, the settlement's Gwich'in Indians had admired his Sioux spirit coat and had questioned him about its history. Having always felt deep sorrow for possessing the famous coat for so long, he had given it to the boy now riding on the sled's runners, telling the youngster to listen as much to his great-grandfather as the missionaries of the town. The old shaman, overhearing the advice, had given him a white wolf puppy in return, declaring the animal sacred medicine.

"What have you named the one my father's grandfather gave you?" The boy stood beside Doll

Girl, staring at the half-grown wolf standing under the white moon.

Eli paused, feeling a little embarrassed. He had pirated the name of a mighty Sioux warrior. His last dog had been killed by the prisoner he had taken at Lake Bennett. He had wanted to shy away from all the painful old memories. He had used the first name that had flashed in his mind.

"Ironclaw! I named him after an Indian." Then he turned away. "Show me how to bed your dogs. We need to get back into the house."

"When will you go back for Doll Girl's mother?" The boy turned and Doll Girl followed.

Eli paused once more. At last he answered, "I need to talk to the woman I live with. We had planned to be married on Christmas Day. She will be unhappy if I leave."

"I understand. Indians are the same." Then the boy spoke to Doll Girl in his mother tongue, pointing at the house.

Eli helped the children carry thick caribou hides into the house after they had tied and fed the dogs. Despite Hannah's protests, he bedded both youngsters on the floor of the storage room, opening the windows to chill the small space with cold air. Then he smiled as both children burrowed under their hides, fully clothed but ready for sleep. Just like the Old West, he thought .. two wilderness-bred Indians unaccustomed to sleeping with stoves, nightclothes, and bed mattresses. He knew they would rest fine till morning.

When he rejoined Hannah in the living room,

he found her sitting in her favorite chair, embroidering. He dreaded her downcast eyes and quivering lip. But then a settled, calm look lay across her face.

"Do you plan to leave in a day or two?" Her voice sounded supple, forgiving.

"I want to. Can you forgive me and let me go?" He sat in front of her and held her hands, surprised by her wise intuition.

"How could I refuse to help that little girl. When I feel angry about you leaving me, I think about all the years I spent without my mother. She died when I was Doll Girl's age. At least I had a father to love me. She's been told her father is dead. You've got to go."

"I thought I'd have to explain . . . tell you why I wanted to go. It seems my worries were misplaced."

"Sometimes you're such a fool, Eli. I knew the moment the boy told Doll Girl's story that you hoped to go. You sat in the kitchen hanging your head, mooning over your old Indian coat . . . and you've been like a caged animal since October. How could I have missed your need to chase outlaws again."

"It will break my heart to go. I wanted so much to marry you on Christmas Day. We should have married last fall, on Thanksgiving—" Then he remembered their daily business during the first weeks of winter. They had opened the mining claims Noodles had helped them find alongside the discovery he had made on a hill called Chickaloon.

When Noodles had first reached the Klondike gold fields, he had learned, along with the thousands of other stampeders, that all the rich pay dirt alongside the Bonanza and Eldorado creeks, the original strikes of gold, belonged to other claim stakers. But the wise old-timer had outfoxed more than one gold rush, and he saw his chance on a hillside nearby. Working with the black man who had floated down the Yukon River with him, he had climbed three hundred feet up and had discovered one of the richest mines of all.

At first all the other miners poked fun and called the place Chickaloon Hill, their spiteful opinion about the likelihood of gold lying so far above bedrock. After joining Noodles, following their own journey to the Klondike, and after the old prospector had shown them a leather poke stuffed with nuggets, he and Hannah had staked adjoining claims. The miners below, seeing additional people dashing around, at last figured they had better shut up and investigate for themselves. Then the great new stampede to the high hills all around had taken place.

"We didn't have time to get married."

Hannah's loud declaration shook him from his memories of their recent good fortune. He smiled. "I never thought we would ever strike it rich in all my days."

"How long will you be gone? How far away is the mountain called Denali?"

"Jesse Peacock said he saw that mountain last summer. The captain of the riverboat he came upriver on claimed the summit was sacred to all the people along the Yukon River. I remember Jesse guessing it lay two hundred miles south of the mouth of the Tanana River. He said no one but Indians had ever traveled there."

"Just the kind of place you'll want to explore first. Will you ever stay at home, Eli?" Hannah's eyes narrowed.

"I will—" He supposed his eagerness had shown on his face. The wanderlust he had felt across the West as a young man, the sweet longing that had tugged him north, lay inside his heart once more. Squeezing her hands, he added, "You know I'm heartbroken when I'm away from you . . . then unwell when I can't find new places. I warned about following an old pilgrim like me."

Hannah's eyes brightened and her mouth curled up. "I know you did. And apparently that's one of the reasons why I love you. I said you should go. Let's quit troubling ourselves by talking about it endlessly. Are you taking Jesse Peacock along? Could the strange man be the prisoner he lost last September on his way back to California?"

"I'll ask Jesse to come along in the morning. Seems possible it could be the same individual."

"I'll feel happy if Peacock doesn't go with you. He scares me! Ever since you came back from Fort Yukon with him, he's not acted right. One day he's normal, the next day you'd think he was the madman himself. And all the darkness of the wintertime makes him sicker each day."

Eli pondered Jesse Peacock's fitness for the journey. Since September his friend had suffered from deep despair. The escape of the killer and the gloomy winter days had seemed to foster queer behavior.

"I think it's cabin fever. The sourdoughs who have wintered here in the past say some men sicken from being trapped indoors for so long. He'll feel better once we're out on the trail."

They walked to the bedroom, holding hands. Eli tossed around in bed, worrying continually. He knew he had to take Jesse Peacock along . . . but what about Hannah's warning? Should he take Doll Girl or ask the boy to join him? Maybe he should take two teams of sled dogs. How many days did it take to reach the mountain? Then he fretted about Hannah's lonely sighs until he slept at last.

In the morning, under a cloudy gray dawn, Eli crunched across the snow to the Lucky Wishbone Café. Each day the miners and townsmen gathered to gossip about the past night's wins and losses, the dance-hall girls, and the latest sickness or death. He supposed his friend Noodles would be sitting in the middle of the men, whooping it up and adding his humor to the first cups of coffee for the day. He thought Jesse Peacock would be there as well, off to one side, sitting forlornly by himself.

"By Jeez, Eli, you hardly ever come in the morning! What you up to today?" Noodles shoved his friends to one side, making room for another chair.

"Old man, I want your help. I need to leave town for a while. Thought you could stay with Hannah, keep her company." Eli saw Jesse Peacock across the room, waving his hand.

"Where you goin'? Awful cold to travel! Goin' up to the mines for a couple of days to check the boys you got workin' there?" The prospector wrinkled his whiskered face.

Sitting down, Eli waved back to Peacock. "No, I need to leave for a month, perhaps longer. A woman is missing."

"You givin' up your weddin' day! By Jeez, Eli, I been waitin' for that party all dang winter."

The men sitting nearby fell silent, except for their clinking cups. Jesse Peacock stood up and walked over, so he could listen as well.

"A little girl came into town last night. Someone busted into her parents' cabin, kidnapped her mother, said that her father was dead. I'm going downriver to see—"

Peacock's voice cried over the noisy coffee cups. "It's the Cannibal. You told me last fall he would show himself. I won't let him get away from me this time!"

"By Jeez, Eli, do you think Jesse's right? Could it be the same crazy killer again?"

"I'm not sure—seems possible—then unlikely. The girl's home is at the bottom of the mountain the Indians call Denali. That's the same high peak

Jesse saw when he came up the Yukon River last summer. I wonder why an outlaw would run that far."

Suddenly a loud voice yelled, "I see'd that Denali Mountain when I come up here, too. I bet it's a thousand miles downriver from here. Biggest darn thing you ever want to see. You ain't goin' to catch nobody livin' round there!"

"Eli—is it that far?" Noodle's forehead creased and his eyes darkened.

"I don't know, old man. I need to look at Jesse's maps and measure the true distance. I hope to start downriver for Fort Yukon tomorrow—"

Jesse Peacock cried out again, "I'm going with you. You promised last fall. You said we'd get the Cannibal come wintertime—you and me together. I'll be ready come the morning."

"Jesse, I want you to come along—and I'm glad to have your company. I came here to ask for your help. Let's sit at an empty table and plan the trip." Eli stood up and stepped to one side, away from the noisy crowd of men now arguing about the mountain, the distance, and the weather.

Then the loud voice yelled once more from the crowd, "It's a squaw that's missin', ain't it? You're chasin' half across Alaskee just for some Injun, ain't you, Bonnet?"

Eli turned around and stared at the man with his black scowling eyes. When the whole café had fallen silent, he called back, "Your blood runs the same red as theirs. Would you like to disagree?"

Finally muffled talk spread slowly inside the

Lucky Wishbone. Noodles shuffled over and sat down next to Eli, joining the hasty arrangements for the following day.

When Eli stepped out of the café to walk back home, amber daylight hung over the town. Hannah's fears about Peacock haunted him, and he felt an uneasiness in the cold air. Jesse had seemed to babble, he thought. And the crippled stub of his friend's arm, blown off in the Civil War, had appeared to jerk around more than ever before. Was it wise to start the trek ahead with an one-armed man as possessed as Jesse seemed to be? Then he wondered if his friend had suffered a head injury when the murderer nicknamed the Cannibal had escaped. In all the years that had passed them by, he hadn't seen Peacock act so peculiar. Admittedly, they had mostly worked far from one another—he in the wild boomtowns, Jesse in the larger towns and cities. Perhaps he had just not seen the man's true character before and had simply overlooked an oddness always there.

As he neared his home, he worried about his next bitter task. Then all the sled dogs broke into a sudden racket at the back of the house, barking about his return. Two small Indian faces peered out through the frosted windowpanes. He watched their little hands rub sparkling clear circles on the icy glass.

CHAPTER FOUR

Medicine

"No!" Doll Girl sat on her chair, sulking, her legs and arms stiff.

"Son, tell her I can't go unless she stays behind. Tell her it's not possible for me to take care of her and a one-armed man, too." Eli knew the Indian girl had good reason to protest. She *had* trekked out all alone. It seemed possible she could survive the return trip better than Jesse Peacock, perhaps even better than himself.

He listened to the boy mutter odd-sounding syllables, interpreting the argument against Doll Girl joining the expedition. As much as he hated confessing the truth to himself, he was leaving Doll Girl behind because if he suffered a calamity in the hostile wilds, Doll Girl would be the only person at home with a useful idea of where to send help.

"No!" The little girl didn't soften her hard face after the boy finished his translation.

Eli knew of one other argument. It would probably strike Hannah as peculiar, maybe even upsetting, but he had to win Doll Girl's agreement and get on with his preparations. The Indians of the North, he thought, might accept customs he had learned from the Sioux long ago. Trading, bondage, and pledges were all an important part of native culture. He would try to bargain his personal sacrifice away.

"Tell Doll Girl she is wrong to come here and ask that I leave my woman for such a long time, then offers nothing in return. Tell her my woman wishes to receive something worthwhile in exchange. She wants Doll Girl and Wahnie to wait here. A person cannot be more fair. Does Doll Girl not see her father and mother saying this is so? Does she not hear them shouting their words to take this generous trade?"

As the boy translated, he watched Doll Girl's dusky face relax. She did know the rules of ancient human law! Now he could get on with his next business; he had to get her to draw a map.

With the boy's help, he hoped to persuade the girl to sketch a drawing precise enough to navigate by. Without such a picture, he doubted if he could find Sleepy Lake and the log cabin secreted there. He judged the upcoming journey like trekking from Montana to Arizona or from the Dakotas to Texas. In any event, his history of wandering the Old West and his background of living off the land, as well, would be put to stiff tests. He had never weathered endless weeks of bitter cold and long, murky days, taking the awful gamble that a team of dogs could carry him so far.

"Doll Girl says she will stay in this house until

the second full wolf moon. That is the end of January. Then she will leave this place forever."

Eli stared into the girl's round, dark eyes. He pictured her marching off downriver, with her old dog Wahnie trotting alongside. Her stubbornness showed plainly on her face.

"Tell her I'll be back with her mother before then. Tell her she should now draw a map to the lake she wishes me to find. And write the names of the landmarks along the way. Do you understand what landmarks are, son?" He shifted his steady gaze to the young Gwich'in boy.

"I know about landmarks. I like to draw maps." The boy's eyes widened.

"Good—just be sure you draw all the details she describes. And let her add other things if she wishes. The two of you must make the best drawing you can."

Hannah brushed past with paper and pencil before he could reach for the items himself. Then her brow wrinkled. "Eli, where will you get all the things you need? The dogs and sleds ... the food? You've never mushed dogs before, and Peacock hasn't either! I wish there was a different way—"

"Now quit fretting—we'll be fine. Let's leave the children alone." He pushed her toward the kitchen.

After they had walked away, he added, "We'll drive the boy's dogs and sled to Fort Yukon. I won't leave that town until Jesse and I have purchased enough supplies and learned about mushing dogs. And I'll ask the boy's elders for advice. Remember, I've lived in winters for most of my life. You shouldn't worry so much!"

"I know . . . but everything has changed." Hannah's frowning eyes fell. "Our wedding day is gone—Christmas is spoiled. At least you have talked the girl into staying with me. I would have worried even more if you would have taken her along."

"Noodles said that he'll live here with you until I come back. He'll be good company for you and the girl. You've seen his antics before. That should make your lonely days pass more quickly."

Hannah's mouth curled up. "I'm glad. He's such an old devil, he'll keep me busy. And I'm sure Doll Girl will learn to love him as much as I do." Then her mouth turned down, and after pausing, she added. "Tell me you'll be careful. Tell me you'll come back to me soon."

Eli reached down and gripped her hands. "I'll be back before you know, safe and sound. Doll Girl's mother will be fine, too." Then he felt her hands tighten and her sad eyes search his own.

In rising gray light the next morning he jumped onto the dog sled's runners and grabbed the back handles. Then he watched Jesse Peacock and the Indian boy crawl on top of the sled's heavy load. Finally he shouted at the dogs.

Startled, disbelieving, he laughed about the dog's hard pace as the long team hurdled downriver toward Fort Yukon. As fast as a trotting horse, he thought, and good enough, perhaps, for as much as fifty miles a day. Then he listened to the noisy music of the dog's pounding paws, puffing breath, and the gnawing noises of the sled's runners sliding over the packed snow of the Yukon River, sounding like the low harmony for all the dog's drumming feet. Lastly he heard the boy's lonely Gwich'in calls echoing between the riverbanks, commanding the lead dog to swing left or right along the trail running downriver, packed down by other passing dogs and sleds.

Flat marshy lowlands, steep wooded hillsides, and distant white mountains lay heaped with all the winter's snowfall, looking waist-high where the winds couldn't blow. Trees, bushes, and grasses, poking above the snowpack, hung heavy with hoarfrost; and every twig and sprout lay coated in clear crystals stuck on by the frosting air.

Then low milky mists blew by as the day turned foggy, hiding everything in wintry scud that seemed wicked and deathless in its murky permanence. Finally an awful stillness settled down and stole away even the huffing breath of the dogs, the hard yells of the boy, and the sled's crunching clatter.

"How many days to Fort Yukon?" Jesse Peacock's shuddering voice broke the silent spell.

The boy turned backward on the sled to answer. "We will sleep four or five nights along the river. Then we will arrive at my home."

Eli contemplated the trip that lay ahead. "Son, will all the trails be as fine as this? If we move as fast every day, we'll get back to Dawson before long. I didn't know sled dogs could run so well."

"Father River always has nice trails. Indian people and mail sleds mush here many times all winter. Other rivers are not so good. Sometimes you will have to break trail, with snowshoes in deep snow. And you must watch out so you don't break through the snow and ice and get wet. You will die unless you can build a big fire fast."

"How do you know where the bad ice is?" Peacock clutched his neck scarf tightly with his lone mitten.

The youngster squinted his eyes. "My father taps with a dry willow stick—listens to the whispers of the river. He watches for the overflow and stays far away from where the beavers live. He knows where the water runs the fastest under the ice and never walks there. You should watch the dogs, too, they know—"

"What's overflow?" Jesse's mitten flew up to his throat once more.

"Water runs on top of the ice but hides under the snow. Very bad! Your feet freeze, dog's feet freeze, sled runners ice up. You must get away fast."

When the boy answered Peacock's question, Eli measured his memories of the wintertime dangers he had faced back in the Old West. High winds, deep snow, and chilling temperatures had been awful hazards he had weathered often. But he hadn't fought off thin ice, overflows, and darkened days before. Nonetheless, winter in the Dakota and Montana territories had been hellish. He felt he could survive the North . . . but he would speak with the boy's great-grandfather soon. The old medicine man might offer useful advice about survival in Alaska.

Suddenly the boy called for the dog team to slow down. Then he yelled, "Mr. Bonnet, you and Mr. Peacock get off the sled and run behind. You must not get colder. When we get to Fort Yukon my people will give you better coats. The ones you wear are very bad. Look—see where the wind blows in around the buttons! You must dress like Gwich'in people or you will freeze to death. Remember the snow spirits will hunt you every day. Only Indian ways will keep you alive."

Eli stepped off the runners and eyed the boy's long pullover parka, hanging knee-length, fringed with fur on the top and bottom and belted with a braided blue sash around the waist. All the boy's clothing made sense: furs and wool, no frontal openings for the cold air to blow through, big stuffed moose-hide boots reaching up to his knees, heavy beaver mittens. Everything seemed appropriate for the iciness hanging over the river.

"Son, by the chilliness I feel already, your mighty winter spirits are after me now!" Then he shivered a little for emphasis. He thought the boy yet looked warm, unlike the dead paleness of Jesse Peacock.

"We will wrap you and Mr. Peacock with caribou hides. Then you will stay warm until we reach my father's home."

Then the boy swung from the sled's load down onto the runners of the dog sled. He whistled the dogs back to their hard trot again, adding afterward, "Run until you get warm, but don't let yourself sweat. If you get damp, you will get even colder."

"Aren't you getting off?" Jesse Peacock's voice puffed through his panting as he jogged to keep up.

"Never let the dogs run without someone driving the sled. If the team sees a moose or wolf, they will run away. You must always hold on tight! If you lose the dogs—big trouble, very dangerous!

Eli eyed the boy again, but for a longer moment than before. Perhaps, he mused, there wouldn't be quite so much to learn from the ancient shaman in Fort Yukon after all. The boy seemed wilderness-wise as well. Instantly he envied the boy's father. How proud, he wondered, must a man feel when he sees his own flesh and blood behave as wisely as the boy had just acted?

Then he couldn't resist—he felt compelled to ask. "Son, what have you decided about your future? Have you thought about your life ahead?"

The boy turned his head and peered rearward. After a moment, he answered, "I will listen to my heart as I grow older. The spirits will decide what to make of me."

Eli blinked. Could such words have come from a mere child, he wondered? Glimpsing Jesse Peacock's surprised face, he then wondered about the boy's uncommon wisdom.

They started a campfire alongside the river when the evening settled down. Hurrying against the smother of nightfall, they fed their dogs, sawed heaps of firewood, and carried fat armloads of spruce boughs to insulate the ground under their tent. Two hours slipped by before the campsite lay ready for the long, cold night.

Then Eli squatted in front of their fire, cooking their supper over the hot orange coals. They had to eat well, he thought. Full bellies meant warm bodies all night. And the northern nights felt much colder than any he had ever weathered before. The awful iciness never seemed to let go, whether one toiled in the daytime or dark. He saw the deadly cold as the greatest hazard of all in the great wilderness they intended to cross. Alaska's winter climate would murder them in a minute, if the cruel conditions ever got the chance.

At noontime during their third day on the river, hard winds suddenly whipped snow back and forth, stinging everyone's faces. Then dark clouds rolled in just overhead.

Hastily, the boy hollered, "We must get off the river and hide ourselves!" Next he pointed to a thicket of green spruce trees standing a little ways from the shoreline.

Eli eyed the storm, peering into the icy gusts. Cupping his mouth with his mittens, he yelled back, "Can't we run a bit longer—get farther downriver before we quit?"

"No. See how the dogs drag their tails. Look at their faces. We must let them rest. Father Winter is angry. We should camp till he sleeps once more."

Leading the way on his snowshoes, the boy

tramped deep inside the spruce woods. Eli followed close behind, astonished by the snug shelter the tall evergreens provided against the roaring blizzard on the river. He then saw the dogs lift their tails and shake off all the snow that had stuck to their furry faces and flanks. The team's quick perkiness reminded him of the pack animals he had used in the Old West. Animals often communicated, he thought, with brightened eyes or wagging tails. He sensed the team felt grateful for being led out of the storm.

The boy hollered again, "Let me show you the best way to camp. We will sleep like Indian hunters tonight."

Once they had bedded the dog team, the boy showed Eli and Jesse Peacock how to build a lean-to with spruce boughs hung over a pole frame, sealed off on three sides but open on the front. Then he helped them bark logs and erect a wall as a shiny reflector that beamed their night fire's heat back into the lean-to. Eli marveled at the comfort of the simple campsite, supplied by the cover of the spreading trees, the heavy boughs they had piled all around, and the leaping flames of their fire.

"Son, the weather sounds bad up above, but we're like beetle bugs down here. I've learned important things from you in the past few days." He then watched Peacock grin happily while he scooped snow into the coffeepot. His crippled companion looked cheerful, warm, and calm for the first time on the trip.

The boy smiled and crawled into the lean-to. "Now it will be easy to throw wood on the fire tonight. We'll sleep with caribou hides and stay warm till morning."

By early dawn low winds sighed through the treetops, rather than the high gales of the night before. Eli roused, woke Peacock and the boy, and broke trail out to the river's channel. Turning down the wide course once more, he shouted for the dogs to pull, then watched as the team lined out for Fort Yukon. The dogs seemed to smell their home's closeness. Their prancing paws and flipping tails danced as they raced through the just fallen snow.

They mushed into the old trading town on the fifth day under sunset skies with purple clouds and ocher light streaking the skyline to the west. Lazy smoke, smelling woody, hung over the middle of the settlement and fogged the log cabins, the clapboard trading post, and the unpainted church, which stood on the river's shore.

When Eli wheeled the sled dogs around, he saw dark human shapes tumble from every building. Then he heard Indian women, children, grown men, and teenagers welcome the Gwich'in boy back. All the other dogs tied around the town burst into howls, their hard wails adding to the commotion brought on by the homecoming. At last, after eager hugs and handshaking between the boy and his people, the curious and friendly villagers began to drift away.

"My father's grandfather sends for you. He says

you are to stay with him until he sees your heart is brave. Mr. Peacock will sleep in my father's home. I will show you both places now." The boy turned to lead the way.

"Can't I stay with Eli—ain't there room for me?" Jesse Peacock's face wrenched into wrinkles.

"No, you will be happy in my father's home. There will be good food and a warm place to sleep. The old one wants Mr. Bonnet to come alone."

"Will your great-granddaddy give us the dogs and supplies we need? Jesse and I would like to leave tomorrow or the day after. We'll be rested by then."

"The old one says he will sing to the spirits tonight. Then he will decide how to help. I will be there so you can understand his words."

Eli followed the young boy. More years than he wanted to remember had passed by since he had last sat in ceremony, listening to the chants and songs and visions of a medicine man. Trance talking and hypnosis of one's own mind seemed ungodly—the evil magic of the shadows in the human mind, he mused. But time after time he had seen Indian rituals work. And their odd seances were no more peculiar than the water witching, or the many other folk remedies he had seen used by frontiersmen all across the Old West.

After he and the boy had sheltered Peacock for the night, they walked to a snow-covered dugout on the south side of the old littered village. Eli ducked down into the low door of the den and crawled inside the bright center. Even though he

saw no fire, just flickering candles, he felt warm
dry air on his face and hands. The ancient shaman
sat across from him in the round room: withered
and brown, like dried wood or prairie soil, naked
to his waist, glistening with grease. Yellowed
ivory hair dropped straight from the sage's skull,
hung shoulder length, and edged his dark gleaming eyes, seemingly not aged like the rest of his
body.

The medicine man threw his arms high and
wide, showing his welcome. Eli had seen Sioux,
Blackfeet, and Cheyenne people sign the same
way with their hands and arms before. Then the
lean fingers of the shaman signaled to undress, sit
down, and eat the stew in the pot sitting nearby.

The boy squirmed past and sat on the other side
of the room. Then the youngster pointed to several
blankets woven from white rabbit hides. "The old
one is glad to see us. You will sleep over there
after you have heard his wisdom."

"Tell your great-granddaddy my heart and eyes
are happy. His land has been kind to me . . . and
I have thought of him many times. Tell him I am
ready to listen to his wishes. The time has come
to repay his gifts."

He listened to the boy murmur Athabaskan dialect. Then he watched the aged prophet answer
back, using his bony hands and arms to decorate
his speech.

"My chief says he has seen the sadness of his little
sister Doll Girl, whose home is alongside the great
sacred mountain worshiped by his Koyukon broth-

ers. A white man is responsible for her unhappiness. He wonders if you are brave enough to find this man and take him away from Alaska forever? More of our people will suffer and die if this is not done. He remembers you telling him about capturing bad people in a land far south of here. He wonders if you will go hunting once more?"

"I will be glad to visit the country of his brothers. Tell him I will catch this white man and send him to a ship made of iron, floating on the bitter waters at the end of the long river we now sit beside. I ask only for the sled, dogs, and wisdom I will need for my journey."

After talking with his great grandfather again, the boy asked, "He wonders why you have brought the one-armed man with you? He says your friend is unwell. And he asks why you didn't bring the sacred wolf dog he gave you for your protection during your travels across our land?"

As Eli thought back, he wondered why he *had* left his dog behind. Ironclaw had just seemed too young to come along. And he had hoped kenneling him with Wahnie would convey the calm habits of the grayed leader. But he did miss him and judged the old shaman felt very disappointed.

"He is back with the woman I live with in Dawson City. He is still learning to be helpful. He is too young—" Eli suddenly recalled his Sioux spirit jacket. "But the boy has returned my old medicine coat that I wore for so long! When I wear my coat, my mind and body stays strong. Its powerful spirits have protected me many times."

During his years of riding the western frontier as a U.S. Marshal, he had worn the Sioux's holiest symbol nearly every day. His life had become mixed completely with its sacred charms and storied good luck, as he liked to describe the coat's powers. He had found himself silently persuaded about its magic through the years. But more than one person had accused him of silly superstitions. Nonetheless, he had simply ignored the disapproval, smiled, and kept his lucky coat close by.

"Great-grandfather still wonders about the man you have brought with you. He remembers him from the past—when our trees turned yellow and our mountain tops turned white. Your friend is the man who cried out at night and spent his days watching the river for no one."

"Jesse Peacock has my promise to help him capture the murderer he lost when the steamboat called the *Victorian* anchored here last fall. We think the white man who kidnapped Doll Girl's mother may be this same evil person. Perhaps our work to catch this killer will help heal my friend."

The boy spoke with the ancient shaman again. Turning back, he interpreted, "The darkness and coldness of our land in the wintertime will not make him better. The old one says you should sleep with your weapons and wear your spirit coat always."

Stunned, Eli stared into the medicine man's black eyes. He hadn't expected such a blunt, harsh warning. After pausing for a moment, he answered, "I have grown much older because I have watched my friends as carefully as I've watched my enemies. Because I have hunted men for most of my life, my eyes are not always shut when I sleep. Tell your great-granddaddy I thank him for his advice."

Then Eli saw the old medicine man appear to understand his answer even before the boy had finished explaining its meaning. Suddenly the bony and withered sage burst into a rattling chatter aimed toward him again.

Solemnly, quietly, the Gwich'in youth translated, "You will find one long sled and eleven dogs waiting on Father River in the morning. There will be food, all the things you need for your journey to the great mountain. The old one says you are to sleep now. He and I will pray for you all night. You will wake up in the morning and feel wise and strong. But do not forget his warnings."

Eli looked into the shaman's gleaming eyes again. He nodded, smiled, and crawled under the white rabbit blankets. As he settled into the fleecy bed, he heard the boy begin to sing and chant in rhythm with his great-grandfather. Then odd clicks from bits of bone, red pebbles, carved wood sticks, and face masks filled the dugout, along with the noisy human sounds. Finally he watched the old shaman take a primitive hand ax chipped from glassy green gemstone, an obsidian knife, and the mummified remains of flesh and hair from a brown leather sack. He wondered . . .

CHAPTER FIVE

Desperation

Waking at last, Eli opened his eyes and listened for human sounds in the inky silence. Hearing none, puzzled, he fished a wooden match from his trouser pocket and popped it with his thumbnail. Murky light danced on the dugout's walls as the white fire flared from the redheaded tip of the match. He found a candle snuffed out during the night, touched it with his tiny flame, and crawled to the center of the den's hollow. Then he saw the ancient shaman who had sung to him the evening before curled up in a corner, sleeping. The old man lay covered in furs, with only his wrinkled head poking out.

Glancing around but not seeing the boy, he found his coat and cap and then crept out of the dugout's tunnel, into the low gray light. The town, mostly unpainted and ramshackle, lay between him and the snow-covered sweep of the Yukon River. Wandering footpaths, beaten down in the snow, ran helter-skelter between the log cabins, clapboard shacks, and drowsy evergreens standing around the town. Muffled household noises resounded inside the settlement's buildings as he walked along. And the village's dogs yawned and eyed him peacefully as he looked for the cabin where Jesse Peacock had stayed the night before.

"Eli, Eli, down here!" Jesse's holler drifted across the wintertime, like the sleepy smoke that trailed from the town's chimneys sticking up all around.

He saw his companion standing alongside a loaded sled and string of dogs down on the river's edge. Turning, he tramped straight toward Jesse and the sled.

Peacock yelled louder, "We're all ready to go! The boy said you'd wake up shortly. Look! we've got an ax, wood saw, snowshoes, caribou hides, food, new winter parkas, lots of equipment. I've stored your Winchester rifle and the rest of your outfit. We're all set!"

"Did you see who loaded this . . ." Eli walked around the heavy sled, wondering about the pile of supplies. Someone had spent many hours, he judged, sorting and packing the provisions for their forthcoming journey.

"I don't know—ain't it something! The boy came back home, woke me up, said to come down here and wait for you. He told me that you would sleep a little more, then you'd want to leave. And he said to tell you not to say good-bye. He and the old medicine man would see you when you get back."

Reminded of the wild chants and songs he had heard during the night, Eli wondered if the primitive ceremony had mesmerized him once more. Whenever he had fallen in with medicine men back in the Old West, he had come away similarly mystified over the effects of the odd-sounding syllables and the steady rattle of the sacred pieces. Somehow the ancient rituals always put him to sleep. And the heavy sleep always rested him completely, leaving him strengthened and ready for his life ahead, just as the shamans forever foretold.

Then he wondered about his companion's fitness. "Are you ready to go, Jesse? We'll have to work long and hard to survive this trip. I want to be certain you feel well ... that you understand what you're facing. We have to cross a thousand miles of wilderness each way. I don't want you to feel you are obliged to come along."

Peacock frowned and wiggled the crippled stub of his arm. "Eli, I feel fine. You said last fall we'd catch the Cannibal together. You promised! What's the use of me sitting in this town or back in Dawson City while you do all the dangerous work? It's my fault the man escaped in the first place. I want to help get him back."

The sharp warnings of Hannah and the ancient shaman flashed back into his mind. His past pledge to Jesse Peacock stood in conflict with the deep worries raised in alarm over his friend's uncommon behavior. But duty whispered and he would follow its call. He would choose to keep his promises. He had done so all his life.

He swung the dog team down the Yukon River,

calling out the Indian words he had learned from the boy. Jesse Peacock jogged in back of the sled, following with choppy, short strides. Keeping the dogs slowed to an easy pace, they traded places from time to time—Jesse struggling to hold on with only one hand. Sometimes they worked side by side, when traversing deep snow, both pushing and pulling on the sled's wooden frame. Afterward, on smooth, fast surfaces, they rode on the sled together, standing on the runners and sitting astride the heavy load, watching as the eleven dogs trotted along.

The Yukon reached ahead in wide sweeps mile after endless mile. When they gazed off toward the far horizons the white tundra stretched out in boundless distances, darkened here and there with black thickets of bushes and trees. Later they found themselves frustrated, seeing riverbanks they had just passed, finding only narrow points of snowy willows and marsh grasses lying in between each turn. They learned cutting across the corners was exhausting. The old traces of trails showed the river's surface was the best road, despite all the extra miles.

At night they camped behind windbreaks and near firewood, hunkered with their sled dogs circled around. After supper they rested quietly in their tent, wishing for tall timber, hoping to get past the wasteland that seemed to grip them forever.

Peacock's voice crept across the tent one night as they lay bundled in their hides and blankets,

"How far, Eli, how far do you think we got to go?"

"We'll get there soon. Don't you remember the distances from your riverboat journey last summer?" Eli then wondered if Jesse had slipped into another depression, brought on by the hardship of looping through faceless lands day after day.

"No, not anymore. The boat seemed faster ... and I could see mountains from the top deck. I remember tall mountains far off. I could see them with my field glasses."

"Jesse, they're still out there, but it's wintertime now. We've had so little daylight and clear weather, you've just missed seeing them."

After a long pause, Jesse asked, "Eli, what if it isn't the Cannibal? What if it's another man?"

Annoyed, Eli rethought his answer several times. What difference did it make? Had his companion slipped so far into deep despair that he had lost his common sense? Whoever had kidnapped Doll Girl's mother needed capture and prosecution. What was Jesse's thinking, he wondered?

Finally he said, "Jesse, even if it's not the Cannibal, we still need to arrest the man. Try to sleep now." Then he listened as Peacock tossed and turned in his blankets, sighing repeatedly in the night.

Two days later they sledded onto long passages of frozen river running between low mountains on each side. Green forests of spruce ran up the steep sides of the heights, providing snug wind-

breaks and plentiful firewood for every camp.
Two mail sleds came by, pausing for a moment
to tell Eli about the open trail all the way to the
Tanana River. Afterward, the government mushers raced off in the opposite direction with their
speeding dogs.

Jesse Peacock began to smile again and his stub
arm appeared to twitch a little less. Then Eli
stalked and killed a fat moose near the river with
a single shot from his rifle. The fresh meat lifted
Jesse's spirits even more and filled everyone's
belly for a change, even the dogs'.

Swinging east in a gray misty dawn, they trotted up the Tanana River, admiring the distant rolling woodlands. Wide, straight river channels
stretched ahead, and they found the mouth of the
Kantishna River in three days, the small island
hiding its opening just as Doll Girl had drawn on
her map. Then they had sledded back and forth
again, around countless corners lying beside
grassy swamps covered over with deep snow that
slowed their pace.

Finally the dead wintry bleakness that had hung
overhead for more than a week disappeared. At
last the great mountain they had talked about for
so long unwrapped from the thick cloudiness.
They stopped and glassed the sacred summit for
an hour, standing spellbound as they contemplated the topmost parts. Denali Mountain stood
south on the compass from their position, soaring
up into the blue skies, just uncovered by the rising winds.

They stood silently and stared in disbelief, their faces tipped up. Could it be true, they wondered, that such a wonderful height existed? Eli had seen high peaks before in the Montana Territory, but this mountain looked two times higher than any mountain he had seen in his past. Even if his expedition failed, he thought, he would treasure the moment for the rest of his life. No other summit had amazed him so.

"Eli, how high do you think it stands?" Peacock steadied himself by clapping his lone hand on the sled.

"I've seen several mountains two miles high, this one looks twice that tall. Even the tops of the other mountains standing alongside are higher than any peak that I have ever heard described by other men. I have a feeling we're looking at the tallest mountain in North America."

"What do you think they'll name it?" Jesse continued to gaze steadily at Denali.

Peacock's question sounded silly to Eli at first but then seemed sensible when he remembered the history of the Old West. Finally he answered, "It has been called Denali by the Indians since the beginning of time. But I suppose some godless politician looking for favors will rename it for some corrupt president who's done no good and hasn't the decency or loyalty to live on this land. The poor Indians that love the mountain so much will be forced off to one side. They won't be given the chance to say a word about the mountain.

Then I have the notion the summit will be spoiled, not left holy like their mighty spirits wish."

"You sound bitter, Eli! What's the difference to you? You crying about the Old West again?"

"Jesse, I've seen one great wilderness plowed under and fenced off by barbed wire. That's plenty for me forever. It's my wish to finish my life in a land where the country doesn't get shot off, cut down, fed to cows, and in general, wasted by the people. Let's leave this land lonely for the old pilgrims like me."

Jesse Peacock dropped his eyes and peered at Eli. Then he opened his mouth to reply, but swallowed and looked back up at the great mountain before them.

A minute afterward, Eli, without speaking again to Peacock, whistled to the team and mushed ahead once more. He meandered slowly back and forth along the river's course, watching the shorelines cautiously. Finally, after two hours of searching, he stopped the dog sled and pointed at the river's shore.

"This is the place where Doll Girl came down onto the ice. See how the recent snows are furrowed low over the tramped-down trail. I am certain these old footprints are snowshoe tracks she left behind!"

"It look to me like an animal did it . . . maybe a moose or some animal like that."

"No. Wild critters wander from side to side, looking for food. Look how this trail runs southwesterly. Straight lines are human tracks. And look—this shoreline appears to be the same as her drawing shows." Eli pulled off his beaver mittens and pointed to the map that he had removed from his parka pocket.

"I guess it looks like the same spot. What now?"

"I need to break trail on my snowshoes to help the dogs uphill. You stay behind the sled—push as hard as you can. Let's go slow. We have a heavy load and the snow runs deep. I want to watch up front, too. I've got to find the first camp Doll Girl marked on her map. Then we can rest awhile and figure out how I can sneak up on Red Shirt's cabin without anyone hearing me till I'm at the door!"

Two more days slipped by as they fought up the scorched hillsides that Doll Girl had sketched in her drawings. Finally Eli found slashed trapline trails coursing through the trees. But then he missed seeing the little trapper's hut on their first southerly pass down the trail. They turned around, backtracked, and eventually found the crude camp hidden back in spruce trees where they hadn't searched before. At last, Eli thought, they lay close to Sleepy Lake, and, more pleasing, under a roof and next to a stove and sturdy walls that would keep out the cold winter winds.

"Eli, how close are we now? Can we get to Sleepy Lake tomorrow?" Peacock's stub arm jerked. His excitement blushed plainly across his weatherbeaten face.

"I think about forty miles. There's one more camp like this . . . then comes Sleepy Lake. I plan to use the dogs until I'm about five miles away, then I'll walk. If there's other dogs nearby and we get too close, our sounds and scent will warn them. I have to get the wind and trees in my favor before I sneak up for a look."

"I hadn't thought about the other dogs! How will we get near enough to catch the man without him knowing we're after him?"

"I'll wait till I have the wind and weather to hide me. Most men will step outside to see what's wrong with their dogs when they first start barking. If I crawl within one hundred paces, I'll have the chance to knock him down with my rifle if he attempts to jump back into the cabin."

"Don't kill him! I want to take him to San Francisco alive!"

"I won't if I can help not to . . . but I can't let him get back into the cabin. If he hides inside, he'll hold us off for a month and freeze and starve us to death. When I yell—if he doesn't stand still—I intend to wound him with my Winchester." Eli pinched his winter-cracked lips and rubbed both of them with salve from his medical kit.

Jesse Peacock paused, then blinked his eyes. "At least shoot him the same way as you shot the other outlaws back in the old days. You shot those fellows in the leg. But you know what I think about your idea of frontier justice!"

Eli recalled the stiff prejudices that he and Jesse had argued about during their long years of working together as U.S. Marshals. Peacock had mostly filled supervisory posts in large towns, while Eli had ridden the prairies and mountains of the Dakota and Montana territories as an ordinary deputy marshal. Jesse hadn't been shot at after he had served in the Civil War. Eli remembered that he had been stabbed and shot several times while on duty. Now whenever an arrest went wrong, he was quick to shoot the troublemaker in the knee. That stopped the dangerous behavior instantly— and tended to stop the man's wrongdoing forever. One-legged cripples weren't competent crooks and mostly found honest work after serving their prison time.

But Peacock had fought against Eli's quick and cruel justice throughout the years. The federal courts had intervened as well. Young, merciful judges began to insist on the same compassion Jesse had preached so often. Eli had sensed the times changing as everyone neared the new century.

Finally, after frowning, he said, "You've never worked in the wilds before. Neither one of us has ever crossed a thousand miles of Alaska with sled dogs to make an arrest. I see the importance of you trusting me fully, following what I say without any of our old quarrels. If we make any mistakes out here in the wilderness, our lives will likely be lost for good. This country is like none other. There's no help for us if we get unlucky or foolish in our ways. Please don't be offended— but I will do what I must regardless of your feelings. But only because I know I can save us, not because of any disrespect for you."

Jesse Peacock blinked again. "I guess I can't find fault with that, Eli. All I want is to catch the Cannibal and get back to California like I should've last fall."

"Jesse, the man we're after may not be the Cannibal. We have no idea who he might be. I don't want you heartbroken if we catch someone else. Our duty is to apply the law—"

"I know about my duty. I simply think it's him. You don't have to preach."

"Jesse . . . I'm sorry to have sounded that way. My desire was to get us ready for our dangerous work ahead, not to make you angry. Let's cook our supper and get our rest. We'll need plenty of it for tomorrow." Turning, he then threw firewood into the small stove that sat in the corner of the log hut.

In the coming morning light, Eli roused and harnessed the eleven dogs once more, Peacock helping him by dragging each sled dog over from its tiedown with his one good arm. When the sky and snow yielded enough light to navigate by, he swung the team again onto the trapline pathway heading south and picked through the tangle of assorted trails scattered around the thick woods. Then, after nightfall had begun to settle down in the afternoon, they found the last trapper's hut, the first camp Doll Girl had said she had used during her escape.

"Jesse, if you're strong enough, I want to rest

here for a little while and mush over to Sleepy Lake and take a look yet tonight. We've got a white moon rising—there will be good light to see by later. And the cabin's bright windows should help me find the place faster than in the day."

"I'm fine—let's keep going. Maybe we can be heading back by this time tomorrow. I'd like that!"

"I think that's unlikely . . . but, with good luck, we should know the hazards we face for the next day or two."

Several hours later, just after glimpsing the lake's silvery surface ahead in the moonlight, Eli stopped the dogs and kindled a small campfire behind a line of trees. Leaving Jesse on guard, he crept down the snow-covered path leading onto the lake from the north. He saw that a foot of snow had fallen since Doll Girl's departure, but the crisscross of the old trails on the lake's surface still showed plainly in the night. Keeping hidden beside the shadowed shorelines, he waded ahead through the deep snow, glassing with his binoculars, complaining silently about the fog and frost that had to be rubbed off the lens every few moments.

At last he identified the cabin's dark shape off in the distance, sitting centered in a clearing out of the woods, along the shore of a small backwater. Creeping closer, he searched the clearing all around the log structure. Lastly he glassed the chimney pipe on the cabin's roof. Slowly, begrudgingly, he concluded no one had lived in the cabin for a long time. Snowdrifts lay frozen against the black smoke pipe.

He tramped straight to the cabin and pulled open the door. Scratching a match, he then stepped warily into the interior through the low woodshed door. He struck another match, found a candle, and quickly glanced around. Frosty furniture, empty shelves, and musty rags lay scattered about the inside. He walked back out and stood under the bright moon. Sensing gloomy emptiness everywhere outside the walls of the structure, he turned back toward Jesse Peacock and the dogs.

"Jesse, there's no one in the cabin. It's been empty for a long time." He watched Peacock jump up in the firelight, his dark eyes rounded.

"Guess I knew my luck would stay bad! Seems things are always against me!" Jesse stared sadly into the dancing yellow flames.

"Let's look on the bright side—we've found a nice cabin for ourselves. Tomorrow we'll find the trail the kidnapper used for his getaway. I've hunted men for most of my life. It's foolish to hope that outlaws will stand still for very long. I think it makes perfect sense that the fellow would leave for unknown places."

"Eli, haven't you looked where we're at? Why do you think we can find anything in this god-awful country? Don't you ever quit wishing for good luck?"

Eli kicked snow over the campfire to kill the flames. Standing silently for a moment, he thought about Jesse's outburst of disappointment. Then, strangely, he felt his Sioux spirit coat under his parka. Turning toward the dogs, he called, "Jesse, quit your complaints and let's get over to the cabin. You forgot, I'm wearing my old good luck charm. Besides, you fret too much! Haven't I always caught the man you sent me after in the past?"

Then he heard Peacock muttering to himself back in the blackness. Ignoring the grumbles, he loosened the anchor rope of the sled and shouted for the dogs to stand up. Before Jesse could catch him, he drove the dogs down to the lake and straight toward the cabin. He thought it would be good for Jesse to tire himself chasing behind on the back trail. Then perhaps his companion would sleep for a change, rather than tossing and turning, like during many of the nighttimes before.

They stayed in the cabin all the next day, resting themselves and the dogs. Eli repaired the sled's damage from its rough travel, then mended their clothing, ripped from brushing by trees so often. As they walked around the one room, tending the cookstove and their bubbling stewpot, they found the home emptied of all the common household items. Then Eli fond the cache standing outside stripped of food and equipment as well. Only a few beaver and martin pelts hung on one side of the small storage room, along with scraps of cloth and canvas strewn on the floor. Puzzled, he stepped back down the cache's ladder, which he found thrown carelessly on the snow when he had first come out.

"Jesse, we have only learned half of the things we need to know. There's a hundred dollars worth of furs up in the cache. Why would an outlaw leave valuable hides behind?" Eli shook his head and hung his parka on the cabin's wall.

"He's taken everything else—funny he didn't burn the place down, too!" Peacock answered from the shadows of the room.

"I've wondered about that as well. Maybe he's planning to come back . . . which would mean he's not far off."

"Like I said last night, what difference does it make? How we going to find somebody around here? Sometimes I can't bear to think where I am. I've never been so lonesome like this, ever."

Eli studied Jesse Peacock. He had seen men before fresh from the populated places, suddenly thrust into the wilderness for the first time. And he'd seen the isolation of the uninhabited wilds chew up those men, swallow their lonely souls until they went crazy. Jesse didn't look well with his head and widened eyes shifting back and forth in peculiar ways.

"Jesse, I'm here . . . don't feel so alone. Let's work as friends and figure out how to find this fellow. Think in sensible ways, don't get discouraged. The man we're looking for is close. I can feel it in my bones."

"You think so. No . . . can't be—"

"I'm certain of it. Listen, why would he carry

off all the cabin's comforts if he meant only to inflict injury and run away when he was done? Why would he leave this cabin standing and not burnt down like you've said? It seems Doll Girl's mother has been kept alive for some purpose, and this cabin left standing for another reason. And why would he leave the furs behind, unless he meant to steal something more valuable?"

Suddenly Peacock's face shone in the candle-light's glow in the center of the room. He jumped to his feet and rushed forward, crying, "There's only one thing worth more than furs in this country—that's gold. There ain't nothing up in Alaska but for those two things. The Cannibal is looking for gold."

"You've thought the same as I, Jesse. But why do you think he would move away in the middle of winter? And, remember, no one can dig for gold until summertime, a long time yet. Tell me why he's moved away."

Peacock's face frowned and he shuffled his feet on the floor. Then he brightened again and answered, "He's afraid Doll Girl made it out and will send her people back. He's hiding in some other place until he can find what he's come after. The mother knows where it is!"

"If you think about three more things, you'll see he can't have sledded south over the top of Denali Mountain. We've already learned he couldn't have run north along the rivers we've traveled ourselves. That leaves east or west. I say we search west for a while."

In the morning they closed the cabin and sledded off, Peacock driving the dogs, Eli breaking
trail and tracking an old trail leading west. Picking
through the timbered uplands under Denali's
shadow, he steered toward the higher slopes,
windswept and thinly covered with dwarf spruce
and alder stands. Reaching the open country
above the timberline at last, he slowed and
flanked the steepness of the lower mountains
fronting the higher peaks beyond.

He rested Jesse and the dogs from time to time
and climbed to the topmost parts of the highlands,
glassing for any sign of human life. He had seen
the faint traces of an old sled trail disappear miles
back, worn away long ago by sweeping winds out
of the north. He searched with his field glasses for
curling gray smoke or black specks looking odd
against the snowy land, standing quietly until he
couldn't bear his freezing feet and fingers any
longer. Then he would jog back down and shuffle
off on his snowshoes once more, searching ahead
for the next horizon to explore.

Up on his third lookout he heard queer rumbling sounds. Clicking, thumping noises ebbed
through the hillsides that surrounded him, muffled a little by the rocky outcrops and deep hollows that dropped off to the lowlands he had just
come up from earlier. He twisted his head back
and forth, wondering what the commotion could
be. Then suddenly he saw the danger race by.
Caribou! Hundreds were running past, bouncing
over the snow with their long, stiff legs. He

whipped around and yelled at Jesse Peacock, screaming to stop the dog team and kicked the sled's anchor hook deeper into the snow. But, in an instant, he saw Jesse had moved away from the sled. He saw his friend standing dumbstruck, swinging his head back and forth also, peering at all the animals racing by.

To his horror, Eli saw the dogs bolt after the stampeding herd, tearing away at full speed. Lifting his binoculars for the last time, he watched the dog team run out of reach.

When he reached the bottom of the hill, Peacock lay sobbing, curled up on the snow.

"Eli, I didn't mean to let the dogs loose. I didn't know the caribou were coming."

"I think you've just killed us, Jesse." Then Eli gazed at the last caribou prancing by, ruining the trail left by the dogs and sled, fatally ending any chance to track their supplies down.

Finally, after a long pause, he added, "I won't give up my life easily . . . your life either . . . but this is the most trouble I've ever faced. We've lost everything—our food, tent, my rifle—"

"Can't we just go find the sled? The dogs can't be too far off."

"I watched the dogs run for miles. There's no way to catch them. If we try, we'll die tonight on these mountains. There's no wood—no way to warm ourselves. We've got to get down to the trees and back to Red Shirt's cabin as fast as we can. Our back trail will be frozen hard before long, so we'll be able to walk without the snowshoes. I know we can make it that far. Then we'll have to decide what to do afterward.''

"We can live in the cabin fine, can't we? Once we get there, we can be warm then."

"Yes, that's true, Jesse, but there's no food. No food anywhere. We're caught in the middle of hungry times in a winter wilderness. What shall we eat to stay alive? We need lots of food to stay healthy in this cold. But my rifle is lost, our ax, everything I need to sustain our lives. Jesse, I'm more afraid than I've ever been in my life."

Peacock rolled over on the snow. Suddenly he screamed, muffled a little by the sole mittened hand held over his mouth. Then awful sobs crept out only to be snatched away by the hard winds that blew by the slope.

Eli stood still, feeling sorry and angry at the same time, yet searching inside himself for the toughness to march away, instead of just slipping into the same despair as Jesse Peacock. Time to start back, he thought. But he couldn't feel the willpower to fight.

PART II

—◆—✦◈✦—◆—

Starvation

CHAPTER SIX

Blueberry

Billy House wasn't fat anymore. His shape had thinned to bone and muscle, no softness anywhere. His name had changed as well. Now his two companions called him Blueberry, but not with the affection of earlier times. As he stood on the Tanana River, looking upstream and downstream, he imagined the name calling would grow worse. He and his friends were starving to death.

"There's been somebody come along here a while back, but they're headin' to that big mountain we keep seein' when it gets sunny." Billy hung his head over the old sled track, marking the snow and ice. He had trapped and hunted in northern Minnesota as a boy—he knew the signs.

"God, we gotta find somebody to help us! We gonna die if we don't!" answered Horace Fincher, his voice bawling. Horace had been on the edge of a breakdown since leaving the Nabesna River.

"Finch, you got to hang on. We're on the Tanana now. It can't be that far to the Yukon River. Once we get there, I know folks are livin' close. They'll have food for us!" Then Billy wondered why his conscience still bothered him when he lied. But it seemed crucial to keep his friends moving, even though he had no perception of the remaining distance.

Oliver Twait's voice joined in, low and mean. "You been tellin' us there'd be somebody to help when we got this far. I ain't goin' no more. You been wrong all the way!"

"Ollie, don't give up. If we stay here, we'll starve for sure. Get up an' let's keep goin' downriver. We've got to get down to the Yukon."

"I ain't movin' no more. This is your fault— ever' bit. We shouldn't have listened to you from the first. I say stay an' wait right here. Hell—Finch can't walk good anyways, his feet is froze."

Billy knew Oliver Twait's diagnosis of Finch's feet described the man's ailment exactly. And scurvy sickened his friend as well. All three of them had suffered daily from the creeping killer, and the disease would murder them soon if they didn't find fresh food. He had grown up working in his father's little pharmacy in Deer River, Minnesota. He recalled seeing plenty of frostbite and sickness back there.

The three of them had joined the gold stampede to the Klondike in January of 1898, each bent on getting rich in Alaska's gold fields. Their original troubles had started when they had found themselves mired in mud, standing awestruck at the foot of the Valdez Glacier, near the port by the identical name. Day after day, foot by foot, they had climbed the steep ice with their sled loads, until at last they had stood on top, five thousand feet above the tidewaters of Prince William Sound. He would never forget, he thought, that wonderful view for the rest of his life, whether he died with Finch and Twait in a few days, or died of old age, after finding better luck. The sight of the distant blue water, countless green islands, and rugged white mountains had been the most beauty he had ever seen.

But on the way across the unmerciful steep glacier, six unlucky stampeders had ruined his cheer. One moment a new friend had been pulling his sled alongside, the next instant the poor fellow was gone forever, having fallen into a crevice hidden beneath the snow. He still shivered when he thought of the deaths. But now it seemed a better way to die than the agony on hand. He and his two friends couldn't stay alive much longer, unless they found fresh meat and fruits to eat. And finding fruit to fight their black scurvy had been the reason behind his nickname. He had become expert at locating berries beneath the snowfall. The frozen little balls had kept them going, although nearly slowed to a crawl.

He stared back at Oliver Twait and thought about how he could inspire the man to keep on. Finch would die first, Ollie next, then himself, if he didn't think of a way to find help. Perhaps if he let the two men rest overnight by a fire, maybe if he shot a rabbit or squirrel, he could get them up again.

"Ollie, build a fire and help Finch the best you

can. We'll stay like you want for a day or two. I'll
hunt in a big circle and see if I can find something ..."

"You do what you want, Blueberry. But get it
out of your head I'm followin' you any longer.
Here's where I'm stayin' from now on."

Turning away, Billy sensed he needed to leave
Twait alone for a while. It seemed clear his companion might snap crazily if he pushed too hard—
then a gunfight would follow. Lately Ollie had
been keeping his rifle near his side.

Lashing his snowshoes on, shoving a handful
of cartridges into his pockets, he shuffled away. It
hurt him to hear Twait's bitter use of the name
Blueberry. He mostly didn't mind the alias. During their journey to Dawson City to dig for gold,
he had found that everyone went by a nickname.
It seemed a badge of honor to have a pseudonym.
And everyone on the stampede across Alaska
tried hard to find an uncommon one that would
be recalled forever.

Several famous nicknames passed through his
mind: Swiftwater Bill, Big Alex, The Evaporated
Kid, Cutthroat Johnson—all famous Klondikers he
had heard gossiped about as the three of them
had moved north toward their goal.

But once the hundreds of men he had voyaged
north with had dropped off the icy summits of
the Chugach Mountains, then onto the Klutina
River on the far side, they had found all the false
names and sweet ideas utterly worthless. Suddenly everyone discovered they had been cheated

by swindlers in Seattle. The chances of reaching Dawson City by shooting the wild rapids of the Klutina, then by ascending the silty, flooding waters of the Copper River, lastly by crossing over the Alaskan Range to the Nabesna, Tanana, and Yukon rivers flowing on the other side, had proved much too slim. The men around him had begun dying by the dozens. Most had found themselves trapped ... too far one way, too dangerous the other.

He and Twait and Finch had chosen to push on. Young and strong, they had won out over the fatal waters in front, seeing others drown one by one. They had won out over the low, rough pass joining the upper Copper River to the headwaters of the Nabesna River as well. And they had successfully run down the Nabesna, then the Tanana afterward for hundreds of miles. But now it seemed the end of their yearlong struggle to reach the gold fields had fallen short by hundreds of miles ... and maybe short by three lives, too.

It had never occurred to them they could run out of food, or that the Klondike would be so far away. When winter had set upon them once more after a fleeting summer, they had begun to suspect the danger. First the canned goods had disappeared. Then the coffee, tea, dried fruit, and other treats had run out. Finally their beans and bacon had dwindled to a few pounds. Yet, no matter how hard they had hunted and how far they had marched downriver, they hadn't come upon more food or human faces. Hunger had turned out to be their only companion.

Suddenly fluttering birds woke him from his haunting daydreams. Canadian jacks, puffy gray-and-white bundles of feathers, flew from branch to branch just overhead. Swinging his Winchester up, he tried to sight one as each bird flew around. How could his heart race so fast just over a small bird, he wondered? Then he remembered buck fever was the name they had called the disorder back in Minnesota. But why suffer the jitters now when he felt so desperate. One or two of the birds would keep them going for at least a day.

Patience, keep steady, he thought, give yourself time. At last he saw one sit down on a tree branch right in front. He aimed the gun sights and pleaded inside his brain. The burst of the rifle shook him, and then shook all the woods around when the retiring blast echoed. Finally an awful silence closed down and two whiskey jacks flew off fast. But the one he had shot lay quivering on the snow.

Leaping forward, clutching the dying bird in his mitt, he turned back toward Finch and Twait. He hadn't felt so happy for days—finally they had a little red meat to eat. They could hold out against the hunger and the scurvy for another day. Smiling, he tramped back onto the river's surface. His friend's faces looked lean, white, their mouths already hung open with hope.

Oliver Twait grabbed the bird and pitched it across the river, swiping it away in a flash. "A damn bird, you come back with a whiskey jack all shot to hell. And you stand here lookin' happy like you got a moose or somethin' like that. Why didn't you just pick berries, Blueberry.''

Stunned voiceless by Ollie's attack, Billy gaped as his other friend jumped after the bird, lurching through the snow. He then watched in silent horror as Horace Fincher quickly tore the bird apart, shoving bloody bits into his mouth like a madman, gobbling everything but a few feathers. Then Ollie Twait began to laugh crazily, splitting the air with his rattling cackles.

That night Billy sat by a low fire, sleeping in slips of time. Nothing seems so lifeless, he thought, so fateful like the hungry wilderness in the middle of winter. And he realized he had to leave his friends, to try to save them, to try to save himself. Loneliness gripped his belly as he contemplated following the sled trail he had seen in the previous daylight. The tracks appeared to be headed for the high, white mountains to the south, away from the Yukon River. The thought of following the old footprints frightened him more than anything he had ever faced. But his wish to stay alive made up his mind. It seemed better to chase the visible prayer than a blind hope. No matter how long or far, he would walk until he caught the men with the dogs and sled. No matter how much he feared walking by himself into the middle of an uncharted forest, he would walk nonetheless. He would rather die by the hand of God than alongside two madmen. Finally, when he saw Finch and Twait fall asleep, he cried, as quietly as he could, muffling his lonely sobs with his hands.

In the morning he watched his two partners rise and stumble over to the fire. After they had woken themselves sufficiently he said, "Finch, Ollie, I'm leavin' to find the men that passed by here earlier. I'm goin to bring 'em back with some food."

Horace Fincher's eyes opened wide, wetting instantly. "Don't leave me, Billy! We can stay here all right! You—you can hunt like yesterday!"

"No—it's time I go. The food that's left will last that much longer if I leave. You got flour, some beans and bacon yet. Might keep you goin' for a couple weeks if you're careful, and Ollie will hunt some more. You two hang in here like Ollie said yesterday. I'll get help and get back as soon as I can."

Twait's eyes narrowed. "You do that, Blueberry. But don't bother comin' back 'less you do find food. You ain't gettin' no more of what we got."

Billy stood up, turned, and then looked back once more. "I said I don't want no food. But I'm takin' an ax and my outfit. And when I get back, you better have helped Finch the best you could. I'm not afraid of you, Ollie. And I'm not puttin' up with your mouth anymore—you understand?"

Oliver Twait stiffened and then slumped down. After a moment of stillness, he muttered, "I'll help Finch like you said. Just go get some food, Blueberry."

He marched away with his pack and snowshoes

strapped to his back, his Winchester balanced in his left hand and an ax clutched in his right hand. Good hiking, he thought, not much snow has fallen since the sled passed by, and the trail seems frozen. He judged he could walk twenty miles every day, maybe a bit more. The big mountain seemed to be one hundred miles away. He sensed his life would last just long enough. But unless he found food on the other end, he would never walk that far again.

The sled track turned off the Tanana, crossed behind a small island, and snaked up a small, winding river. On his second day out, he began to see scattered signs of wildlife. Beaver houses sat mounded with the snow here and there, otter slides ran up and down shorelines, and old moose trails wandered to willow and birch trees. He felt torn between the choice of hunting or keeping hard to his pace ... his belly gnawed with hunger and terror. If he slowed, hunted, and failed to find food within a day or two, then he would surely be condemned to death. He didn't have strength enough to hunt and travel as well. Keep walking, please keep walking! his mind whispered. He broke an icicle off a long row, hanging like snakes on a tree limb and crunched little chunks with his teeth. But his belly just seemed to hurt more.

In the settling dark on the third day, while sitting by his fire watching sooty shadows dance on snowbanks, he at last saw his luck change. Food! Why hadn't he noticed earlier? Why hadn't he looked around?

Just outside his firelight a little mound sat inside an open circle cut among the marsh grasses. Muskrat houses—muskrats lived nearby! Plump, red bodies as fat as duck, and weighing about as much! He had eaten one as a boy on a dare by his friends, and had been surprised by its tastiness, even though his stomach had turned over with disgust back then. But a muskrat would taste just fine now, and whatever roots he found inside their house would taste even better. Biting down on his bottom lip hard to steady himself, he crept forward. If the house had stayed alive in the winter, he would hear disturbed splashes when he stepped close. And when he cut the house open with his ax, the hollow inside would feel warm and smell musty, stinking of weeds and life.

The house steamed through the little tunnel he chopped into its interior. He could see the misty curl of fog puff out, even in the darkness. When he reached through to the center he felt the two hand-sized escape holes down to the riverwater and the flat grass platform sitting in between. Packing the tunnel tight again, he ran back inside his firelight, searching, his heart beating wildly. Food—he could kill nourishment in just a little while!

Darting his eyes back and forth, he found the willow tree he needed. He ran, bent the branches over, and cut off one with his ax. Jumping back to his fire, he skinned, sharpened, and shaped the straight shaft into a crude harpoon. He then carefully hardened the point above the hot coals of his campfire, finally pricking his finger and confirming that his spear was ready.

Sneaking back, he opened the house once more, aimed the point of his spear to plunge through the inside, and packed the house against the freezing air again. He would have to wait, he thought, freeze, stay silent—but the discipline would be worth his life.

The telltale animal sounds ebbed through just after he had begun to shiver uncontrollably. But his shaking helped drive the spear through—then fatal peeps let him know he had a muskrat pinned inside the house. He tore open the entryway again, grabbed the wriggling little body, and flipped his fresh supper out in an instant. Food at last! He cried and laughed, and then shivered with chills and hunger.

He salted and stewed pieces of the skinned carcass over the orange coals of his fire, steadying himself against eating raw meat and rushing his first decent meal in weeks. Nibbling on the roots he had robbed from the muskrat's den, he sensed stomach cramps and sickness would weaken him if he didn't stop his common impulse to gorge himself. He had learned enough selling medicines for his father to appreciate the dangers of starvation and scurvy. And his belly would trouble him if he didn't feed it slowly and let it digest the soft and nourishing food over time. At last his mixture of muskrat and wild roots seemed done. He blew on a spoonful, then swallowed cautiously. It tasted awful, but he didn't care.

He slept four hours, rekindled his fire, and ate again. When he woke up the following day, after hearing morning birds, he felt much stronger, renewed for a change. The tiny chickadees that had disturbed him flitted around, begging for their share of the food. Smiling, happy for their noisy company, he fed them leftovers from his kill and wondered why the little birds seemed so unafraid. Then he understood, they hadn't seen a man before.

He speared three more muskrats before midday, then marched away as fast as he could to make up for the lost time. Each little rat meant at least two meals, plenty to reach the giant mountain ahead, and even partway back if needed. The pathway in front appeared hard and clear. His hope lifted, his legs felt lively.

In the yellow twilight he found the sled track swinging up toward a burned-off forest. Judging that he would at least have the dusky light from a winter moon, and seeing only blackened remnants of spruce trees to walk through, he turned uphill, without stopping again. A few more miles tonight, he thought, and tomorrow I'll find someone.

After a breakfast of roasted muskrat meat and more sharing with the friendly birds, he set off once more. He noticed the bit of additional daylight now that Christmastime had come and gone. What was it, he wondered, the middle of January. Striding longer, higher, he saw a great, dark woodland far ahead.

He camped another night in the wasteland of fire-killed trees. Then, before noon the next day, he stepped among dark evergreens, barren cottonwoods, and white birches. A fearful silence fell down. He followed the sled trail, sorted back and forth through tracks, then headed off again toward the high, shadowy mountains, now seeming close by. Suddenly he saw something hidden behind a few trees—a little log hut with woodsmoke curling from its top. He stopped—

"Hello—in the camp—hello! Is anybody home?" His voice didn't carry as clear and strong as he wished. And why feel so afraid, he wondered?

Then he blinked, horrified, as a tall, pale man pushed through the caribou skin door and stood silently. The stranger looks as hungry and cold as Finch and Twait, he thought. And he looks so hopeless.

CHAPTER SEVEN

Partners

"Where's your dogs and sled?" After asking, Billy worried about his foolishness, if there had been any dogs they would have barked long ago. He then wished he had sounded more neighborly, rather than forgetting to say hello.

Eli stared back, his eyes rounded with thankfulness greater than any time in his life. The young man in front had a rifle—and snowshoes to hunt with as well. Now he had the chance to keep Jesse Peacock and himself alive. He wondered where the newcomer had come from, and why the man looked so starved himself.

"Young friend, it appears my luck has been no better than yours. My companion and I lost our outfits and walked back this far. You appear to have suffered the same kind of trouble. But you have a rifle and snowshoes—which are things I need."

"My name's Billy House—what's your?" Then Billy saw a one-armed man, haggard and worn, stumble out of the hut.

"Eli, has somebody come for us? God, do they got any food?"

"We've been found by someone in the same predicament as ourselves, I think." Then Eli stepped forward to offer his handshake. "Billy, my name is Eli Bonnet, this is my companion, Jesse Peacock. We're U.S. Marshals on duty—but in grave danger right now. Tell me why you've come."

Billy couldn't help thinking he should share his food with the hungry, one-armed man. And he wanted to eat again as well. He shrugged off his backpack and held it toward the man called Peacock.

"I got two muskrats I killed two days ago. They taste pretty good when you stew 'em slow. But I ain't got no vegetables."

Jesse Peacock slumped onto the snow in front of the hut and broke into lonely cries. Billy stood in puzzlement over the human sounds. He couldn't tell if the words sounded sad, or if they sounded insane.

Eli stepped forward and lifted away the canvas pack. He had eaten possum as a boy in the South before the War between the States. He hadn't tried eating muskrats, but he had eaten with the Sioux in the Dakota Territory many times. Dog had been one of their favorites and hadn't seemed so bad when he had tasted the meat. Now he would eat dog in an instant if he could get some. Then the young man's apology for not having vegetables struck him as odd. Why would a person feel regret for not having vegetables in the face of a wintertime famine? He supposed Billy House had lost part of his common sense from his hungry times.

"Billy, come in and rest. You've surely come from Providence, leastwise that's what an old prospector friend of mine would say. Don't let Jesse concern you, he'll strengthen in a while. Let me put one of these critters in a pot for soup. With you here—if I can borrow your snowshoes and Winchester, I can save us all. There's food around in the woods, but I've had nothing to hunt with but my Colt Peacemaker. I've gathered a couple rabbits and four squirrels—but there's no fat to them. I need to find moose and caribou—then we can all get well again."

Suddenly Billy remembered his two friends back on the Tanana River. They hadn't had any new meat to eat since the gut-shot bird that Finch had gulped down. He needed to bring them fresh food like he had promised. He shouted, "I got to save those muskrats for my friends. I guess we better not eat 'em after all."

Turning, Eli studied the youthful stranger behind him. He quickly realized he had fallen in with more than one desperate man. He wondered how many men there were. He began to fear why Billy House had tracked him down.

"Billy, you need to get your mind clear and tell me your business. What's this news about friends?"

"Me and two friends been tryin' to get down the Tanana River to the Yukon so we could get to Dawson City for gold. We run out of food. Finch's

got froze feet and my other friend don't want to
walk no more. They're starvin' to death. I got to
get back with food for them. That's why I followed you—I thought you'd have some!"

With his heart sinking, Eli stopped in silent horror, brooding over his newfound disaster and the
hopelessness of feeding five hungry men in the
middle of an empty wilderness. Gathering food,
killing enough wild game necessary to feed one
or two people looked favorable. Hunting up
enough to keep five men alive seemed impossible.
Yet he saw no other choice. An honest person
could do no less than try his best. But his secret
voice kept whispering that he felt so helpless.

He reached back and shook Billy by the shoulders. First he had to get a common understanding
between them, then he could devise a plan to help
the others. "Billy, listen to me, you've got to eat
and keep strong. You and I appear to be the only
hope for anyone, including ourselves. If we eat,
we might gather enough strength to save our
friends. Without food, you'll never see the Tanana
again—nor will I. Now come inside, we need to
rest and plan an escape."

Billy followed, hanging his head and staying
quiet. Eli pointed to a camp stool and then pulled
two frozen muskrats from the pack he had carried
inside the trapper's hut. He laid one rat close to
the little tin stove in the corner. Then he began
cracking open the moose bones he had found earlier under the snow, as he had begun to do before
being startled by his new friend's call.

Billy House stared, his eyes hollow. "What you doin' with them bones?"

"I found a few moose bones outside. Some have marrow inside, frozen and good. There's nothing better as food than marrow. I learned that from the Sioux and Blackfeet long ago. Tonight we're having fried marrow and muskrat soup. How does that sound to you?" Eli smiled, feeling somewhat cheerful for a change.

"Awful good, I ain't ate much lately. I got salt and pepper I brung, do you want some?"

Now Eli couldn't help himself. Even though his awful fears still persisted, he laughed. "God bless you, Billy, God bless you. You'll never know how good salt and pepper sounds until you've had none of it for a month. Tomorrow's troubles look smaller to me already!" He laughed once more despite worrying that he had lost his common sense, too.

That night, after eating, Eli wrote to Hannah and pinned his letter to the inside wall, above the hut's door. The end of January seemed near. Additional bits of light each day and persistent cold, clear weather had signaled the arrival of late winter. He knew Hannah would search for him when she saw the end of the month . . . and Doll Girl would start out as well. The little girl's spirit and endurance had made an unforgettable impression. He only needed to keep himself and the others alive for one more month, then help would arrive. But he had to post a letter just in case. One could never be certain in the wilderness—and he wanted

Hannah to know what his troubles had been all about.

He had scratched his message on scrap paper with a pencil stub he had found, writing:

Dearest Hannah,

We are in great danger. I've lost count of the days our sled and dogs, food and equipment have been lost. We've walked back this far, and we'll push toward the mouth of the Kantishna River tomorrow. I pray we'll find you there.

If we miss you somehow, please go on to Sleepy Lake. I'm sure Doll Girl has come along— she will show you the way. Ask her to help hunt and keep plenty of fresh meat waiting. I shall return to your side soon. Please remember my love for you.

A young man named Billy House has found us here. He tells about two friends now on the Tanana who are starving as much as Jesse and I. I must go down to help. I intend, again, to see you running upriver to find us. But it's important for you to know about my new friend's crisis, and that I have no way of judging my days ahead. I will try to save these men, and I will try to wait for you as well. But please remember my wishes and wait for me as I've asked, if we miss our rendezvous.

During your stay at Sleepy Lake, please take guard against any stranger. Trust Doll Girl. She is Indian and will know many things. Rely on her in this great wilderness. I realize she is just a little girl, but you must remember she knows the ways of the true people of this land, and they have walked this ground since the beginning of time. Listen to her always. She knows how to survive in this faraway place.

I must leave you now with my love and my remembrances of yours. I shall see you soon, I promise with all my heart—

Eli

Afterward he slipped under the hides he had fashioned into blankets back at the cabin on Sleepy Lake. He thanked his luck that the kidnapper had left Red Shirt's furs behind, hanging in the cache. Without his makeshift covers, he and Jesse would have frozen to death many days earlier on the outbound trail. Now, at least, they could stay warm at night.

He listened to Jesse whimper in the darkness of the trapper's hut. The despair his companion seemed to feel every day, his failure to hold up against the hardships, and his fatal outlook had begun to wear thin. Constantly hearing words of gloom seemed an uncommon burden for any man. Yet he had to endure Peacock's sickness and keep striving to save everyone. Hannah and the old shaman had warned him. It seemed time to remember that it had been his own idea to bring Jesse along.

In the morning he led toward the upper reaches of the Kantishna River, hoping to complete their march overland in less than three days. If Billy's information proved correct, they stood the chance of reaching the muskrat marshes downriver before their strength gave out. Then, perhaps, more of the little water creatures could be harvested. They had found a few animal traps hanging around the trapper's hut, and Billy claimed he knew how to catch the remaining animals.

Stomach churning with the hopes of more food, he wondered about Billy's quiet resolve to save his friends. If only Jesse Peacock could have shown the same pluck, speed, and resourcefulness, he thought, they would be in better shape. All down the mountains to Sleepy Lake, then across the timbered lands to the first and second trapper's camps, Jesse had cried, balked, and fought against the sensible advice about how they might save themselves.

They pitched a hungry camp that night, after it had become so black they could no longer see the trail. Eli banked their fire, then worked with Billy House to gather more wood for the nighttime hours ahead. The young man had remained noiseless all day, tramping along with his head down, his pace as fast as Eli's. Peacock had dragged behind, whining, complaining every mile of the way.

"Mr. Peacock's been a city man all his life, ain't he?"

Eli paused to answer. It seemed important to explain Jesse's sickness carefully.

"Jesse has lived in San Francisco for many years. He came up the Yukon River by steamboat last summer to arrest a killer I'd captured the winter before. On his way back down the river, he lost the prisoner at Fort Yukon because of foolishness and bad luck. The man beat him, knocked him cold. Jesse has never seemed well to me since that time. I worry about him a great deal. We've worked together for many years, though in different places. I've always worked on the frontiers, Jesse in the towns. This journey has been hard on him. It's my fault, I believe. I should have left him behind."

"I'd be grateful if he'd quit with his whinin' all the time. I listened to enough of that from my partner Ollie Twait."

"I'm sorry ... but I remind myself Jesse's not well. Perhaps your friend suffers from the same sickness. Nowadays most men lack the strength to live with the hardships of a wild land. You must remember the mind works in odd ways when one finds himself hundreds of miles away from other people. Loneliness breaks hearts and saddens souls."

"Ollie ain't sick—he's just mean. All he does is call me by my other name, but now he makes it sound stupid. It was his idea to come this way, too, but he's forgot about that. He blames me for starvin' us to death." Billy crouched and piled firewood in his arms.

Eli, holding up a firebrand so he could see, thought he could see a little wetness in the young man's eyes. "Billy, what other name do you use?"

"I named myself Blueberry when we started at Valdez. Everybody wanted one that was different."

"I like that name, Billy. Most folks in the North

use something other than their birth names. It's part of the culture in this land. Would you like me to call you by that name."

Billy House stood and turned back toward their camp with his armload of wood. "I guess I'd like that . . . but Ollie's gonna make fun if we make it back."

"I don't think so. Let's get back to camp." Then Eli glimpsed a smile on Billy's face as they turned back to their fire.

They dropped onto the channel of the Kantishna River a day after the time Eli had hoped, Jesse having slowed them further. Up hills and through deep snow, he and Blueberry had pulled Peacock along, one man on each side. Then, finally, weakness had silenced them. No one had strength remaining to say anything, each man left with his worry about making his next step. At last they plodded downriver and found better conditions for walking, the surface turning windswept and hardened like an old packed pathway.

The weather changed from below zero temperatures and blue skies that reached back beyond the great mountain, to snowy days, a bit warmer and cloudy gray. They saw no wild game as they trudged along—only old moose tracks here and there. And each night they listened as hunting wolves howled, sounding close by, sounding as lonely and hungry as themselves. And when the wolves wailed Jesse Peacock darted around their camp, his eyes rounded and white.

"Do wolves eat people?" he asked after the wolves had sung for an hour one night.

"I've never heard of it. You should rest, Jesse, you're in no danger. Blueberry and I have the rifle, and a pistol to boot. I might even try to eat wolf if I got the chance."

Eli recalled hearing contradictory stories from the Indians in Canada. They had claimed their ancestors had been hunted down by wolf packs long ago. Their legends told of their struggle against the hungry predators back then. And they had shown great fear of the grizzly bear also.

Blueberry stared hard at Peacock. "We ain't in no danger from the wolves, we're in danger of starvin' cause they're goin' to eat every moose and caribou there is if we don't find 'em first. I'm like Eli, I'd eat wolf right off if I could shoot one."

"I guess I would eat some, too . . ." Peacock slumped down, his head hanging low.

"Get some rest, Jesse—you, too, Blueberry. We've got a long ways to walk tomorrow. There'll be food for us downriver." Eli turned to his spruce bough and beaver blanket bed.

On the afternoon of the following day they marched onto the frozen marshes Billy House had found earlier. Eli asked Jesse to cut firewood and clear Billy's old campsite by kicking the snow aside. Then, frustrated by Peacock's complaining, he lost his temper and reminded his companion of his one good arm and two normal legs, and that he had better use them to help them survive.

Otherwise, he said, he would leave him behind the next day.

Two hours later he knelt alongside a muskrat house they had set with a trap. "Blueberry, I think we've caught something!"

The young Minnesotan crouched down. "I think we can get a half dozen or so before we trap 'em out. There ain't but seven houses here. Generally you can figure two rats a house. I got some before—I think that's all that's left."

"We've got supper for a change—maybe Jesse will now quiet down. In the morning, if our luck continues, we should have food for your friends. With the equipment you say you've got back there, and with one more pair of snowshoes, you and I can head out and hunt. Then our fate will change—I know it!" Suddenly Eli worried he had begun to babble also, indicating his own giddy anguish.

Then, when he looked up, he saw another trap anchor wiggling nearby. He turned, pointed, and grinned at Billy House. "God bless you, Blueberry! God bless you for knowing how to trap these little critters! They taste as good as duck!"

By noon of the next day they had stuffed six skinned muskrats inside their packs, having eaten two they had caught the night before. At last their pace picked up because of their fuller bellies. They marched with their heads down, bent on reaching the Tanana River and Blueberry's friends as soon as possible.

Gray days crept by, warmer ones with infre-

quent snow pellets spitting down, telling of a coming storm. Eli shifted his eyes back and forth,
searching for moose, rabbits, anything edible. He
wondered about Alaska's winters, looking so
black and white and seeming so noiseless it hurt
his ears. Only the crunching of their boots
sounded, but even that human sound ebbed fate-
fully into the emptiness. Death seemed to haunt
everything—no color or cries, nothing—an odd re-
quiem for Mother Nature herself. Then one night
savage calls speared the deep silence. Their hidden enemies had trailed them again.

Blueberry looked up from their evening fire. "I
guess the wolves can't find food neither. Don't
leave much hope for us."

Eli sat with his head down, thinking. He then
frowned at his new friend. "Blueberry, don't get
discouraged. I've walked hungry lands before.
Optimism is our best medicine. I've learned that
from my old friend named Noodles. By his advice
I've learned that better times always wait just
ahead. Besides, I'm wearing my medicine coat—it
has never let me down."

"I've seen you wearin' that fancy Indian jacket.
How come you got it on?"

Jesse Peacock picked up a willow branch and
poked at the dying embers on the edge of the
yellow flames. "Eli's been superstitious ever since
I hired him back in the Dakota Territory to be my
Deputy U.S. Marshal. He shot some Indian's horse
down so he could take it. He thinks it's got magi-

cal powers. I think it's silly for a grown man to dress that way."

"Jesse, my luck stays near me when I wear my spirit coat. I suppose I am superstitious, but most folks are. The Sioux shaman who owned this jacket had ridden safely into many battles. Even I missed him after taking good aim. With all the bullets that had been shot his way, I thought this coat must have what all Indians call strong medicine. It's served me well for many years, and I'm going to keep it forever."

Blueberry looked up once more, his face wrinkled. "Do you really believe it can help save us?"

"Just as soon as we do our part properly, Blueberry, but no sooner—it can't act alone." Then Eli stared into the dancing flames, spreading his fingers to warm his hands.

The following day they saw the tent ghosted in a snowstorm, with a shadowy figure nearby, sitting hunched over by a small fire. Gray smoke also darkened the stooped man, crouched by himself in the rolling puffs. When they tramped near enough for the man to hear them walking, he turned and stared, his face lean and eyes vacant of any brightness.

Then the dark shadow yelled, "I see you didn't come with any food, Blueberry. I knowed you wouldn't. It was you who got us into this trouble in the first place. Even a fool would have guessed you'd come back empty-handed."

"Twait, we come back with four muskrats left over. That's enough for a couple good meals. You had more time to hunt than me. What'd you get? I don't see nothin' layin' around."

"There's no game to hunt. Now you've been stupid enough to bring two more starvin' men back with you. Well, you and them ain't gettin' what little flour I got left—none."

Eli stepped forward and stood above Oliver Twait. "Your behavior is bad and I'm out of patience. We'll all share equally or your share will be none. For the few words you've spoken, you've offended your partner and the two friends he's made. It's time for you to shut up and listen, I've come here to save all of us."

Twait shot straight up, threw his arms and hands against Eli's chest, and kicked out a foot to trip him backward. Jumping away, Eli grabbed the man by the arms. Heaving sideways, he threw Oliver Twait off balance and onto the snow beside the fire. Then he pounced on the man, like a cat, pinning him by kneeling on his chest.

"Big mistake, Twait, you're not quick or strong enough to better me in a fight! And you've made the mistake of attacking a U.S. Marshal. Eli then slipped his right hand under his parka and pulled out his lawman's badge.

Oliver Twait stared at the silver star, his brow creased, eye sockets widened. Finally he cried, "Get off! I'll quit with what you say. You're hurtin' me and I ain't well."

"From now on say please when asking for things. And when you use your friend's name,

Blueberry, speak respectfully, do you understand?"

Twait paused, then nodded his head for an answer. Watchfully, Eli stood up, letting the man roll over, stand, and brush off his clothing.

Suddenly Blueberry stepped close by. "Where's Finch? Where's he at?"

"He's in the tent. He can't hardly get around no more." Oliver Twait turned away and walked back to his fireside seat.

Blueberry ran to the tent. Eli followed, worried about the news of the sick man, near death. What could be done if there's a man down, he wondered? His medical kit had been lost, and there weren't any doctors for a thousand miles.

When he stepped inside the tent and knelt by Blueberry, he saw the sick man lying flat on his back. Fincher's skeletal face, waxy white, was set above a ragged old blanket. He reached for the sick man's wrist and searched for a pulse. Horace Fincher opened his eyes and mouthed a few weak words.

"Billy, I see you come back. I knew you'd bring help for me."

"You're gonna be all right now, Finch. I brought some food. You want to eat now?" Blueberry's voice quivered and his eyes turned humid.

"Whatever you want, Billy. But I don't feel so hungry or cold anymore." Then Fincher's lips curled a thin smile.

"This is my new friend Eli Bonnet. He's come to help us. Let him look you over and I'll start cookin' a nice stew for you to eat." Blueberry slipped out of the tent.

Eli pulled down the sick man's blankets, unbuttoned the coat underneath, then opened Fincher's dirty shirt and underwear. Next he listened to the man's chest. The heart beat sounded normal, but deep congestion wheezed inside the chest cavity. And every rib and bone lay wrapped in blackened skin. Scurvy! The lack of fresh vegetables and meat, the nutrients from those foods had been lacking for too long, he thought. Without good food and care, he knew Horace Fincher would die in a few days.

Moving down to the man's feet, he pulled off both boots and examined the toes of each foot. Frozen, then thawed, then frosted again, he fretted. It seemed clear each foot would have to be amputated or gangrene would set in eventually. The man's future looked dim . . . near its end.

He redressed Fincher, covered him once more, and slipped out of the tent as well. When he reached the campfire he saw Jesse Peacock slumped alongside Twait. Blueberry sat on the other side of the flames, readying the muskrats.

"Blueberry, when you finish your stew, first feed Fincher as much as possible. The only chance we have to save his life will come from forcing food down his throat. Afterward, we'll share the remainder equally."

Blueberry looked up, his eyes still wet. "Do you think we can save him. Has he got a chance?"

Eli hesitated. The only hope for Horace Fincher

lay with the luck of finding fresh meat. At last he answered, "In the morning you and I will take two rifles, the sled, snowshoes, and gear to hunt for a week, longer perhaps. If Providence will help out, as my old friend back in Dawson City might say, we'll find a fat moose. And I believe my luck is set for a change."

Then he felt the unsettled gazes from angry eyes—an odd mix of hatred and hope, faith and fear. My Indian medicine needs to change soon, he mused, otherwise one of these men will try to kill me.

CHAPTER EIGHT

Madness

Jesse Peacock and Oliver Twait watched as Eli and Blueberry faded around a bend in the Tanana River, heading out to search for moose and caribou. The two hunters had risen before first light, readied the sled for their journey, and pulled away under a white dawn.

Jesse sat gazing upriver after the two men had disappeared, wishing he knew what to do. He didn't want to starve to death. God, he thought, could a man who insisted on wearing a Sioux spirit coat and another named Blueberry ever find food? He doubted it.

Then Ollie Twait's voice broke the silence. "You know they ain't never comin' back. We're gonna sit here and die if we don't do something!"

Twait's voice jogged Jesse from his melancholy. He didn't like the man, but Ollie seemed to be his only friend. Horace Fincher had sickened so much he could hardly answer back when asked questions. Jesse knew he would go completely crazy if he didn't have someone to talk to, someone to listen to all his fears.

"I don't know. Eli's come through for me before. He's been all over the Old West. He's one of the few men that's lived to tell about it. Maybe things will work out."

"You were cryin' yesterday that we're all gonna die. Now you want to sit here and wait for what—a miracle? Those two are gonna to save themselves. They ain't gonna save us."

Jesse felt his heart sink. Twait's preaching sounded sensible, but what could the two of them do, he wondered. He frowned and looked at Twait. "We're not strong enough to hunt. I don't know how to anyway. Don't we have to wait?"

"Wait for what, a sure way to die? Well—I'm not waitin' no more. How far is it down to the Yukon? You come up from there before, didn't you?"

"I don't remember exactly, maybe we're a week from there." Jesse worried. They had no food.

"Is there any people down there?"

"Just some dog sleds running back and forth. They carry the mail all the time. They run upriver as far as Dawson City. I don't know how far downriver they go. A long ways, I think."

"Let's go. We can make it for week. I know we can."

Jesse stared, face wrinkled, eyes squinted. "Maybe you can—but I doubt it. I know I can't. We're not strong enough to pull Fincher along anyway, let alone all the stuff we need to take along. We just can't move without food."

Both men sat staring at the fire, each inside his

own thoughts. Jesse worried back and forth over Twait's idea to leave for the Yukon and the statement that they would die if they didn't try to save themselves. The ebbing life of the orange fire in front and its ruffling and popping stirred his belly into greater dread than he had ever felt before. God, he thought, I don't want to die!

Twait's voice surprised him again. "Go get more wood, the fire's gettin' low!"

"Why don't you go get it? You got two good arms, I only have one." He turned and faced Oliver Twait, feeling his silent fear of the man once more.

"You haven't got wood once since you been here. It's your turn—now go get it. I ain't askin' again. You can drag in some dead wood just fine with your one arm."

Jesse stood and walked away from his fireside seat, looking back once. Turning up the shoreline nearest the tent, he felt the weakness of last few days sink through his limbs. He stumbled to a log through the snow and sat down. Hanging his head, he rested. What to do, he wondered, what to do? He didn't want to sicken like Fincher. But what else? His brain shrieked with terror. He wanted to scream his dread of starving to death.

At last he rose again and found a dry spruce snag close by. Pushing, he broke it down, then pulled it back to the campsite. As he slogged down the shore past the tent, he saw Twait coming through the canvas door.

"How's Fincher doing, is he any better?"

"He's dead." Twait ducked his head and sat back down near the fire again, his breath puffing a little.

Jesse stopped, his mouth hanging. One of them had died already. He realized he would be next. He seemed to be the weakest one remaining. Dropping his firewood, he stepped away from Twait and ducked into the tent. Fincher lay rumpled, his blankets scattered, body jerked into odd angles, and eyes rolled back with tiny blood vessels standing out in the whiteness. And his neck looked broken, throttled, with thumbprints yet pressed on the waxy skin around the throat.

Panic-stricken, he crouched along the dead man's side. His years of law enforcement came rushing back. He had witnessed murder before. Twait had killed Fincher. The man had committed murder while he had gathered firewood. He jerked his head around. Would Twait come for him next?

Then, feeling unable to endure Horace Fincher's death dance any longer, he crawled to the door and peeked out. Twait still sat by the fire, staring straight ahead, stonelike. Jesse felt his mind wildly burst. He coiled himself to run, his mouth set to scream all the madness he felt filling his brain.

"Come out here, Peacock! I know what you're doin' an' what you're thinkin' about. I got a gun—you don't."

Jesse crept through the flaps, circled the fire, and then sat down across from Oliver Twait. Tears streaming, shivering, he stayed soundless, wondering what it must be like to be killed.

Twait glanced across. "You want to live . . . or you want to die?"

"I want to live. I want to get out of here! Why'd you have to kill him?"

"You did it—you're the crazy one. You think Bonnet is gonna believe I did it if he comes back. You're the one that's been acting nuts ever since you come here."

"But I didn't do it—you did." Jesse couldn't control himself, he broke into a fit of bawling and moaning. He clutched his head with his one arm and rocked himself, his mind feeling empty of clear reasoning.

"No, Peacock, you did. I just saw you come out of the tent. When Bonnet gets back, I'm gonna tell him. You know he'll want to see you hung."

Jesse continued to rock, unable to argue. My God, he thought, Twait's right. He had, in fact, acted like a madman several times in front of Eli. He'd cursed, complained, and threw fits continually since losing the dogs back in the mountains. The best he could hope for seemed like the situation of one man's word against another. And both Eli and Billy House had seen his behavior for days upon days. Maybe he had gone insane in the past. There appeared no other explanation.

At last he looked up and asked, "Are you going to kill me? Is that what you're planning to do?"

Twait's face stayed plain—his mouth hard. "No . . . not as long as you do what I tell you. If you listen, keep your mouth shut, we both can live. We can get down to the Yukon River and get one of those dog teams. Then we can get out of this godforsaken country. We can run downriver to St. Michaels and catch a ship. You been there before, ain't you?"

Jesse nodded his head. If he could only get back to San Francisco, the place he had come from less than a year before, he stood the chance of recovering his sanity. Once he was home, he could strengthen and come to grips with dealing with the murder that had just taken place. But the same fateful end waited for both of them if they tried to walk down the Tanana River for a week or more. They would both surely die of starvation, he thought. They just didn't have the food to make the trip.

Twait's eyes darkened. "Well, ain't you been there? How far is it down to the Yukon?"

"I came upriver from there on a steamboat. There's always ships sailing back and forth to Seattle and San Francisco. I don't remember how far ... maybe a thousand miles, maybe more. But it doesn't make any difference, we haven't the food to even make it down to the Yukon from here. We'll die before we ever get there."

Twait never moved his dark eyes off Peacock. "You might die if you don't want to eat, but I ain't goin' to starve. When Fincher cools, I'm gonna eat him."

Jesse Peacock threw up. Both of them must have gone mad, he thought. My God, he screamed inside his brain, what kind of hell has seized me. Could he possibly eat a man's flesh to save himself, he wondered. But then if he didn't, he knew Twait might kill and eat him as well. Suddenly he felt numbness in his head and all through his body. The world is insane—everyone is insane. There must be no other life for him but madness.

CHAPTER NINE

Freedom

The late owl's cry nudged Jesse from his fitful sleep. Where am I? he wondered. When he opened his eyes, he remembered. Oliver Twait lay on the other side of the dying embers of their past night's campfire, watching.

The winged hunter cried again as he rolled from his fireside bed and pitched more wood onto the glowing ashes. He couldn't bear to live in the dark any longer. Fire, sunshine—he had to have strong and clear light all around. Then he watched Twait appear to fall back to sleep.

They had sledded seven or eight miles after Twait had butchered the body of Horace Fincher. Jesse had tried not to watch, but he had seen some of it. He had retched over and over, but his empty stomach had heaved nothing except clear liquids. Then the hollow inside had felt larger than ever. And the acid in his throat had given him a painful reminder that he was starving to death.

After their short run downriver, they had built a fire. Then Twait had cooked and eaten human flesh. He had watched, not sick now, his stomach aching, his mouth tasting the imagined flavor. He hadn't eaten any himself, but he knew he would. He had reached a point in his reasoning where nothing seemed uncommon.

Nonetheless, he realized he still had a spark of sanity inside his brain. The chastened idea that he had dropped into the abyss that man would crawl into just to stay alive lay vividly in his mind. Man always thinks he can live more righteously than the savage animal, he reflected, but he will slither lower than a common snake to save his life.

Twait's eyes opened once more. "I got the gun, you don't!"

"I'm not thinking about you, I'm thinking about eating." Jesse glanced toward the sled they had packed and pulled behind. He stood up, walked to the sled, and ripped off its cover.

"I knew you would—I knew!" Oliver Twait laughed, his mad sounds spearing into the blackness of the night.

At daylight they smothered their fire and sledded farther down the Tanana River. Jesse felt a little bounce in his step, a renewal he hadn't expected. But he kept glancing backward, fearful of seeing a lone shadow back in the haze. Now he knew what the old outlaws must have felt like across the Dakota Territory, when Eli had chased them. One sensed he would be tracking somewhere behind, forever following, striving to catch up.

"Why you lookin' back all the time, Peacock? Bonnet and Blueberry ain't followin' us. I bet they ain't even alive. Keep yourself draggin' this sled. The sooner we get down to the Yukon River, the sooner we get away. Then it won't make no difference whether you think Bonnet is chasin' us or not. We'll be long gone!"

"You better worry some yourself. I know Bonnet isn't dead. We can only hope to outrun him. But like you say, if we get a ship to take us away from this godforsaken land, we'll be safe. I've listened to him enough lately, he loves this land. He won't leave it. We just better hope we can walk faster than he can, or we'll get hanged if we don't!"

Then Jesse felt Twait pulling harder, faster. He picked up his own step as well, his recent words passing through his mind again. God help us, he thought, if Eli is still alive. Then he shivered with dread. How stupid does one get to pray to God after what he had done. He had sat and ate the meat of man. If he prayed to anyone, it had better be the devil.

Stopping often, they ate more of the flesh of Fincher. And each time Jesse rushed the same words through his brain. Eat or die—walk or die! The haunting message helped, so did the nourishment. After resting for an hour or two, he'd find strength to pull again. And he and Twait walked their miles in a little added light every day. The glow seemed to fill them with hope, and with the food they now had to eat, they felt fit to make their march.

Suddenly, the horror that Oliver Twait planned

to murder again pierced Jesse's soul. The moment the two of them reached the Yukon, Twait wouldn't need him to help pull the sled any longer. And the first musher to pass by would be killed soon afterward. Ollie would want the man's sled and dogs to run downriver with, and why carry an extra man's weight when you needed to run from the law?

As they approached an abandoned Indian fish camp standing near the river's edge, he saw his chance. He recalled seeing the place once before, back when he and Eli had journeyed upriver. Eli had refused to stop and raid the cache standing high on four peeled spruce poles. But they had talked of the likelihood of dried salmon being stored inside. And they had talked of the ability of the Athabaskans of Alaska to cross great distances with only a moose-hide pouch of the nourishing fish. Twait must want something different to eat as much as he.

"Ollie, you know what that place is?" Peacock watched the killer's face for signs of knowledge.

"Well . . . some kind of Indian camp, I guess. So what?"

Jesse sensed a spark of hope. "It's a fish camp. Eli Bonnet said there would be dried salmon stored there when we came by before. Let's get some. It'd be better for us to eat than what we been eating."

Twait swung his stride sideways, pulling quickly to the snow-covered campsite. Jesse looked at the man's face again, searching for more signs. Ollie's mouth hung open, salivating, and his eyes gazed up, beaming. Now, Jesse thought, if a bit of carelessness and a bit of sleepiness could take place, an opportunity might come by.

Dried salmon did lie above, stacked like split firewood in the little log hut. Twait threw out several, then shinnied back down the ladder. Jesse smiled and helped as much as he could, trying his best to win the killer's confidence. That night he felt another spark of hope once they had settled themselves inside the shack built near the cache. Twait appeared a bit less wary. And, best of all, the man's burps and yawns told of a full belly and his need for sleep. He knew Ollie had become accustomed to odd human noises at all hours, and to the clunk of additional wood being thrown onto their night's fire. Twait's dark, gleaming eyes didn't seem to stay open for quite so long anymore. Perhaps a bit of snoring, grunting, and a rustle would sound the same. Then those eyes could be smashed shut forever.

In the middle of the night he woke as he had all the times before when their fire had burned low. But this time he stayed silent for a moment and opened just one eye, peeking. Twait lay across with both eyes closed, rough snores sawing out of his nose and mouth. Finally, snorting and snuffling himself, he sat straight up, reached to one side, and tossed a length of firewood onto the orange coals in front. Ollie's eyes snapped open and stared. Jesse immediately dropped his head and snorted again, pretending to nod off for a moment. He wobbled his head and snuffled louder, picking his head up as if he had just awakened once more. Then, on purpose, he reached for a long, heavy pole of wood he had kept close by. Twait's eyelids fell shut, his rifle tucked under his round belly, his breathing ragged. . . .

Then Jesse leaped, not caring about the hot coals burning his knees and Twait's fatal cries. He just hit down and down. And when Ollie's head looked mashed, when the blood poured out of his nose, mouth, and ears, he sat and laughed. He laughed until he filled the woods with his gladness for his freedom at last.

The next morning he pulled away, with the leftover fish he and Twait hadn't eaten, one ax, the rifle, and his sleeping roll. He knew he would reach the wide Yukon River within two or three days, and then his escape from the cruel wilderness and Eli Bonnet would be close at hand. Once on the river's ice, he planned on flashing his marshal's star at the first musher unlucky enough to come along. But he wouldn't kill the man as Twait would have, he would just steal his dogs and sled. Mushers lived rough lives—they knew how to survive. They could wait for help better than he.

On the third afternoon he stepped out onto the frozen Yukon, tears streaming down his face, his mouth laughing crazily again. For the first time in many days, life looked brighter, more possible and worthwhile. Once he got possession of a fast team, he would race downriver. It seemed impossible for Bonnet to catch him now. He lay too far in front—he had the headstart. And, perhaps, Eli might even guess the wrong direction to follow.

He heard them coming first, in the low light of the morning, yelps and cries echoing upriver in the still air of the fine winter day. He stepped next to the beaten sled trail, running up and down the Yukon's course, and waited. The musher would stop. Alaskans always stopped to help lonely strangers. It seemed a matter of principle on their part, a regulation to be observed by anyone wanting to be known as a sourdough across the great land. If a person didn't stop, you lost your reputation and badge of courage.

"What in tarnation are you doin' here by yourself in the middle of this river?" The red beard and blue eyes of the tall musher shined in the hard sunlight.

"My name is Jesse Peacock. I'm a U.S. Marshal. I'm afraid I have to confiscate your dogs and sled." Jesse flashed his U.S. Marshal's badge.

"Tarnation—you can't do that. This is government mail for Dawson City. If I don't haul this load there, I'll lose my job in a city boy's second, that's for sure."

"I'll give you a letter to show your employer. Now get off and unload your sled so I can get on my way. I must get upriver at once." Jesse lifted his rifle higher, hoping to persuade the man to hurry.

"Well, why don't you just jump on! You don't look fit to mush anyway. You look worse than the little Indian girl I picked up earlier this winter.

Mail don't weigh nothin' at all, I got plenty of room."

Jesse felt his temper break a little. "Mister, I'm not asking again. Do what I say. I said I'd give a letter. Someone will come along in a day or two, you and your mail will be fine. Why do you want to argue with me?" He lifted the Winchester rifle higher still.

The red-bearded face paled. Throwing down his snow hook, the musher bounded off the sled runners. Turning, he yelled, "Now hold on—quit gettin' mad. You got to understand my hesitation to give up my dogs and sled. I don't want trouble, just give me time to get my stuff."

"Well, wait a moment before you unload. I want to run back up the Tanana about five miles. There's another U.S. Marshal following behind me. He might be sicker than I am. You meet him and help out."

The tall man stopped still, his face wrinkled and eyes squinting. "I sure don't know what's goin' on. This is awful peculiar. By golly, been a weird winter." He then stepped back on the rear of the sled and impatiently waved for Jesse Peacock to climb on the load of dirty white sacks that read U.S. MAIL.

Two hours later Jesse turned the dogs downriver on the dead run. He doubted whether his nonsense of delaying Eli Bonnet would work for long, but even a few hours would help. And there seemed the possibility that Eli might turn upriver. Certainly he would spend time helping the musher with his government mail. That's Eli, he thought, always caring for the disenfranchised, the lost souls of the land.

Suddenly the ship back to San Francisco, back to his warm home, looked likely. He yelled for the dogs to run even faster, and smiled for the first time in a long while.

CHAPTER TEN

Food

The lonely tap of a woodpecker stopped him among the trees. The rattling raps sounded once more, then, at last, Eli saw a little movement down below. Just a patch of brown different from the other colors of the forest, but something that moved when the rest of the distance remained lifeless and silent. He stood riveted, staring, telling his mind to recall the habits of the hunter: stay quiet, calm, move only when the quarry looked the other way. His heart pounded inside his head, racing, impeding his hearing when he needed it the most. Again he forced himself to wait—his life depended on it—Blueberry's and two other men's lives as well. Behave like the cunning varmint, he thought, like the wily Indian and the winged hunter above. Wait, watch, strike only after the wary animal has dropped its guard.

When a noisy wind brushed by him, he stepped forward, cursing the sounds of his snowshoes. If the moose heard him, the brute would disappear in a flash. This appeared to be an old fat bull, accustomed to being hunted by the best—the hungry wolves of the land. And this bull had picked his position carefully. He had good visibility, plenty of cubbyholes to back into so he could fight for his life, and best of all, thickets of birch and willows close by.

But Eli saw weaknesses. The animal hadn't thought about humans and watching up on the ridge and the fatal aim of a rifle in the hands of a famished man. When the wind came by again, he stepped once more.

The blast of the Winchester echoed in the hills around him. He knew Blueberry would hear the shot. He also knew his friend's weary but grinning face would come tumbling down the hillside soon, tracking the snowshoe trail to the kill. And he thought the young man would weep a little. Starving men's souls couldn't be expected to stand firm against the sweet happiness of finding food at last. He wiped his own tears away. He had saved the day, just as the morrow had looked so grim. He and Blueberry had worked down to a few hours of lingering strength—then they could have hunted no more. His magic coat had worked. . . .

He skidded downhill, tramping sideways, stomping each snowshoe against the slope while he held on to brush to slow his descent. Walking over to the downed animal, he stood looking down, awestruck. Nearly two thousand pounds of weight lay at his feet. As he knelt to bleed the carcass, he shivered in anticipation. He could hardly wait to taste the heart. They would boil that piece first to gather energy for the ordeal ahead. A long day's work lay in front: skinning, cleaning, hanging the meat that they couldn't carry on their return trip high up in the trees so that wolverines, foxes, and wolves couldn't steal it all. The birds would eat some, he thought. But he felt a little needed to be shared with them. One had saved his life.

"Eli—Eli, did you shoot somethin' to eat?" Blueberry's call carried through the woods, then echoed down the slope.

"Come and see." Eli grinned, thinking of the happiness just ahead.

In a few minutes he heard the young Minnesotan puffing overhead while yanking the sled downhill, through the trees and alder brush blocking the way. They would struggle mightily to make it back up, he reflected, and it would take another full day to return to the river. But the thrill of seeing the faces of Twait and Peacock would make it all worthwhile.

When Blueberry pulled close enough to see the great brown shape in the snow, he called again, "Eli, you found a moose. My God, look at all the fresh meat." Then while trying to spring forward on his snowshoes, he fell flat on his face in the snow.

Eli laughed, then felt sorry for his friend's weakness and clumsiness. "Take it easy, Blueberry, this moose is ours forever, and we have plenty of time."

Blueberry rolled to a sitting position. "Can we

eat right away? I don't feel good. I could build a fire here close by . . ."

"Come help tip this animal up a bit so I can begin skinning, then you can build your fire. We'll boil and eat the heart, that will be the best nourishment for us at first. We have to be careful and not eat too fast. Otherwise, we'll cramp up and sicken. And you need to go slow so you don't hurt yourself with the ax. We'll camp overnight and start back in the morning."

"Eli, you don't know how happy I am." Then the young man wept, mopping his tears away with the backs of his fat winter mittens.

Both men worked all day gutting and skinning, cooking, then pitching camp next to the pile of meat Eli had cut away piece by piece. In the waning daylight they trimmed a tall spruce tree, so they could climb its branches like a ladder. Then they began to hide the meat they couldn't haul back on their sled.

"Go slow so you don't slip—take your time. Remember you're weak. Don't fall." Eli tilted his head up, worrying, watching as the Minnesotan climbed.

"I'm fine—now look out below." Blueberry dropped a rope so he could pull up the chunks of meat to hang in the tree.

Eli peered up again. "The birds and pine martins will eat some meat. I hope not much. It will take four or five days to get back to Peacock and Twait and Fincher. I hope a wolverine doesn't come along. They can climb. If one does, he'll rob all our stockpile and spoil what he can't eat. The Athabaskans call them the devils of the land. They say that wolverines are the spirits of ancestors gone bad. They tell about families who starved to death because of a raid on their cache."

"Eli, this land is the meanest I've ever seen. But I guess I love it best of any. Don't really know why. It's near killed me several times. I'll always stay. Maybe it's the challenge. I just hope I find gold someday."

Smiling, Eli continued staring up. "Blueberry, of all the friends I've made, you're the one I'll pray for the most. And trust me, you'll get rich in the end. A young man like yourself always succeeds. It's because you never give up."

"Thanks, Eli, but I think I should tell you I've thought of quittin' a lot lately—been so hard. Thank God you shot this moose."

Eli dropped his head, and then decided not to tell his friend the truth. It seemed best to keep one's own doubts a secret. Sometimes it's better to let friends see nothing but hard determination, he thought. The masquerade might influence them to better spirits.

In the early gray of the next morning they began the hard pull up the steep hollow where Eli had felled the moose. With full bellies at last, their strength crept back. Yet reaching the top exhausted both of them to the point of weary shivers. Then, resting in the afternoon sunshine, they cooked and ate once more. With full bellies for the third time since the previous day, they turned toward the Tanana River, along their backtrack, across the rolling hills standing in the way.

When the setting sun darkened the trail enough to blind them, they pitched their camp on a hill among birch trees. They slept like mummies, not waking all night, tired out completely by their heavy load and long, hard days.

They struck the wide Tanana again on their second day and camped on its shoreline under a late sun. Just before sleeping, Eli judged that he and Blueberry would pull back with their fresh food for Peacock, Twait, and Fincher before the next nightfall. In a week or so everyone would be healthy enough to move forward, he mused. And he would see Hannah coming upriver then. She wouldn't let dog mushing and winter camping stop her from searching for him. He had found her devotion included an undying pledge to take part in his life. He also knew Doll Girl would be urging a rescue as well. He even pictured his old friend Noodles coming along. He heard the old man's hoots and cackles in his dreams.

Eli stopped in his tracks the next afternoon when they had rounded the bend in the river hiding their old campsite. Looking anxiously backward at Blueberry, he saw the young man's face cockeyed, one hand shading his eyes while he peered ahead. The tent, the fire, every sign of human life had vanished. Instead, six black ravens danced on the snow, croaking and pecking at a bloody smear. And two lean foxes stood staring back, poised to dart away.

"They must have killed a caribou or moose themselves ... gone downriver afterwards ..." Blueberry's voice drifted into the winter's silence.

Eli waited to reply. He shivered, yet he felt sweat drizzling down his sides from pulling so long on the sled. What has happened to all three men they had left behind, he wondered? What's wrong?

"Blueberry, stay here. I think things have gone wrong for our friends." Eli dropped the tow rope and ran forward toward the ravens and foxes.

When he reached the abandoned campsite, he froze. A skeleton lay on the snow in front of him. The skull's empty eyes gaped out, a spine and ribs snaked down, and broken bones stuck out from the hollows of the hips. Bits of flesh still hung here and there on the corpse. Nonetheless, the birds and animals had nearly picked everything clean. And a circle of paw prints and bird tracks had beaten the snow flat—and bloody red.

Eli shuddered, searched around, then stepped forward and knelt beside the bones. Some seemed gone, then the skull's front teeth told who lay alongside him. Fincher! The sick friend of Blueberry's had been left behind. But why? Searching again for the missing arm and leg bones, he wondered? Could the foxes have carried those limbs away? But why would they have done that? Both foxes had appeared too hungry to have bothered with hiding food.

Searching further, he saw the old fire pit, with blackened embers and gray ashes yet settled down in the snow. A flattened area lay across from him, and scattered remnants of spruce boughs showed where the tent had sat, and how it had been torn down in a hurry. Then he saw the tracks of two men pulling a sled downriver toward the Yukon. Suddenly he knew what had happened to the missing human parts. Blood drops stained the trail where the footprints led away. Cannibalism! My God, his mind shrieked, Peacock and Twait had taken Fincher's flesh to eat. Suddenly he wondered if they had killed him, or had he simply died?

The Old West was full of tales of men eating other men. He had heard them all—Alfred Packer butchering his companions during a quest for gold in Colorado, the Donner party in their attempt to cross the snows of the Sierra Nevada, and last, the arguments back and forth about Indian warriors gulping down the bloody remains of their enemies. He pushed the silent horror of those past stories from his mind. It appeared he had the same awful madness here before him.

He turned back toward Blueberry and wondered what to say. If he told the truth, his young friend would surely break down. If he didn't say anything, the facts wouldn't change. Tramping back, dragging his feet, he decided to tell. The time had come for the young Minnesotan to learn about the savage ways of the new frontier and the ugly sins of men who had faced hungry times. He had seen similar kinds of desperate acts in the Dakota and Montana territories, across Arizona as well. Goodwill aside, it seemed time to inform Blueberry to harden up, at least if he planned on staying in Alaska very long. This wouldn't be the last time either of them would see the awful jeopardy men faced while living off the land.

"Blueberry, there's horrible news. Your friend Horace Fincher is dead. His remains are lying—"

"Finch is dead! My God, the varmints are eatin' him!" Blueberry's face paled, his eyes and mouth widened, then he began to step forward.

Eli reached out and stopped the young man from walking to the skeleton. "Blueberry—listen to me. Stay away—leave your poor friend alone. You don't want to see him now. He's gone forever and it's best you remember him the way he lived before. He's still your friend—but he's gone for good!"

Blueberry turned away and sobbed. Finally, after a moment he said through his tears, "We gotta bury him, Eli. We can't just leave him lay there!"

"Blueberry, we can't. You know as well as I do the ground is frozen, the ice and snow lay deep. We have no means to bury him. It hurts me to say this, but we have to walk away. We have to let the critters of the land have him. But his spirit will be free afterward. It will cross over to the big mountain behind us. Think of him resting there!"

Blueberry turned back, still crying. "What we gonna do? I don't feel like going on anymore."

"We need to move on and leave this place. I want you to look the other way. When we get downriver a few miles, we'll pitch camp and rest until you feel strong again. I learned long ago about tomorrow. In the morning the sun will rise and warm us once more. It will begin to brighten our lives. We'll find the strength to live on."

At last the Minnesotan nodded his head, then he hung it down. Eli picked up the sled's tow rope, thrust half across to Blueberry, and kept the other half for himself. He pulled down the Tanana without looking back, tugging the heavy sled and his friend along. After he judged they had walked five miles he noticed a shoreline facing south, one that would catch the morning beams when the sun first peeked over the distant mountains. A high slope of gravel stood nearby, a hillside that would catch the rays and heat things in front. This will be a good campsite, he thought, the best location we've had all winter, a warm place for healing, a place to plan our future.

Late at night as their fire snapped scattered volleys, and as its yellow light cast quick, dancing shadows on the bank behind them, Eli looked up and studied Blueberry sitting on the other side. His friend had quieted himself, but he still wiped his eyes now and then. Deep thoughts seemed busy in the young man's mind, and his sadness lay plainly on his face.

"Blueberry, would you like to leave this place in the morning? It's a nice place to stay if you wish."

"I'm gettin' better and thinkin' of catching up with Twait! I think he did somethin' bad to Finch!"

Eli paused, thinking about the suspicions he had had about the death of Fincher. But the wild creatures had eaten all the evidence. Human parts appeared to be missing, and drops of blood had stained the snow. In addition, Jesse Peacock hadn't posted a message. But perhaps cannibalism was the only crime. And cannibalism wasn't against the law—at least not against the laws of man.

"Blueberry, we can't be sure of anyone's guilt at this time. I agree we should follow. But Twait and Peacock could have abandoned this place just because Horace had passed away. He was very sick when we left the camp to hunt. Starving men do strange things. Perhaps our friends are downriver . . . waiting."

"Why'd they leave—what'd they have to eat? Their best bet was to wait for us to come back with food. You need to tell me why you didn't want me to look at Finch back there. I know somethin' is bad wrong. You need to tell me what you seen!"

Eli's heart sank. His young friend did have the right to know, he decided. "Blueberry, maybe Peacock and Twait took parts of your friend to eat. I'm not absolutely sure, but it looked that way."

Blueberry broke into sobs again, his cries filling the night. Eli sat still, hanging his head. Sometimes, he thought, the truth felt so wrong, yet lies would never do. The young man across from him would have found out sooner or later, then what. . . . As much as it hurt, the horror had to be told. Now the two of them could reach beyond the evilness at hand. They could chase down Peacock and Twait together. As heartless as it seemed, he had done the right thing.

After a long, sleepless night and after a cautious silence between them, they began their early-morning work of breaking camp. Blueberry marched around, pale-faced, his lips pinched hard and thin. Eli watched the Minnesotan, then decided his friend's face showed grim determination. A silent pledge had been made—they would follow the bloodstained trail until they caught their companions.

They tramped downriver along the shorelines, trudging by the snowy islands and over the ice, stopping only for a few hours each night. Up again early every morning, they ate, reloaded, then grabbed the tow rope of their sled and stalked ahead again. Both knew they could catch up. Both thought they would find out about Fincher.

Eli saw the trail swing toward an Indian fish camp he and Peacock had passed earlier in the winter. Stopping, he stared with an odd sense of doom circling his soul. Something seemed very wrong. What could it be, he wondered? Animal noises drifted across the river's ice.

"Blueberry, get the rifle for me. We've gotten ourselves close to danger. Something—"

"Eli, look!" Blueberry pointed.

Suddenly a dark brown animal jumped through an opening of the camp's rough shelter. The wild-

eyed creature tore back and forth in front, snarl-
ing, warning them to stay back. Dusky hues
streaked its body, which looked to be the size of
a small bear. But this thing appeared quicker and
more dangerous.

"What is it?" Blueberry's arm stayed straight.

"We've met our first wolverine! Walk slow. Get
the rifle. This critter isn't a bit afraid of us. If he
comes across the ice, we'll get badly hurt before
we have a chance to kill him!"

The young Minnesotan slowly dropped his arm
and stepped backward once, then again. When he
stood near the sled, he pulled his Winchester from
the top of the load. Then he crept back to Eli and
handed him the rifle.

"Didn't know they was so big . . . and mean."

Eli dropped his mittens on the snow, then
raised the Winchester. "Watch out! I'll walk closer.
That animal is bouncing around so much, I'm
going to need a better shot. You should step back
and get the other rifle. We may need both before
we're done."

He inched one foot forward, paused, and then
slid the other foot forward. Ten steps, twenty,
thirty, he counted each and measured the distance. Less than a hundred yards, he thought, but
that still looks too far. He lifted his leg once more.

The wolverine charged with a wild growl.
Streaking along, it bounded across the snow in a
flash. His rifle exploded. He missed. Flipping the
rifle's lever down and up, he jacked the action for
his next round. Then he heard another shot and

saw snow fly up behind the blur of fur now close in front. Blueberry has just missed, he thought. Aiming, swinging down, he froze his mind's eye on the target and squeezed the trigger again. A hit, but the devil animal kept coming. But slower. Bang! He heard another miss by Blueberry. Levering his rifle the third time, he aimed once more and killed the wolverine a few steps away.

"Eli, you got him. I thought he was goin' to chew you up for sure. Never thought that thing could run so fast." The young man jogged to the bundle of brown fur.

"Don't you dare pick him up. I don't think he's dead yet."

They waited, and then walked to the wolverine after it had quit its last kicks. Keeping his rifle ready, Eli poked the animal with his foot, feeling for any signs of life.

"Blueberry, stay here and start skinning. I need to look inside the hut. This critter acted like he was guarding a kill. I'll call you when I know."

Turning, Eli walked to the shack up on the shore. Creeping, listening, he peeked in the doorway. He then gagged when he saw the sight inside—another skeleton. But this body was not yet gnawed clean. Hair, clothing, and leather pieces lay scattered on the dirt floor. Intestines dangling from the half-eaten body. Its face looked chewed off. He counted two arms. Twait had been killed by something . . . or someone. Finally he saw the bloody block of firewood, with human skin still mashed onto its surface. He understood why only one set of tracks led away. He turned and walked back to Blueberry.

"More awful news. Ollie Twait's body is inside. I think Peacock killed him with a club."

The young man's face whitened, like the snow. After a moment, he whispered, "I'm gonna go an' look. I want to see for myself. Both were goin' crazy—appears Peacock got there first."

"Blueberry, you stay here. There's nothing to be gained by looking inside. It's an awful sight—I couldn't bear it. And I've seen worse back in the Old West!"

"I'm goin' to do it, Eli. I gotta toughen up someday. If you can do it—I can learn, too!" Then Blueberry stomped toward the hut.

Eli knelt beside the wolverine and finished skinning the carcass. He glanced now and then at his friend walking around the rough hut, then watched as the young man stopped and stared inside the door. Suddenly the Minnesotan turned and marched back, mittens over his mouth, but his face plain and straight.

"Eli, I see that Peacock must've found somethin' else to carry along to eat. Maybe dried fish. I saw some bones that looked that way. And I see'd he threw off Finch's arms, maybe didn't want to eat them anymore."

Eli looked up in amazement. "Blueberry—good job. I missed those things."

"Can I climb up and look if there's fish in the cache? If there is, I want to trade some moose meat for what we need. Ain't good for us to eat nothin' but meat all the time. I want somethin' else, too."

In spite of the wolverine, and in spite of the dreadful sight lying nearby, Eli's mouth curled into a smile. "That sounds good to me, Blueberry. It's old sourdough law to leave behind payment. I'm proud of you, go get it done."

They pulled away an hour later, leaving Twait's body just as they had found it. Both men knew any attempt to bury or hide the corpse would prove worthless. The hungry animals of the wilderness would smell the grave, dig, and scatter the bones nevertheless. They realized they now were walking a land with little mercy—a land ruled by gluttonous wolverines and weasels, foxes and wolves, shrews and mice, creatures big and small that fed on flesh, never caring where it came from. Providence had willed the world that way from the very beginning. Only fools pretended there was a better world. Final judgment would let no part lie around unused. Wild creatures lived without the holy cross.

When they reached the last few miles of the Tanana River, they stopped, surprised again. In the lonely distance lay an odd gray mound, with a human shape sitting on top. A smoky fire blazed nearby, fanning against curling mists of low scud. Then the hunkering figure looked their way, waved, beckoning them to come downriver.

As they neared the campfire, a tall man stepped forward, offering his hand. "Been here three days waitin' for you, was about ready to give up."

Glancing at the U.S. mail sacks, Eli shook the man's hand. "I'm Eli Bonnet. This is Billy House—call him Blueberry, his choice. It seems you've become acquainted with a one-armed Marshal named Peacock."

"Took my sled and dogs from me in a city boy's second. First time I ever got scared of a lawman. He was pretty quick with that one arm, pointin' that Winchester. But he did tell me to wait and help you. Though he didn't say nothin' about Blueberry."

Then Eli asked, "Did he say which way he intended to go?"

The red-bearded man combed his whispers with his fingers. "Yes, sir. Said he was headin' up to Dawson. Surely peculiar though, he wouldn't let me drive him there. He didn't look well. I said I was goin' anyhows. But it didn't make no difference, he wanted my dogs real bad and looked like he'd shoot me to get 'em."

Blueberry shook the tall musher's hand next. "Good thing you gave 'em up. He's killed one man and ate another."

Dark, tired eyes flared above the musher's nose, then his mouth flew open. "Tarnation, I've heard of men eatin' one another, but never knowed it to be true. Can't imagine bein' that hungry."

"I can—we been that way ourselves lately. Eli shot a moose and saved us in the last hour. Now we got plenty, you want some?"

The musher squinted at the sled sitting behind Eli. "Tarnation, that sounds good. I got plenty of food, but nothin' fresh. You boys come over by my fire, we'll cook and make plans. I gotta get this mail down to the Yukon and catch another sled headin' upriver. I suppose you boys want to come along."

Eli turned toward the fire, tugging the heavy sled along. What should he do, he wondered? He sensed Peacock had wanted to throw him off for a day or two. But his former companion had always acted so crazily it seemed impossible to predict what he might do. And Hannah would be coming down the Yukon River in a little while.

After their meal each man clutched a handful of tow rope and pulled toward the Yukon, leaving the mail bundles behind. Eli led the way, head low against his load, and down against his uncertainty. Which way had Peacock really gone? And did he and Blueberry have the strength to chase him? His duty as a lawman, his young friend's duty as a friend seemed compelling. But the mountains behind still held Doll Girl's mother and her kidnapper. There was a responsibility there as well.

"What you thinkin' about, Eli?" The Minnesotan's voice broke away from his panting breath.

"What I should do? Should I wait for Hannah— let Peacock go? Should I turn back and try to find Doll Girl's mother once more?"

The tall musher swung his head back and forth. "You two ain't fit for the trip back to that big mountain. You'll both die if you try. Then what

good are you to anybody? I been in the country
a long time. Listen to common sense."

Eli dropped his head lower. The mail carrier's
prophecy frightened him, and seemed wise. He
had watched Blueberry's face change to a ratty
beard with bones beneath. His own facial features
must look the same. It appeared the savage wilderness of Alaska had won this time. It had beaten
him back toward civilization and the common sus-
tenance of man.

All three men marched back onto the Yukon
River in a hard snowstorm blowing east. Eli
stopped and peered into the blinding wind coming upriver. Then he turned and stared downriver.
Which way, he wondered . . .

PART III

Searching

CHAPTER ELEVEN

Prophecies

"Noodles, take this gold and buy two sleds and twenty dogs. Then buy everything you can think of to keep us safe while we search for Eli." Hannah lifted a syrup can full of nuggets and carried it to the old man.

"By Jeez, I got plenty of gold, more than I'll ever live to spend. You keep yours, maybe you'll need it someday. I'll pay for everythin' we need. I owe Eli for savin' my life." Noodles shook his head so hard his white whiskers flew out from his chin.

Hannah frowned, then decided not to argue with her elderly friend. "You pay for half. I'll pay the other. Let's not waste time."

Doll Girl skipped to Noodles's side and hugged his waist. "I get to go, too. I know about dogs and sleds."

Hannah looked at the girl. Doll Girl did have the only worthwhile experience with sled dogs. "Yes, I think you should go. Now both of you dress warmly, it's twenty below outside. I want everything ready by morning after next." Smiling, she wondered sometimes who seemed more the child, Doll Girl or Noodles? Both had grown so close they acted like grandfather and granddaughter. And for two months they'd been underfoot like two rascals.

The winter daylight had grown longer; January had come and gone. Hannah worried that she might have waited too long to start the search. She had filled her idle time by schooling Doll Girl in English and math, and the little girl had been an outstanding student. Noodles had hung around, learning more about speech and numbers himself, but hadn't shown any change. He still hooted and cackled, yet spoke the same old way.

All three had missed Eli being home for Christmas, and for New Year's Day as well. They had walked to a huge celebration downtown on that day; Doll Girl coming back wide-eyed and grinning, all her pockets full of treats from Noodles' friends. It hadn't been an unhappy winter, but now she felt despair. Eli seemed overdue by a few days.

Noodle's forehead furrowed. "Don't you think we should ask somebody else to come along? You and I don't know much about mushing."

"I think we'll be fine. You and I camped out all last winter during our travels to this place. Doll Girl can teach us how to drive dogs. If we add another person, we'll need even more supplies. We can carry the most by keeping our load to just the three of us."

"Wahnie and I know all about mushing. Father

River is long and wide. It will be easy at first. Travel won't be difficult until we reach the Kantishna, the crooked one flowing from the spirit mountain."

Hannah sensed her other worry. "Doll Girl, are you sure you remember the way back? I don't want to get lost."

The girl's mouth fell open; her eyes grew humid. "I can never get lost, and Wahnie would take us there even if I fell asleep. He is very wise."

Hannah felt sorry for her doubt about Doll Girl's skills. "I shouldn't have asked—I'm just frightened. Now go and show Noodles how to buy the best dogs. I'll order the food, then you can see if I have what we need."

The misty eyes brightened. "Don't be afraid, Wahnie and I will take care of you."

Hannah felt her own eyes grow wet. She had learned to love the little Indian girl like her own daughter. The child's courage and spirit seemed so special for her young age.

"I know you will. Now run for your parka and help the best you can. We have two days in which to get ready."

Noodles and Doll Girl tugged home noisy, disorderly sled dogs throughout the afternoon of the first day. Hannah marveled at the dark-eyed child's wizardry with the savage brutes. She watched in awe as the small girl pushed and tethered, with Noodles' help, all the dogs into two rows strung across the snowy yard. And when any dog became too troublesome for Doll Girl, her grizzled old friend Wahnie would jump in and a fight would break out. In a matter of seconds, the disobedient dog would yield and obey.

Noodles assisted the best he could, his cackles and hoots filling the outdoors. He seemed to enjoy handling the sled dogs, quickly learning the methods from Doll Girl. By nightfall the two of them had finished assembling two complete teams. Then they bedded each dog on wild hay they had carried home for that purpose. At last the racket of the day began to ebb, and, Hannah reflected, her neighbors could live in peace once more. She had seen her next-door friends, their hands on their hips, glaring across, not a bit happy about all the hubbub.

The following day they bought two new sleds constructed by Athabaskan Indians for heavy freighting. They added harness straps, extra harness, coils of hemp rope, leather socks for the dogs' feet, and canvas covers for each load they planned to carry. Then they bought axes, saws, tents, bedrolls, and caribou hides to carry along. Lastly they ordered food for themselves and their dogs to be delivered to their home. Working late into the night, they finally completed their preparations. Then each of them fell into bed, exhausted from their two days of hard work.

In the yellow light of the next morning they began to load their sleds and harness their teams. Hannah had supposed Wahnie would head the front of one paired column of dogs, and she had planned on tying Eli's dog Ironclaw in the right-hand position, just behind the old gray leader. The two dogs had been kenneled together for over two months, and she thought it would be the best way to teach the young dog about the skills of leadership. But Ironclaw wouldn't come to his assigned position. Hannah shouted and chased him around the yard, trying to catch him. Doll Girl and Noodles stood close by, laughing, amused to see Ironclaw dash to the head of the second team, then out of reach, each time Hannah tried to pull him back.

Finally Doll Girl stepped forward and caught Ironclaw by his neck. "You must let him lead, he won't pull unless you do!"

"Isn't he too young? He's had no experience, and I'm afraid he'll get into fights with the other dogs. I don't want to see him hurt."

Doll Girl smiled and pulled the young dog to the front of the other team. "He will watch Wahnie and learn. And he is big enough to make the other dogs behave. He's strong and smart like my old friend. Follow me with your sled and watch how he pulls, how fast he runs. You will see he acts just like my dog."

"How will I know what to do? I've never mushed dogs. Ironclaw has never led before. Are you sure this is safe?"

"All sled dogs know what to do. They love to pull, that is what they are born to do. You step onto the runners, hold the brake down, then watch and listen as I yell to Wahnie. After you hear what I say, tell the same things to your dogs, they will obey. Ironclaw will learn from Wahnie as we go along. You will, too. Just remember to hold tight, the dogs will go very fast, at first, until they grow tired of running."

With painful doubt in her breast, Hannah stepped onto the rear of her sled and waited, her right boot jammed down hard on the sled's brake, locking it into the snow. She watched as Doll Girl jogged over to her own sled. Twenty dogs squealed and yipped, hopping up and down, all eager to race away. Only Wahnie, at the front of the first sled, and Ironclaw, at the head of the second, stood steady and soundless. Each leader trembled, each one looked back eagerly at their masters, but both dogs stood their ground, waiting for their master's command. Then Doll Girl grinned and yelled to her dog, "Wahnie, go!"

Both teams tore off like a shot down onto the frozen Yukon, snow billowing behind. They swung around to the west, never looking back once at their drivers. They ran as twenty-two dogs thrilled to be free, thrilled to be off again on an adventure. With their tails streaming back, each dog flagged his joy over having been chosen to haul along the river. They were on the loose again, with their drivers riding behind, with their leaders running in front, to chase the reaches of the Alaskan wilds into which they'd been born with their hodgepodge of wolf and husky stirred into one.

Then, at last, they slowed to their willful trot, their everlasting pace, which chewed the miles away. Fifty miles a day, sixty miles a day, they could keep to it always. Just give us some water,

just give us some food, they said, then we can go
on forever. They grinned their unwearied persistence, their tongues lolling out as they loped
along, their love of life dancing in their eyes.

Hannah couldn't help it—she laughed and cried
at the same time. With head winds stinging her
face, with her tears freezing on her cheeks, she
clung desperately to the sled handles, thunder-
struck by the speed and power of her dogs. Thinking she had never gone so fast, her heart leaped
with the excitement to be off again on one more
great search for Eli Bonnet, much like the one she
had gone on once before. She wondered if there
could be something buried deep inside her which
compelled her to chase after the man she loved
two separate times within one year's duration.
Perhaps, she thought, I've come to love this land
as much as he. Maybe the danger and the distance, the immortal mountains, and the endless
forests have mesmerized me, too.

She watched as the Yukon River slipped by. It
coursed between boggy flatlands, snow-covered
and windswept. Marsh grasses stuck out above
the snowfall, along with willow bushes, with
weeping, leafless branches, for as far as her eyes
could see. When the brighter part of the morning
came, the sun crept up on top of the skyline, and
then low mountains stood out, both on the northern and southern horizons. And the dogs kept
running west, sweeping back and forth mile after
mile on the loops of the river.

Experimenting with the foot brake, she stepped

down hard. Instantly, Ironclaw and the other dogs behind him glanced back, each dog flashing frowning eyes at her, telling her not to slow them down without good reason. But she had learned about the brake's drag, and sensed its value for stopping the sled when she wanted. Then she worried again. Doll Girl hadn't told her the command for stopping the dogs. Could it be like reining back on horses, she wondered?

Finally she relaxed her grip on the sled handles, sensing her balance on the balls of her feet. The dog's pounding paws, the sled's gnawing noises on the snow's crust, and the creaking of its wooden frame as it twisted and swayed on the trail, began to sing a song.

She listened carefully. Yes . . . the rest of the wilderness lay silently. Just she and her dogs, along with Doll Girl and her team, made music in the winter stillness. She then recalled her past year crossing northern Canada, when the land had seemed similarly forsaken. There appeared to be something sinister about the snow and cold. The elements endeavored to hide other living things from human eyes and ears. Everything sleeps, she mused, burrows away from the hardy souls who dare to come into the frozen bush.

After only two hours on the trail, she watched Doll Girl wave her right arm toward the shoreline. Then Hannah saw the little girl turn her dogs to the same riverbank. Next she heard the girl yell, "Wahnie, stop!" Ironclaw immediately trailed behind and stopped as well. Then the young leader stood still, with the other dogs behind him behaving the same way, though a few lay down.

Doll Girl threw out her sled's snow hook and kicked it down into the snow's crush. "We make tea now." Without waiting, she then waded into the woods, searching for dry firewood.

"By Jeez, little girl, how'd you know I was 'bout froze to death just sittin' here on this sled. My old bones need to move around a bit to keep warm." Noodles followed Doll Girl through the trees.

Hannah stomped her own hook down. She walked along petting each one of her dogs, then she hugged Ironclaw with both arms. "You've grown up before my eyes and I've missed it, my friend. We'll find Eli together, you and I, won't we?" She heard the young dog whine, just like he always did when he heard his master's name.

Doll Girl returned to the river's ice with an armload of wood. "We will live the same as my father and mother, when I camped with them when I was little. We will rest the dogs often, eat good food, stay warm and dry always."

Noodles shuffled back and dropped his firewood. Next he shoved a handful of birch-bark scraps he had ripped from several trees under his woodpile. Striking a match, he cupped its flame from the wind with his hands, then touched the kindling with the tiny yellow tongue. In a moment an orange flame licked up to the dried sticks stacked above.

"By Jeez, mushin' is the best way to travel across this land. At this rate we'll be to Fort Yukon in a jiffy." The old prospector added larger pieces to his brightening fire.

Hannah reached under her sled's canvas cover and pulled out a tin kettle. She filled it with clean snow and crouched beside Noodles at the fire's edge, perching it above the flames. "Doll Girl, how far is it to Fort Yukon? Will we get there tomorrow?"

"No, it will take at least two more days. It's far." The little girl joined them and warmed her hands.

"Do you know how to find the boy who brought you to Dawson City? I want to see if he knows what might have happened to Eli."

"We will talk to the ancient one instead. He is a very wise shaman. The spirits speak to him as they fly over the mountains. He will know how to find Mr. Bonnet."

Hannah gazed steadily at Doll Girl across the fire. The little girl's belief in spirits hadn't weakened a bit, in spite of several days of Bible lessons. Hannah wondered if she would ever be able to bring Doll Girl to the church with an acceptance of Jesus Christ as her savior. That hard stubbornness on the child's part had been the only frustrating part of their relationship.

"Doll Girl, you know I don't believe in spirits. Why do you test me so?"

The girl beamed back. "You will believe after you listen to the old one. If you think there is only one God, why can't I believe there are more?"

"Because that's not what the Bible says." Then

Hannah felt sorry, thinking she had snapped needlessly.

Noodles frowned. "Hannah, we need to parley with the old medicine man and learn what he knows. I 'spect he's like me—seen a lot of country, done a lot of things. He'll give us good counsel, if nothin' else." The old man rattled the pot on top of the fire to settle the melting snow.

Suddenly Hannah remembered Eli describing the same medicine man from his first journey to Fort Yukon, back in the past autumn. She deserved her old friend's admonishment, she thought. The sacred elder would surely know something of value to use in their search.

"I'm sorry, Doll Girl. I'll be glad to visit with whomever you wish. All I want is to find Eli as soon as possible. I'll gladly talk to anyone who can help."

At noon on their fourth day they pulled to the front of the dugout belonging to the ancient wiseman of Fort Yukon. Doll Girl immediately crawled into the tunnel leading inside, then she popped back out and motioned for Hannah and Noodles to come in. When Hannah reached the hollow of the hut, shining yellow with candlelight, she stared in silent fear at the skeletal figure in front. Noodles crawled in last, gesturing to the shriveled sage with hand signals.

"By Jeez, the old devil knows the Indian signs I learnt crossin' the Old West!" Noodles winked at Hannah, his eyes dancing.

"What did he say?"

"He wondered how old I was. When I told him, he said he couldn't remember bein' so young." The old prospector cackled about the shaman's humor.

"Ask him about Eli. I want to leave here as soon as possible. We can get a long ways downriver yet today."

Doll Girl slid forward on the dirt floor. "I'll do it. He knows my language. It is nearly the same as his." She began murmuring odd syllables to the old Indian.

In a moment she turned back to Hannah. "The old one says the ravens said that we would come here. He said danger waits for us near the great mountain. He wonders if we are strong."

Hannah felt her fear deepen. Then she wondered why. The withered Indian couldn't possibly see into the future. Yet she wondered if he knew anything about Eli.

"Ask him if he knows where I can find Eli? Does he know if he's well?" Then she felt the sharp, dark eyes across the room focus on her. Indian eyes just like Eli had described to her in the past, seemingly able to see into one's soul.

After another throaty exchange with the shaman, Doll Girl interpreted once more. "He says Mr. Bonnet is like the wolf running across the land. He will come back when his hunt is over."

Hannah supposed her two questions had been answered, albeit in an unusual way. Eli had warned her that Indians dealt differently with life's issues. They measured mankind's deeds against animal behavior, or as compared to nature's forces—the wind, the water, and the sunshine. They might describe man as acting strong like a bear, or weak like the summer wind, however a human event might suggest a description. Eli must be off on some wild-goose chase, she thought, which made perfect sense. He had always been the wanderer. But she wondered why the wrinkled sage had warned her about danger near the mountain called Denali.

"What danger waits near the big mountain?"

Doll Girl spoke again in her mother tongue to the shaman. After a moment she turned back to Hannah with round, fearful eyes. "The old one says the spirits are angry because my father's bones are lost. He says the white man who kidnapped my mother is still searching for me. He warns that this evil one will kill again."

Hannah stared at the little Athabaskan girl. Why would the kidnapper look for a child, she wondered? Glancing at Noodles squatting next to her, she saw the seasoned prospector's full blue eyes also widen. Turning back to Doll Girl, she asked, "Why would that man want you?"

Before Doll Girl could open her mouth to answer, the ancient shaman shook his bony, clawlike hand at her. Then he quickly murmured curious human sounds. Doll Girl instantly dropped her head, and after a single moment she answered, "I cannot say. It is a secret that I must try to keep. Please don't ask me to tell."

Hannah sat still, flabbergasted. The inside of the

dugout fell silent, except for breaths like falling whispers. At last she decided the medicine man didn't matter enough to stay any longer. She had learned Eli seemed well. She had been fairly warned of a dangerous man waiting ahead. It's time to go, she thought. For whatever reason, she felt compelled to journey on toward the great mountain she had heard about so much. She turned and crawled back out into the wintertime.

Doll Girl and Noodles crawled out behind her. All three stood soundlessly looking off toward darkening skies downriver. Hannah reached over and hugged the little Indian girl, wanting to comfort both of them from the fateful jeopardy they had been warned about. At last they walked to their sleds without speaking again. Somehow they sensed their need to run farther west, regardless of their fear over what lay ahead.

CHAPTER TWELVE

Skeletons

They ran twenty miles beneath an uneven, graying sky. Just before nightfall snow began to blow along the river's surface, until its course became a lost trail. Hannah alertly followed Doll Girl in the dusky light, seeing the little girl beckoning from the back of her sled. Finally she saw Wahnie swing wide toward a windbreak of riverbank with trees on top. She chased close behind, but without having to shout or wave at Ironclaw, at the lead of her own sled. The young dog knew the time had come to find shelter.

All three worked feverishly to pitch camp in the dancing light of their bonfire, which whipped back and forth in a blizzard now slanting overhead. Their encounter with the shaman back in Fort Yukon had persuaded them to mush later than usual—an unspoken bargain having passed between them to run as far away as possible from the withered old prophet. His farseeing powers had frightened everyone into an uneasy silence.

When at last Hannah felt able to talk about their troubling visit with the medicine man, she crouched by her two friends beside the fire. "I'm not afraid to go on. That old coot couldn't know the things he said!" She stirred their supper flipping her wrist.

Noodles' face wrinkled. "By Jeez, I don't know. I ain't sayin' I'm scar't to go on ... never been scar't of nothin' but Providence, but that powwow was enough to make me take heed. We best be careful as we go along!"

Doll Girl's black eyes met Hannah's. "I'm not afraid either. But we must believe what the old one said—he's very wise. Grandfather Noodles is right, we need to act like Indians the rest of the way. If we watch, the spirits will tell us when there is danger."

Hannah continued stirring their food, thinking over her common impulse to pretend she felt unafraid. Then she decided to tell the truth. "I shouldn't have said I'm not afraid. I'm really scared to death. I don't know how to live outdoors like you two. I need you to help me learn. We'll be fine then, don't you think?"

Doll Girl hugged Hannah. "Wahnie and I will take care of you like I said before. Grandfather Noodles will help also."

That night they huddled together under their caribou covers, Hannah on one side of Doll Girl and Noodles on the other. Each lead dog slept inside the tent as well, adding their body heat to keep the deadly cold away. The wind thundered outside and flopped the canvas walls up and down, upsetting their rest and keeping each of them tossing, sleeping only in slips of time.

As Hannah lay waiting for sleep, she thought back to the shaman's quick outcry back in the dugout. Why had he interrupted Doll Girl so suddenly? What did he and Doll Girl know about the kidnapper and his presumed search? What persuaded them to keep secrets? It seemed Doll Girl knew why the stranger still hunted. . . .

But it wouldn't be helpful to pursue the secrets. She knew Doll Girl well enough to realize the little girl wouldn't violate a trust without good reason. She would have to rely on the child's common prudence. Doll Girl and Noodles had grown to be like family, and like a sister, she would have to wait. And besides, it might be only silly curiosity on her part, just as silly as the old Indian who had frightened her so badly. At last she fell asleep, happy to have Ironclaw and Wahnie lying nearby.

At sunrise they found hard blue skies and deep cold outside their tent. Hannah, when she first saw their sled dogs peeking out from under snowdrifts covering their bodies, marveled at the animals' abilities to curl up and sleep untroubled by the wintertime. She had learned to admire the dogs more than any other creature she had ever seen work. Smart, tough, loyal, seldom unhappy, their worth amazed her. No wonder, she thought, the Indians and Eskimos and sourdoughs of Alaska measured their lives by the value of their dog teams. They provided the sole means to cross the boundless wilds all around. And, as revolting as it seemed, she had heard you could eat them, too.

"Today we must protect our eyes!" Doll Girl's voice knifed the icy air of the morning.

Hannah, surprised, turned to face the Indian girl. "What's wrong? It's a nice day, except for the cold!"

Noodles hooted one of his odd calls, then said, "By Jeez, I know what's wrong."

Doll Girl laughed, as she always did when her adopted grandfather teased and played. Digging in a leather bag Doll Girl had carried along, she held out three narrow masks with thin slits for seeing out. "We need to wear these. If we don't, our eyes will get sick from the sun."

Snow blindness. Hannah recalled reading about the awful hazard back in Dawson City. Many men had sickened to the point of losing their eyesight completely in the Alaskan winter. The sun's glare burned the eyes until they reddened, watered, then swelled shut, leaving their owners blind, maybe forever.

After pulling on their masks and wrapping woolen scarves over their noses and mouths, they began to mock each other. The three of them looked like freakish creatures, with their faces hidden by masks, scarves, and fur-fringed hoods, and with their bodies bundled in long parkas and high, fat moose-hide boots. Then they called out muffled, funny names and chased each other around the snowy river. For the first time in days, they forgot their fateful purpose for a little while.

Two hours later they restarted their journey along the Yukon's rough surface. Wahnie led the way once more, but now across new snow, piled like waves on a hardened sea. Plowing along, the old leader picked his way; sometimes he cut corners, pulling across swampy grasses; at other times he trotted in wide sweeps around river bends, coming close to places he had just passed. Watching the long strings of sleds and dogs in front, Hannah searched the great flatness, which seemed to grip them inside its very belly. She had never imagined such distances of winding channels, fields of willows and grasses, stands of runty trees, and tangles of driftwood, stacked here and there. An unending riddle, she mused. And she wondered how the old dog up front knew his way. And she wondered what would happen when the weather clouded again. Could Wahnie keep on?

That evening they sat by their dying fire watching northern lights chase sharp stars blinking above. Hannah had seen the magic glow before, but not beneath a moon-free sky, with yellow, red, green, and blue frosting the night. She and Doll Girl huddled together and cooed about the bright colors. Noodles, alongside, sat hushed for a change. Finally they crawled under their hides and blankets inside their tent, whispering about heaven's ways.

Day after day they ran farther downriver. Clear and cold, cloudy with snow falling, windy or calm . . . they kept on regardless of the weather. Finally they reached beyond the flat wasteland that had appeared so endless, sledding between low mountains treed with green spruce, spreading up the slopes. Countryside color, instead of black and white, Hannah thought as she gazed around. And she saw Doll Girl and Noodles teasing and laughing.

"By Jeez, I bet that was the biggest swamp in the world!" Noodles poked at their night's campfire, building up the flames.

Hannah smiled widely. She guessed she felt the same relief as the old prospector. "Doll Girl, I still wonder how Wahnie finds his way. It doesn't seem to matter whether it's cloudy or clear, he always knows where the best trails run. No wonder you love and trust him so much. I hope Ironclaw learns to be as clever."

"Ironclaw will never forget the way back now. He will remember it forever. He and Wahnie are the best leaders in Alaska." The Indian girl's eyes brightened, as they always did when she talked about the two lead dogs.

"How many days till we reach Kantishna River?"

"We will arrive there soon." Doll Girl looked back to the fire, suddenly appearing lost in thought.

Hannah supposed the little girl had just remembered her home and her mother back on Sleepy Lake. It seemed unusual, too, that Doll Girl never spoke of time elements like others. Eli had explained previously that Indian people told time by the passing of seasons, the migrations of the caribou herds, or by the deaths of ancestors. They didn't think it important to count individual days, one by one. They always dealt in uncertain terms of time.

And strangely enough, Hannah recalled, she had forgotten the number of days that had passed since leaving Dawson City herself. It seemed so long ago, it puzzled her. Why hadn't she counted, she wondered? Had Alaska washed away her regimen of when to get up in the morning, or when to eat or sleep?

Several days later, under a lowering sun, Wahnie pulled around a left-hand turn and cut between the mainland and three hulking islands, standing midstream across the river's course. Soon afterward Hannah saw Doll Girl's sled appear to be headed opposite from their original direction down the river. We're on the Tanana now, she thought. Doll Girl had described the Tanana River, flowing in from the east, and she had said it ran as wide as the Yukon, at the junction.

The next day she saw Doll Girl gesture toward a small log cache standing onshore, with a bark-and-log hut built nearby. An awful place, Hannah thought, but at least we won't have to raise the miserable, cold-stiffened tent tonight. Smiling, she sped up Ironclaw and her dogs to catch the sled ahead.

After Doll Girl and Noodles had anchored their dogs on the river's edge, they stood side by side and waited for Hannah to pull up.

"By Jeez, we can sleep in somethin' different tonight. I'm sick of stringin' up the tent every night. What you think?" Noodles grinned through little icicles, hanging like tiny snakes from his whiskers.

"That sounds good ... I'm so tired of fighting with that frozen canvas cloth each night, I could scream. Perhaps we can hang up some hides to make it a little more cozy than it looks."

Doll Girl wandered in a circle, climbed the shore, then stood looking around. In a moment she yelled back down, "Someone's been here. I can see old tracks covered up by snow. This is the last place Wahnie and I stayed when we walked to find someone to help my mother!" She walked toward the shack standing nearby.

Suddenly sharp screams filled the air. Noodles grabbed his Winchester rifle from the sled next to him and bounded up the shore, Hannah chasing behind, both stunned by Doll Girl's wailing cries. They ran to the open door of the shack, seeing the Indian child standing just inside its doorway. In the gray light of the hollow lay white gleaming bones—a human skeleton lying under the light of the setting sun.

"Little girl, get out of there!" Noodles scuttled sideways and peeked inside while Doll Girl bolted outside.

The old man crept through the opening, after seeing nothing more than human bones. Then he stepped back out, his face long and flat.

"Hannah, take Doll Girl back down to Wahnie

and bring back my lantern. ı want to look around some more."

"Is it Eli? Hannah's cry speared the fearful stillness that had settled around.

"By Jeez, Hannah, quit that and do what I say! Do it now! This ain't the time and place for you to act like some weak city girl. Now get, I tell you." Noodles' old blue eyes hardened.

Hannah turned back to her sled, dragging Doll Girl along by one arm. Pulling a coal oil lantern out from under the sled's cover, she ran back, leaving the Indian girl waiting behind.

Noodles snatched the wire handle of the lantern, fished for matches under his parka, scratched one, and lit the wick. Then he stepped back inside the hut, the light's yellow shine casting unsettled shadows on the walls.

"By Jeez, mighty strange in here."

Trying to steady her voice, Hannah peeked through the door. "Is it Eli . . . please tell me?"

"No, No—I don't believe so—too small a fellow, front teeth ain't right. But I ain't figured out somethin' yet. There's too many arm bones layin' in here. I guess we know it can't be Jesse Peacock anyways. He ain't got but one. There looks to be four in here. Somethin's mighty strange."

"Let's leave here at once. This is awful."

"No—we need to stay. We need to look around in the mornin', when it gets good and light. You, Doll Girl, and me gots to figure what's goin' on if we can. Ain't natural to find one dead man and a part of another . . . nosiree."

"But there's nothing but bones. Bones that must have been here a long time. Some Indian person, perhaps." Hannah stared at the old prospector, bewitched by his settled, calm face as he poked at the skeleton.

"Hannah, I'm an old man. Been across the West—now come clean across North America. I can't remember all the skeletons I see'd in my life . . . lot's of 'em, I guess. This pile of bones is fresh. Look here, the meat's just been gnawed away by hungry varmints not long ago. Now itty-bitty critters is chewin' on the bones. This here man ain't been dead but for a month or so."

"I don't want to stay in there!" Hannah stepped back from the doorway and shivered. Silent horror sickened her when she thought of trying to sleep inside the ramshackle tomb.

"Well, you're goin' to. That's the way it's got to be. Hannah, you got to get over bein' squeamish and scared. It ain't goin' to bother me none. And I bet it don't bother Doll Girl much, neither. You got to remember you're in the middle of the biggest wilderness in the world. It ain't smart to pass up comfortable surroundings when they come by. Besides, like I said, we gotta look round in the mornin' light. Now go down and get our stuff. I'll get rid of these bones!"

Hannah turned away from the front of the hut, a little numbed by her friend's hard words. She walked back to Doll Girl and the sleds. What has got into that old man, she wondered? She had never seen him behave so willfully; she had never heard him speak so deliberately. Then she thought it appeared to be her own fault. She had acted like a little girl—perhaps even younger than Doll Girl.

By the time she and Doll Girl had trudged back with their arms full of camping gear, Noodles had cleared the floor of every bit of the bones. Shivering again, Hannah stepped inside and began to spread their hides and blankets and set down their kettles and skillet for their night's fire. Peering around, the hut reminded her of a wickiup that Eli had described being used by the Apaches of Arizona. The structure had been built standing room tall, rounded enough for six or eight people, and stood like a thatch of wood poles, sheets of birch bark, and layers of spruce boughs, all woven together into a crude structure. Toward the center, near where the skeleton had been, lay an old ash pit, deliberately placed below the center of the ceiling, which had been left open for the rising smoke of fires.

"By Jeez, don't look so bad now, does it?" The old prospector popped back in with an armload of firewood.

Hannah looked around once more. Noodles had left the lantern hanging high; its glow soothed the inside, with its steady beam. But an ubiquitous gloom still seemed to hang about, haunting her yet.

"I feel better than before . . . and I'll stay like you want. Just remember all this is new to me. I am the city girl, you said, and it will take me a while to become accustomed to the sights you've seen for so long. But give me time, I'll grow stronger as time passes."

"Maybe I shouldn't've been so hard on you. I just get old and cranky sometimes, when I'm scared myself. Findin' bones along a trail always did upset me mightily." Then the old man hooted and cackled, like he always did when he felt relaxed again.

Doll Girl broke the silence she had kept after her original screams. "The old one said the spirits were angry. We need to keep Wahnie and Ironclaw close by. They can see and smell the evil ones coming. Grandfather ... you should keep your rifle ready, too."

Hannah and Noodles gazed steadily at the little girl. The girl had appeared guarded and resolute often ... but not quite like now. Hannah felt her silent fear settle deeper.

That night she lay listening to the secret noises of the night. Now she knew the sounds of mice—their tiny peeps, their little feet scurrying across the floor. Then she heard a late owl hoot and the lonely howl of a wolf, far away. The fire's sooty shadows played across the hut's walls, whenever she opened her eyes and wished she could fall asleep. Quite a day, she thought. First time on the fabled Tanana River, first time she had ever seen the skeleton of another human. She pictured her life back in San Francisco as a girl, then as a young woman. It had never occurred to her before that she would find herself in such straits. She listened to the old man snore, the little girl sigh. It seemed important for her to show more backbone, just as she had in the past.

In the morning, while she hauled and packed their overnight gear on the sleds, Noodles and Doll Girl searched around the shack. Then the old man leaned the ladder against the nearby cache and Doll Girl climbed inside, then slid down. Next they meandered around the river's surface out front, with Ironclaw and Wahnie sniffing the snow. Suddenly both dogs stopped and pawed at a small bump on the river's ice, digging out the remains of an animal. Finally they walked back to the sleds.

"By Jeez, Hannah, the dogs found a dead wolverine without his skin. Doll Girl says it looks like some men come along here not long ago, left some moose meat, kept on downriver toward the Yukon. Appears right to me, though so much snow has fallen, it's hard to tell. Don't suppose Eli and Jesse come chasin' an outlaw the other way, do you?" Noodles brushed his beard with his mitten and squinted his eyes.

Hannah stood quietly. She stared ahead, up the Tanana, then back down toward the Yukon. Which way to go ... which way to Eli, she wondered?

Doll Girl's voice sounded, low and wistful. "I need to find my mother."

"And you shall—soon. I think it's best to keep on. Eli is most likely still ahead. Let's keep going!" Hannah turned to her sled, motioning with one arm to harness up and head out. Her soul sensed

the Tanana and Kantishna rivers seemed wrong
. . . but right for the child she loved so much.

Day after day the dogs trotted upriver, Doll
Girl pointing out where she had fought off the
wolves, where she had camped each night on her
way out. At last they neared the mouth of the
Kantishna . . . then old Wahnie refused to follow
Doll Girl's shouts. He pulled toward a flattened,
snowy hollow, barely visible under the recent
snows. When he reached the side of the odd depression, he sat down.

Doll Girl stood still on her sled's runners, staring down. Hannah stopped Ironclaw close behind,
anchored, then walked forward and stood beside
the girl.

"What wrong? What is it?" Hannah couldn't
understand the problem. Then she thought she
could see something as well.

She walked to the center of the low, packed-
down area and kicked at the small object sticking
up. Suddenly she realized, and jumped back, crying out.

"It's more bones. Lord, please not Eli." Then
Hannah held her mittens over her mouth.

"By Jeez, get away and let me see." Noodles
rolled off his sled's top and bounced to Hannah's
side, kneeling down on the snow. He began to
paw out bones with his mitts, like a burrowing
animal.

After a few minutes the old man stood up,
glancing down at scattered bones. "It ain't Eli. It

ain't a woman. It's a fellow whose got missing arms and legs!"

"The man in the shack—he had too many. This must be where those bones came from!" Then Hannah's face paled as she began to understand why.

"You two best get a grip on yourselfs. Don't start cryin' and screamin' now that you figured out what's goin' on. When men get hungry in the wilderness, they do crazy things. It's just the way things is . . ."

Doll Girl, her face plain and calm, stepped from her sled, then next to the bones. "My father and mother told me stories of my ancestors, before the white man came to Alaska. Sometimes they would eat each other to grow stronger, because the other person had been a powerful enemy. Sometimes they would eat each other to stay alive. It's the way of Indian people. White men think they are better than the wolverine, but they are wrong."

Hannah's eyes widened. She stared fiercely at the Indian girl. How could Doll Girl act so cold-hearted now? Cannibalism seemed the worst of all the mortal sins! Eating the forbidden flesh of man meant hellfire forever.

"Doll Girl, men are put on this earth to rise above the behavior of creatures. How can you say men are no better?"

"Men are only equal to other animals, they are not more important. Indians believe people are the same as the bird or the tree to Mother Earth. Why would the great spirit love a man more than a flower?"

Noodle's faded blue eyes flared. "By Jeez, I can't believe you two! We got two skeletons layin' along our trail and now you're arguin' about religion! One day you're both screamin' off your heads, then the next you're both preachin' the gospel, accordin' to Injuns an' the Good Book! Stop it, I say! We gotta figure out what's goin on, 'else we might end up with little critters chewin' on our bones, too."

Hannah hung her head. The old man had correctly characterized their behavior. She supposed each of them had become muddled in the aftermath of seeing death haunting their trip. Even Noodles appeared to act differently now. He had stopped hooting and crackling as much as before.

"I'm sorry—you're right. Doll Girl, did you know of any other strangers living near your home, when the kidnapper busted into your father's cabin?"

"No. That is why my father and mother lived so far away. They did not wish to see any whites. They did not even wish to see other Indians. We came out from the great mountain only to trade. Father always seemed angry."

Noodles peered at Doll Girl, his face wrinkled above his whiskers. "What was he so mad about?"

"The Koyukon people didn't believe in him. White men were more important to them than him. He was the last shaman . . . but no one cared."

Hannah and Noodles exchanged glances. Then they stared at Doll Girl. Hannah wondered if her old prospector friend sensed the same thing. It didn't seem like an explanation; it didn't feel like much at all. But somewhere in the words of Doll Girl lay an answer. Perhaps the child didn't really understand the riddle she lived with every day. They would have to journey on to find the truth. . . .

CHAPTER THIRTEEN

Shadows

Wahnie led them up the Kantishna River, away from the Tanana River and the secret crimes hidden along its frozen length. Hannah, glad to be underway again, followed closely behind the old leader's sled. She prayed they would find Eli soon, safe and well. Perhaps he's simply waiting ahead at Sleepy Lake, she thought. She wondered if he knew of the two dead men back in the snow?

Then the awful stillness of the boundless land began to affect her. Suddenly other people seemed so important. . . . And all she had were Doll Girl and Noodles. Those two didn't feel like adequate companionship to keep the painful longings away. Her deep discontent felt the same as homesickness, but much blacker and more insidious. It had suddenly come upon her, just as they had turned up the winding Kantishna—when she had wondered where the nearest people lived and towns lay.

Thankfully Noodles had repeatedly told her to expect the peculiar malady. He'd also told her Doll Girl wouldn't catch it, for she had been raised

as a child of the wilderness. Additionally, he
wouldn't catch it, he had gotten over the disorder
long ago, as a young tenderfoot prospecting the
West. But she would suffer the sickness, he fore-
cast, sometime during their long journey.

The best cure for the watery gloom seemed to
be common sense and companionship, if you were
lucky enough to find some. If not .. some people
went crazy while others dashed back to city life.
Only the strongest hearts could find happiness in
the solitude of the wilds. Only certain kinds of
folks could find peace in the shade of the woods
and under the sun of the clearings.

That night she listened quietly to the noisy voice
of the hasty veteran and to the soft tones of Doll
Girl's answers. It helped to soak up human
sounds, after her long day of riding the sled alone.
Then she felt she couldn't endure it any longer.

"Noodles, could we change sleds once in a
while? Perhaps I could ride with you from time
to time ... or with Doll Girl if you'd rather."

The grayed prospector peered over his coffee
cup with a steady gaze. "By Jeez, you been struck
by the lonesome sickness, ain't you?"

Hannah couldn't answer. She broke down unlike any other time in her past life. Feeling blue,
not having any idea of Eli's whereabouts, exhausted from living outdoors every day—then the
skeletons—she let it all pour out. Ashamed, unable to stop, she sat muffling her sobs with her
hands, dabbing her tears away.

Her two friends jumped over to her side,

hugged her, then murmured soft words she really couldn't hear. Finally she felt herself growing weary of her hopeless crying. She looked up and stared at their fire.

"I'm so embarrassed. I tried to harden up as fast as I could in this endless . . ."

"By Jeez, Hannah, you're doin' fine. It's been gray and cloudy for days now. As soon as it gets sunny, you'll feel better right away. I warned you about feelin' lonesome, then forgot to do anythin' about it. I been havin' so much fun ridin' with Doll Girl, I plumb forgot you been alone day after day. Tomorrow you ride with her. I can mush Ironclaw just fine. It ain't goin' to trouble me none sleddin' all alone. I crossed the Dakota Territory by myself. I never really had a friend till I met Eli back in Arizona."

The outburst from Noodles struck Hannah as funny. She smiled a little, then wiped her tears away again. "I love you two so much. I'd be lost without your help. It never occurred to me when I began this adventure back in Dawson City I would be so afraid at times. I guess I'll be the *cheechako* of the North forever."

Doll Girl frowned with her dark eyes. "What's a *cheechako*?"

Hannah and Noodles exchanged glances. Slowly they began to giggle, each breaking away from the sorrow of the past moments.

"By Jeez, little girl, it means newcomer. It means Hannah's a greenhorn in the wilderness."

Doll Girl smiled and shook her head. Hugging

Hannah once more, she answered, "You and Iron-claw not beginners anymore. You have come far!"

Two more days passed under snowy skies. Then the sun broke through the grayness overhead and shot wandering beams down on angles. Bit by bit the overcast faded to curling mists, mare's tails up high, with deep blue higher still. Next the mountains to the south began to uncover. One by one they threw off their coats of clouds, leaving their white slopes glistening in the brightness all around.

At last Denali came out. The great mountain stood before them in all its glory. Hannah and Noodles stopped their sleds and stood with their heads tilted up, silenced by the sight. Its topmost part filled the sky with its rounded summit, stony sides, and eternal snows. Resplendent beyond belief, it soaked color from the heavens, leaving soft indigo painted above.

God has spoken, Hannah thought as she stared. It's now clear why the Indians of this land worship this peak. Then she wondered if any man would ever be able to touch its top. No, no! she decided, they would be struck dead if they did. Perhaps Doll Girl's spirits did descend from the mountain after all.

"Doll Girl, I can't believe you grew up below this mountain. I wonder what it must be like to wake up in the morning and see such sights. Now I understand your love for Alaska. If I die, I want my soul to rest on its crown. No one can sleep closer to heaven!"

Doll Girl frowned, her eyes still peering up. "Someday I must carry my father to that mountain. He cannot rest until he sleeps on its side."

Hannah and Noodles glanced at each other, their eyes sharing the moment. One more puzzle had been thrown in their way. What did Doll Girl mean by the fateful words she had just spoken? Hannah felt the hair prickle on the back of her neck.

They continued up the crooked Kantishna, their moods lifted by the sunlit mountains ahead. Hannah shook away her foolish pining of the past days and began to learn more about the frozen world around her. She sat on the sled listening to Doll Girl describe their surroundings.

The little girl pointed out snow-covered beaver and muskrat houses, trails where moose had lumbered along, dragging their feet, the odd tracks of otters and mink as they hunted, and the holes left behind in the snow by the hunting owls as they pounced on squirrels or ptarmigans from above. Then she saw wolf and fox tracks, wolverine and weasel tracks, and the stealthy prints of lynx, as they stalked after their prey as well. Soon she began to see the dissimilarity of the signs and how Doll Girl could read the lives of the creatures that shared the forest.

Hannah found it difficult to imagine growing up in Alaska as a child. The closeness with the creatures that lived alongside made sense, but living year after year without much friendship with other people puzzled her. What must it be like to go for months and months and not to see another living soul? She knew Eli, Noodles, and Doll Girl had often lived that way, but she wondered if she could. Standing alone in the midst of the wilderness a thousand miles or more from any other person seemed horrid and incomprehensible. She doubted if she had sufficient courage to live that way by choice.

At last Doll Girl pointed to a trail running toward low hills, lifting higher and higher until they became the rough mountains fronting Denali. Progress slowed as they picked their way along a narrow path leading through trees, over snowbound bogs, up hillsides, and through barren woods which had burned away years before.

Two days later Doll Girl pointed to a squat log hut hidden among the drooping boughs of several fat spruce trees. "There is my father's trapline camp. I slept there before I walked to find you." Then she yelled for her dogs to stop in front.

"It looks so tiny." Hannah wondered why trappers build their shelters so small.

"My father had many of these to stay in while he traveled through his land in the winter. They are simple to build and easy to keep warm. We will sleep inside tonight."

Noodles sledded alongside and threw out his snow hook. "We must be gettin' close to Sleepy Lake by now. Ain't this the place you said we'd find first." He waded through the snow and opened the hide door of the hut. "By Jeez, Hannah, come quick! There's a letter from Eli hangin' in here!"

Jumping from her sled, Hannah raced for the hut and pulled the folded letter from above the low door. Opening the paper, she read quickly, then hung her head. "Somehow we missed seeing Eli when we came up the Tanana River. He's in trouble and needs our help."

The old prospector snatched the letter from Hannah's hand and read the message himself. Looking back, he saw her sobbing again.

"Hannah, I think from readin' this here letter, Eli was gone to someplace else before we ever turned up the Tanana River. I bet he's chasin' the fellows who's killed them men we found lyin' on the river. It's his duty and you know Eli."

Hannah nodded, then quietly answered through her tears, "I know ... and I think you're right about what he's done as well. But he needs help. What can we do?"

"We gotta keep on to Sleepy Lake like he writes. We can't never 'spect to hunt him down in this country. We maybe couldn't find him even if we knowed which way to go. Let's stay the night and go on tomorrow like we're supposed to. That's our best choice."

"Doll Girl's heart will be broken. I know how much she hoped Eli would be waiting with her mother ahead. What can I say to her? She's so little and needs her mother so much."

Noodles slowly shook his head, then hung it down like Hannah. "The truth will be best. She's

not so little as you think . . . maybe can take bad
news better than you. We gotta keep on. We'll
figure somethin' together once we get to Sleepy
Lake. Now let's unload and stay the night."

After the bad news Doll Girl grew silent and
deliberate. She willingly helped with the camp
chores, but her face sat pinched and pale below
her parka hood. After Hannah and Noodles had
settled themselves inside the tiny enclosure, she
stayed outdoors near Wahnie for a few minutes,
standing beside him. Both gazed off toward Denali, now rosy from a red, setting sun. Then, just
before nightfall, a wolf pack howled close by, stirring all the dogs from their beds. Jumping against
their lines, all of them growled and howled back,
joining the wild chorus.

When Doll Girl stepped through the door, she
slowly pulled off her long parka and hung it up.
"I have left Wahnie and Ironclaw loose for the
night. They will sleep outside and help keep the
wolves away. The hungry ones will kill and eat
our dogs if we are not careful. Grandfather Noodles, you need to keep your rifle ready." Then she
stared at Hannah with her Indian eyes. "If you
know how, you should try to help, too."

"Eli taught me over a year ago. He bought me
this rifle in Dawson City." Hannah pointed to her
Winchester lever action she'd leaned in the corner.

"By Jeez, Doll Girl, I watched her shoot one
time. She ain't as good as Eli by a long shot, but
she's as good as me." Then the old prospector
grinned with his toothless mouth.

"When they come you will think they are ghosts. My father has fought them before. They are quick, like shadows. Every winter they killed and ate our dogs!"

Hannah watched Doll Girl's purposeful ways as they readied everything for the coming nighttime. The little girl arranged so she lay farthest from the door, but nearest to the tin stove, so she could feed it with minimum effort. Noodles lay next to the door, bundled against the cold drafts creeping along the floor. Both Winchesters sat on each side of the little hollow, cartridges inside their barrels, hammers set on half-cock. And a lantern hung handily for lighting, near the door.

Just after they blew their lamp out, Hannah scrunched around beneath her blankets and caribou robes, sighing with the worry she felt for the night. Then she remembered her life as a girl back in San Francisco . . . and her recent chore of living in the same clothing day after day, with a loaded rifle leaning nearby. She sighed once more, shaking her head in amazement on her makeshift pillow.

Doll Girl's voice crept across. "You should sleep now. Wahnie and Ironclaw will tell us if we need to wake up."

Hannah smiled, then whispered, "I love you, Doll Girl. I'm all right." She smiled again, hearing the little girl fall asleep, then the old man snore.

Total blackness, warmth, dreaming—what's that—Hannah questioned in her mind, as her eyes shot open? Two throaty growls sounded outside.

The inside of the hut lay stone quiet. Doll Girl's gentle breathing and Noodles' snorts stopped on the stillness that had settled down.

"By Jeez, Hannah, light the lantern quick. I believe them varmints are sneakin' round out there!" The old prospector rolled to his knees, fumbling for his rifle in the dark.

Then all the dogs began to yelp, crying sharp wails just outside the hut. Noodles, Hannah, and Doll Girl bounded through the doorway, stopping in front, peering back and forth. A white moon hung above, casting a picture of shadows, moonshine, and dimness among the dark trees. Suddenly a pale shape darted between the dogs, instantly appearing like one of them.

Doll Girl screamed and ran toward the dogs. "Don't shoot, don't shoot—come with me! We have to chase him away before he chews the ropes apart."

Hannah and the old prospector followed, both confused by the jumping dogs and the Indian girl beating around between them, her arms like windmills. The tumult of howls, yips, barks, and screams filled the night's freezing air.

Suddenly a lone shadow dashed back to the trees, followed by Doll Girl's loud cries. "Shoot him! Shoot him now!"

Noodles' rifle split the night air with an explosion, adding its awful blast to the rest of the commotion bouncing through the woods. Slowly the uproar faded, then washed back in echoes, floating from the hillsides, standing off in the distance.

Hannah held her rifle ready, unsure of what to do. "Doll Girl, come here, are you all right? My Lord, don't run away like that again. You could have been killed by that thing. Was it a wolf? Did you hit him, Noodles?"

"By Jeez, no. That varmint ran quicker than lightning. Hannah's right, little girl, what'd you go jumpin' over there for?"

"Wahnie and Ironclaw were beside me. I wasn't in danger. The wolf knew he would be killed if he tried to bite me. He ran away instead."

Noodles yelled at the sled dogs, trying to calm them down from their yips and howls. Carrying his lantern among them, he examined each dog's leash. Next he walked along the tracks left behind by the fleeing wolf. Finally he hung the yellow light on a dead branch on the far side of the campsite, leaving its shine near where the wolf had escaped.

"By Jeez, them sly varmints ain't goin' to sneak up on us again. Hannah, go get me another lamp, I'm goin' to hang another one out. I'll sit up the rest of the night and wait. You two get back to sleep."

"Are you sure you've had enough rest. I could watch first." Hannah worried about the old man's well-being.

"I'll be fine—it's toward mornin' anyways. Old coots like me don't need much sleep." The old prospector levered his rifle and set the hammer on safety again.

Doll Girl turned to a woodpile nearby. "If we

build Grandfather Noodles a fire, he can stay warm while he watches. It will help make our dogs happy again, too." She called out in Athabaskan for the dogs to quiet down.

The following morning dawned clear and blue for as far as their eyes could see. As they seesawed back and forth up rugged lands lifting away from the trapline hut, they glimpsed bits of distant country stretching back to the rivers they had journeyed along days earlier. Great uneven patches of green, black, gray, and white spread northerly, painting a wilderness of heavy evergreens, barren trees, and frozen waterways. The terrain stood broken, pitching and rolling into ten thousand hills and valleys, bogs and tree lines, and a wintertime that seemed everlasting.

Intent on reaching Sleepy Lake before dark, they drove the dogs hard all day. During their quick march, Hannah impatiently watched the lazy circle of the sun as it swung westward, at last sinking behind Denali and the Alaskan Mountain Range. Then a pale amber evening settled, casting a honey-colored hue over the countryside in front. Finally she saw their destination just ahead. A long reach of white ice running off between the sides of a gentle valley, lying peacefully in the yellow of the setting sun.

Led by Wahnie, the dogs leaped into a race down onto the lake and across to Doll Girl's old home, sitting on the far shore. Yipping, flipping their tails, every dog seemed to sense the end of their long journey, the end to their daily toil of wading through deep snow and pulling heavy sleds. They could rest for a while, sleep in little log kennels, safe from the wolves, warm and snug for a change.

"I have never come home to a lonely cabin before." Doll Girl stood in front of the cabin, grimly staring up at the cold chimney sticking up through a snow-covered roof.

"By Jeez, we'll fix that in a hurry, little girl. Let's grab some wood from that woodpile and get a fire started. By the time we get the dogs bedded and the sleds unloaded, the place will be nice and warm. After we eat, I bet things will look better for us." Noodles bounced off through the snowy yard toward heaps of firewood stacked nearby.

Hannah followed close behind. She called, hoping to cheer the Indian girl, "Old man, in the morning I'm chasing you out. I'm going to build a big fire, heat water, and Doll Girl and I are bathing and washing our hair. I can't bear to live in these clothes for another day." Turning her head, she saw Doll Girl still gazing soundlessly at the log cabin standing empty in the darkening forest. And she saw tears dripping down the little girl's face, now barely visible in the shadows of the coming night.

CHAPTER FOURTEEN

Jeopardy

"Eli would starve to death before he would violate man's law. I figure he found the two dead men same as we did. He's chasin' who's killed 'em. Somebody come along, did those two fellows in, then run off. Eli's after them—I know it." Morning sunbeams slanted through the cabin's front window and highlighted Noodles' face, weather-beaten from his awful trek to the foot of Denali Mountain. His bony fingers stiffly clutched his coffee cup, and his aged eyes searched Sleepy Lake.

Hannah's own ideas nagged her; she sensed something more evil than coincidental strangers. "I believe Jesse Peacock killed and ate those men. Since the first time I met that man years ago, I've always thought him weak and corrupt. And he seemed so irrational when Eli asked him to go along."

"Maybe that Billy House did it. Might've been him. Men go crazy when they're starvin' to death. Nobody wants to die!"

Hannah read Eli's letter again, then slowly shook her head. "No . . . any man who would try so hard to save his friends wouldn't kill and eat them in the end. Jesse did it, I know!"

Noodles shifted his gaze to Hannah, then lifted his coffee. "I 'spect you're right now that you made me think on it. But still could be strangers we don't know about. In the meanwhile we gotta do what Eli says. Tomorrow we start to hunt like he wants. We need fresh meat for the dogs anyway."

Doll Girl's voice chirped from across the room, near the crackling stove. "I know my father's best hunting place. We can go there. A moose will be hiding in the willows, and we can chase him out."

"By Jeez, I hope we can chase him right to our sled. I ain't young enough to pack moose meat through all this snow. Those critters look bigger than horses!"

Hannah listened halfheartedly as the old prospector and little girl discussed the next day's hunt. Eli's written instructions made good sense, but she felt so unsettled by not knowing his whereabouts. And his warning to stay vigilant spooked her to her very heart. She realized the time had come for her to take responsibility for her own well-being more than ever before.

Yet she sat in the middle of a savage wilderness all alone, except for an old man and a child. She wondered if true bravery meant doing things in spite of inexperience and fear. Dog sledding, hunting moose, total isolation—what had she gotten herself into? Could she learn to be the sturdy pioneer fast enough to sustain their lives? God—she felt so afraid!

At least, she thought, enough winter had passed by to yield a little more sunlight. What was it, March already? The sun climbed higher every day and the weather felt warmer, much different from the thirty- and forty-below-zero-temperatures she had fought so long. She had wept silently when she had first seen her face in the mirror hanging on the cabin wall. Her appearance had shocked her—cracked lips, red-and-black skin, and scabs over frozen flesh. What would Eli think if he saw her now? Perhaps he would say she would never look beautiful again.

They spent the rest of the day bathing themselves, washing and mending clothing, settling into the cabin for a lengthy stay. Hannah found herself amazed by her acclimation to the dangerous cold. Whenever the cabin became heated, she felt stifled. She began to walk about the inside clothed only in her long woolen underwear. Noodles laughed and teased, but soon afterward he undressed to the same cooler garment himself.

The following morning they mushed the length of Sleepy Lake into a blinding sun. Doll Girl and Noodles led the way, with Hannah following with the heaviest sled. After the end of the snow-covered expanse, they took turns on snowshoes breaking trail for the dogs, up through bottom lands choked with young birch and willows. Finally Doll Girl pointed to the tops of low ridges stretching along their path. They fought uphill through the trees and underbrush, found a look-out, and pitched an impermanent camp to hunt from for a day or two.

After they had readied their campsite, Doll Girl waved toward Denali. "We will hunt by walking these hills toward the Great One. Wahnie and Ironclaw can come along, but the other dogs have to stay. They are too noisy." She then turned from the camp on her snowshoes, her careful footsteps hushed by the deep snow.

"You follow way behind, Hannah, and keep quiet. I'll stay close and plug the first critter I see." The old prospector's blue eyes gleamed in the low winter light.

Hannah waited until she could barely see her two friends and the two dogs ahead. Then she stepped onto the packed trail and tried to walk soundlessly, feeling hard breezes on her cheeks. In a moment she recalled Eli's past stories about hunting wild creatures. Doll Girl and Noodles had stalked upwind so they couldn't be scented, she mused, and they will be able to search far ahead as they creep along. If they're lucky, they will sneak up on a moose feeding or sleeping below. Then she felt a little jealous for being left behind.

Two hours later she saw Noodles signal her to stop and stay back. Disappointed and curious, she stood noiselessly, wondering. Suddenly the winter-time shook with a rifle shot, then another and another. Five times the woods echoed with gunfire, frightening her to shouldering her own weapon.

What, for goodness sakes, is that old man shooting at, she asked herself?

Then hoots and cackles drifted downwind to her. Whatever had happened, she thought, the old man must have succeeded. He must have killed something. She began to shuffle forward on her snowshoes toward the human sounds.

"By Jeez, Hannah, we got one. It saw us and started runnin' away, but I got 'im anyways. Sure is tough killin' one with my thirty-caliber, it ain't powerful enough for big critters."

Picking her way through the snow and brush, Hannah crept to the side of the black shape sunken in the snow. She stopped still, shocked by the size, and feeling a little sickened, too, by the sight of death. Then she wondered why Doll Girl appeared to be acting so strangely.

"Doll Girl, for Lord's sake, what are you doing?"

The Indian child quit chanting her mother tongue and chopping twigs off the nearby underbrush. "I'm thanking the spirits for this gift. I'm covering the moose's eyes so he can sleep. We must treat his spirit well, so his brothers will live here again. Then there will be food for us next time we hunt."

Hannah stared, nonplussed. "You go through rituals each time you kill something?"

"Yes, each animal is a friend who we live with every day. We must treat them with respect. If we do not, they will all run away and my people will starve." The girl began to sing and cut twigs again.

All afternoon Noodles and Doll Girl pulled, hacked, and cut until they had butchered the moose into small pieces. Hannah helped the best she could, her face cockeyed, feeling watery inside her stomach at the sight of so much blood and guts. She had never seen an animal dismembered before—meat gathered from its true source. Lord, she thought, if Eli could see me now, blood up to my elbows and spattered on my face.

They retrieved their teams and drove back for their butchered moose, just as long shadows fell across the woods. The moment the dogs scented the fresh kill, they began to tear toward the waiting meat piles. Hannah shivered in terror as she braked her raging dogs. Then she whispered a quick prayer as Doll Girl ran to release Wahnie and Ironclaw from their lead lines. Next she watched as the little girl stood shoulder to shoulder with the two leaders, defending the meat, crying out warning calls. In a single instant the child had saved their hard day's work from the hungry dogs.

That night, after feeding the dogs, they fried liver slices over the dying embers of their campfire. Lounging for a change, they recounted their day's hunt, then praised Doll Girl for her bravery in front of the savage dogs. Hannah began to envy her little friend's boldness, her ability to jump to the rescue each time, with her hands swinging high. What things must she have been taught, she wondered, to have enabled the child to act with such gray wisdom. Then she remembered Eli's letter and his description of Doll Girl as a part of the wilderness. He had written about the land and its true people. And he had said to stay watchful of the ways of the Indian.

Suddenly Hannah felt compelled to behave courageously herself. "Doll Girl, do you know this country well enough to guide Noodles and me, if we searched for your mother?"

Before the Indian girl could answer, Noodles' cry speared the night. "By Jeez, Hannah, Eli's life may depend on us waitin' for him at Sleepy Lake! We best do like he asked in his letter. It's a bad idea to do otherwise." Then the old man frowned.

Doll Girl paused before answering Hannah's original question. At last she said in her small voice, "Grandfather Noodles is wise to say we must wait. I have often wondered why the stranger came to my father's cabin. Now my dreams have shown me. But we are not strong enough to go there. Only Mr. Bonnet can take us, and he must wear his spirit coat."

Hannah and Noodles sat still, dumbfounded, peering at the little girl, who, in turn, sat gazing steadily at the fire.

Finally Hannah broke the deep silence. "Doll Girl, what are you saying? Why must Eli come along and wear his medicine jacket?"

"Only shamans can walk in sacred places. Mr. Bonnet wears the spirits of the ancient ones. He has strong medicine like my father, and like the old one back in Fort Yukon. We must wait for him.''

Later that evening Hannah lay wide awake, listening to the whispers of the bright, snapping blaze they had kindled for the night. She had learned to love the wild dance of their campfires banked high against the long, cold nights. The flames leaped up in rhythm, mostly colored orange, but sometimes with yellow, blue, green, and red fingers swaying as well. She now knew the kinds of wood that made the difference, spruce burned one way, birch another. Alders burned in spite of being freshly cut; willows wouldn't burn at all. Dry cottonwood disappeared in a flash, wood dripping with sticky sap lasted the longest.

It had become clear to her that primitive man had first used fire to soothe his soul while he had watched deep shadows hunt for his very life, just beyond his circle of light. Human life had begun around the fire. The recesses of the human mind had filled while he had huddled near its sanctuary. No wonder Doll Girl believed in spirits and powers unseen by man or beast. But why wouldn't the child explain her riddles, she wondered?

The next morning they harnessed their teams to their heavy meat-laden sleds and turned back to Sleepy Lake. They mushed along, following the frozen trail they had left behind the day before, proud of their bloody prize.

Wahnie saw the danger first, just as he dashed downhill and around a corner hidden by thick brush. He had seen the dangerous enemy once before—a moose that had decided to claim the packed path for himself. Weighing nearly a ton, the bull would never give up the trail without a fight. And the old dog realized the stupid team would give him one.

The bull stood in the middle of the way, hornless now that most of the wintertime had passed. He waited with his ears flattened, his front hooves ready. Wahnie, wise enough to leap aside, immediately used his longest harness line to get under the low limbs of a giant spruce, crouching himself against the pull of the other dogs. In a single instant the team, except for the two dogs that Wahnie had saved because they were fastened close behind, charged the moose, tipping over the trailing sled in their crazy attack. In a blur the bull jumped into the tangle of dogs and began to kill and cripple them one by one, striking out left and right with his kicking feet.

Noodles and Doll Girl spilled off the sled as it flipped sideways, tumbling head over heels into the deep snow. Then they popped up on their hands and knees, their hoods and parkas covered with snow, their faces just as white because of the noisy horror of the awful fight nearby. They scrambled for their lives, back toward Hannah, crying for her to stop her dogs.

But Ironclaw had already seen the danger. The young leader skidded sideways, then darted back into the dogs running behind. He slashed with his teeth, raging up and down the line, forcing each team member to cower down and stay motionless on the trail.

Hannah jumped off the sled. She threw out her snow hook and stomped it down in the same instant that she yanked her Winchester out of its leather scabbard, which was tied on the side of her sled's handlebars. She ran ahead beyond her dogs and stopped just as Doll Girl, and then Noodles tore by in their hasty retreat. Calming herself, she drew a deep breath, let half out, held still, and stared down the sights of her rifle. Hold steady, aim, squeeze—magically her mind recited Eli's words over and over. The blast of her rifle shook her. The moose fought on, striking one dog after another, but a little slower now. She flipped the lever, jacked another round into the barrel and sighted again, praying for a fatal shot. Bang! Her rifled barked again, but it sounded so feeble. Then, to her horror, she watched the bull turn and charge, head on, front hooves pawing the air.

She watched the ugly head bounce toward her, with bloodshot eyes bulging out frightfully. Then her fear slipped away. Now everything seemed so slow and dreamlike and surreal. She levered her rifle once more and aimed. How could she miss, she wondered, since the giant moose had gotten so close. Bang! The Winchester smacked into her shoulder again. Then she felt a much greater blow and heard her own loud scream.

CHAPTER FIFTEEN

Showdown

Suddenly Eli saw a puff of snow kick off the Yukon's surface. Then he heard the rifle shot roll down the river, even before the icy dust settled. He fled for the shore, wildly sprinting for the trees and hollering for Blueberry to run for his life as well. Glancing backward, he observed the young Minnesotan catching up, terrified by the deadly sound. Another bullet buzzed overhead, noisy like a reckless bumblebee, followed by a second report, echoing down the distance.

He had been shot at countless times as an adolescent. Joining Stonewall Jackson's army as a boy of twelve, he had served as one of the youngest soldiers in the Confederacy. When his commanding officer had found out that he could shoot markedly better than blow a bugle, he had been reassigned to a sniper unit. And Union infantrymen had hated snipers most of all. The instant you touched off your fatal shot at any unwary soldier, the whole of the blue army fired a rattling volley back your way. He could still hear the savage hums of the minié balls cutting through the trees in which he liked to hide. It had paid to be a quick and nimble youngster back in those days, able to dart up and down the gray trunks of oaks like the wily squirrel.

Diving into the snow behind a tangle of dead trees washed ashore by spring floods, he peeked around and saw Blueberry close behind. He appeared safe, too, from any more rifle shoots aimed their way.

"I think we've found Jesse Peacock, though I'm confounded why he would be holed up here. He's in that cabin three hundred paces up the shore. But why would he quit running and lay for us here?"

Eli judged that they must be a mile or two upriver from the Indian village of Nulato. He had been told of the trading post, the homelike comforts throughout the little town. He and Blueberry had hoped to enjoy those accommodations for at least one night. Nevertheless, now they seemed pinned down by Jesse's errant gunfire.

"I ain't never been shot at before. I don't like it much. I'm pretty scared." Blueberry eyed the place where the shots had been fired from.

"We're lucky Jesse made the choice of a fool, or else we'd be dead or wounded. Most men shoot too far, too soon. I suppose fear is an impediment to their common sense when it comes to a gunfight." Then Eli wondered why he lay preaching at his young friend. It sounded silly.

Blueberry snaked next to him by sliding on his

belly. "What we gonna do? We'll freeze to death if we stay here. Maybe it ain't Jesse!"

"I don't believe just anyone would shoot at two strangers walking downriver . . . except for a madman. And we only know one of those!"

Poking his head above their barricade, Eli studied the low gray cabin in the distance. One window, one door, each facing south—the log structure appeared to have been constructed from spruce trees a foot or more thick at their sawed-off ends. It would take cannonballs or a blazing fire to break through, he thought. A diligent woodsman had evidently raised the cabin.

"Blueberry, our cover is safe and filled with dry wood. Gather some and build a small fire. We'll hide here till dark, then I'll sneak into town. Someone will know why Jesse tried to bushwack us instead of keeping the lead. I'm puzzled. He could have easily outrun us. We have no dogs to keep up. Odd behavior, I think."

"He ain't got no dogs up there either. What do you suppose happened to them?"

"My guess is when Jesse mushed into town, someone recognized the team as belonging to the mailman. I have a notion the villagers stole the dogs back, then chased him away."

Blueberry pushed off his belly to his knees and pointed to the frozen river they had just run off. "I sure wish I had our sled and my rifle. At least I could eat and protect myself. What if he walks down here and shoots us? You ain't got nothing' 'cept your pistol."

Eli grinned and gently shook his head. "You've ate half a moose already. I think you won't starve by nightfall. And Peacock knows that I'm a better shot with my Colt than he is with a rifle, so you shouldn't worry. We're safe as beetle bugs for now."

They improved their fortification by heaving more logs on top and stuffing wood pieces into gaps in between. Blueberry crawled around and started a blaze to warm themselves beside. Then he seated himself on a tree stump.

After a long silence, he asked, "Eli, how far do you suppose we've walked?"

Eli shook his head again, then frowned. "Hundreds of miles. I haven't walked so much since the War Between the States. When I served with Stonewall Jackson as a boy, he'd march us thirty-six miles a day, rain or shine. Surprising how far a man can march when duty calls."

"Is that why you don't look very scared when you get shot at—'cause you soldiered in the Civil War?"

Memories of the bullets that had always missed by a little passed through his mind. Men did become accustomed to being shot at, he mused. You learned, after a while, that the shots you heard meant you had lived to see another day. Your brain inevitably resolved that the true shot that killed you could never be heard. A secret peace then settled in your head. You found your own careful aim seemed the thing that really mattered. He had sprinted from the river by instinct. And he had run away knowing few men could hit a moving target.

All across the western frontier, the Indians, then the outlaws had popped away at him with their rifles and pistols. That, too, had shaped him. He had won his Sioux spirit coat during a gun battle. As older age had come along he felt less afraid than ever. What had happened, he wondered? He hoped that he wouldn't turn into a hasty fool himself someday. Fear acted as the great elixir of life! He needed to keep some inside.

In a few hours the black of night fell. Blueberry crept back to the center of the river and recovered their sled and equipment. They let their campfire ebb, then kicked snow over its embers. Eli then readied himself for his hike to the nearby Indian village.

"Blueberry, you'll get chilled waiting without a fire, but no one can walk within rifle range without you hearing them. Stay here and listen. You'll be safe. I'll be back in three hours. Listen for two hoots from an owl."

"What if a real owl hoots? How will I know it's you?"

"You'll hear me crunching on the snow's crust just afterward. I doubt if a true owl can walk quite like me." Eli smiled, imagining he must have reddened his friend's face with embarrassment.

He turned away into the lonely night. Silvery light gleamed through curling clouds hanging high up against the moon's crescent, shining frosted brightness to see by, away from the shoreline's sooty shadows. He crunched along the river's snowy surface, thinking of his trek from the mouth of the Tanana. It had torn him apart to choose the pursuit of Jesse Peacock, rather than wait for Hannah and Doll Girl. And he knew Noodles had insisted on coming along. They were like family, and his heart missed them. Were they waiting at Sleepy Lake, he wondered?

Another mail sled had come along just after he and Blueberry had reached the Yukon River with the mailman who had waited for them on the Tanana. Then he and Blueberry had borrowed supplies, waved good-bye to their new friends, and turned downriver, guessing that must be the direction Jesse Peacock had gone. Later they had met an Indian family sledding upriver, finding out, in fact, that a one-armed man had been seen, mushing west toward Nulato. Day after day and hour after hour they had chased him, always hoping for a mistake, or an act of God that would slow him down. Now it seemed Providence had listened to their prayers.

Barking dogs warned him that Nulato lay near. At last he saw scattered yellow lights shining through the blackness hiding the shore. He found a beaten trail leading from the river's snow, climbed the steep, rough beach, and followed the track until it wove among a few log cabins and clapboard buildings. Picking out the largest, with two attachments appearing to be storehouses, he walked up and pounded on the front door, next to a flag pole. Then human sounds crept through the wooden planks of the dark doorway.

Suddenly the door swung wide open and a square, brown-bearded man leaned forward, clutching a flaring lamp. "I told you people a thousand times to leave me alone at night. Now get away, I say."

"I'm Deputy Marshal Bonnet. I need to learn about a man who's running from the law."

The huge man thrust his head forward. "Well now, ain't this somethin'. Can't believe a lawman has come to the wilderness, after all these years. Lord be the keeper of us all, I say, just wait till the Mighty One sees the need. Come in here, mister. Be you praised always."

Eli eyed the man when he stepped inside, smiling about the noisy welcome. The large room smelled of dried furs and beans and tobacco. A trading counter lay across the openness, dividing the room. A white dog sat staring, but with friendly eyes. Then he saw an Indian woman staring as well, her eyes black like those of a hunting hawk.

The bearded trader burst out again. "You're Eli Bonnet, I wager. You're after Lucifer's disciple, and God bless you for it. This land has gone on too long without David and his mighty coat."

"It appears you have me at a disadvantage, sir. I'm surprised to have you greet me by name. Please tell me yours." Eli offered his right hand for a handshake.

"I'm Simon Paul. This here little woman is my

wife, Calico Woman. Seventeen years I been here, trading with the Koyukon people. They're like my family, but you got to treat them like children. Anyway, you can't move across this country without them knowing it. Not possible. No sir. We got a good moccasin telegraph out here."

"Then you can tell me about the man who welcomes strangers with rifle fire, upriver from this place. My friend and myself would have rather met you first."

The burly trader squinted his eyes, then raked his beard with his thick fingers. "I'm awful sorry to hear that. I been keeping folks away from there for days. That one-armed fool took over old Sasutna's cabin after we chased him out of town. He's burrowed in and we don't know how to get him out. We ain't gunfighters, and we don't want to burn down one of our homes in winter."

"His name is Jesse Peacock. Sadly this land seems to have driven him mad. At least, unwell enough to do senseless things. I've chased him down the Tanana—now this far down the Yukon. I had worried he would reach a seaport and get away before I could catch him for the wrongful things he's done."

The big man broke into hard laughter. His barrel chest shook with spasms. Finally he said, "Mr. Bonnet, that's what finished him off. That's when he lost his remaining wits. Hellfire, the only seaport is Saint Michaels. The ocean water is froze and it ain't thawing out till June. I told him he couldn't get away from God ever—and the law neither." Simon Paul began to laugh again.

Eli left the trading post and the God-fearing proprietor after an hour. He marched back up the Yukon's channel, staying on the far side, away from the cabin Peacock had seized. When he judged himself near Blueberry again, he called like the great horned owl, then crossed to rejoin his friend.

When he saw his friend's shadow in the dark, he said, "Blueberry, start a fire and let's pitch camp. It seems we have ourselves in the middle of a Mexican standoff. Leastwise, that's how my old friend Noodles would describe this problem."

"What did you find out? Is it Peacock, like you said?"

"Yes . . . and more unwell than ever. The town's trader said the villagers stole back the mailman's dogs and sled when they figured who really owned them and what had happened. Then they chased Jesse out of town. Seems he wasn't sense-less enough to start a gunfight with a band of angry Indians. But he did walk back up here and force an old woman out of her cabin for revenge."

Blueberry struck a wooden match and ignited wood he had gathered during his long wait. The rising flames cast an odd glow on his rough face, which was bearded and weathered from his hard winter of living outdoors. When his campfire began to sputter, he sat down once more.

"Eli, why did he stop instead of keepin' on downriver? He could have got away."

"No one knows why he stopped ... perhaps just to see people for a change. And I learned he couldn't have escaped our pursuit regardless. The west coast of Alaska doesn't thaw till summer. There's no ships until then."

Blueberry stared across the orange flames leaping high into the night, his eyes dark and hollow. Then he slowly shook his head. "I'm the reason you didn't wait for your friends. I'm sorry, Eli, we should have waited, took care of your first duty, then gone after Jesse. It's my fault we've done wrong. I shouldn't have begged you when you was tryin' to make up your mind on what to do."

"Feel no fault, Blueberry. I'm responsible for my own decisions. I chose ... it seems wrong now. But we'll not know about that till later on. It never occurred to me Jesse couldn't get away. I didn't know the coast of Alaska stayed frozen until June. Now we'll finish our work and head back and find Hannah as fast as we can."

The young man continued to stare. "How we gonna get Peacock out of there?"

"I don't know. The folks in the village don't want the cabin damaged. The trader said there's enough dried salmon and firewood there to last till "kingdom comes," in his own words. You lay down and sleep. I'll take first watch. Perhaps by morning, I'll think of something."

Eli watched his friend throw his bedroll beside the fire. Then Blueberry crawled inside his blankets and pulled up the covers, his eyes still dark and hollow. At last he said, "I'll try to think of somethin' myself." Finally he fell asleep.

When bright light woke him, along with Blueberry's noisy morning fire, Eli sat up and rubbed the sleep from his eyes. He felt rested, in spite of his short night's rest. Most times dawn seemed like his favorite time of day. The smoky fires, the lively sounds of bacon frying, the new sun rising, and lastly the sweet songs of morning birds starting their days had always gladdened him.

"Blueberry, I've thought of a way to fool Peacock. With good luck, no harm will come to us, or anyone else."

The young Minnesotan turned his head, blinking to clear his eyes from the rising gray smoke. "I was just thinkin' of coverin' up the stove pipe and smokin' him out."

Eli laughed, recalling the hazards of cooking over open flames. "I tried that once in the Montana Territory. Had a fellow cornered in a cabin just like this. I stuffed a blanket down the stovepipe and jumped off the roof, ready for my man. Unfortunately he had seen that trick before. He quickly threw a bucket of water into the stove, dowsed the fire, busted out a window for fresh air, and commenced firing. It took me two more days to get him out."

Blueberry smiled, then asked, "So ... how are we goin' to get Peacock out? I don't want to get shot—you neither."

"I can think of only one thing that will make him leave that cabin. That's the same dogs and sled that he had when he mushed into Nulato. I aim to see that he gets them!"

Blueberry stopped blinking his eyes. "Eli, why would you let him run away again?"

"I intend to be on the sled!" Then Eli laughed, seeing his friend's widened eyes and open mouth.

After eating their breakfast, they built a scarecrow of sticks, stuffed coat, and cap. They poked the figure above their tangle of logs, positioning it to look like a man watching the cabin. Eli then crouched behind their bulwark, keeping Blueberry and their human shape barely visible to Jesse Peacock, whenever he might look in their direction.

"Move our stuffed friend now and then, so Jesse will think I'm still here. Continue to do the things you would if I really were around. Keep a fire, stay low, pretend to talk to me. I'll crawl away carrying my snowshoes, staying behind brush and trees. When I can, I'll cut through the woods, back to the Indian village. Watch for the sled and dogs late this afternoon."

Blueberry rubbed his nose with his mitten. "How you goin' to get somebody to drive dogs up to that cabin. Won't Jesse kill them?"

Eli pulled his Colt from under his parka and spun its chamber, looking for live rounds. He squinted his eyes and grimaced. "If he opens the door or window and I see a rifle, *I'll* kill him." Then he crawled away.

Two hours passed before Eli reached Nulato again, sweating from crawling and snowshoeing through the surrounding timberland. When he broke out into the clearing behind the trading post, he kicked off his snowshoes and marched to the front of the structure. Stepping inside, he saw Simon Paul standing with four Koyukon Athabaskans, all peering at red fox furs.

The moment the heavy trader recognized him, he called, "Mr. Bonnet, you appear wet and winded. Have you come to tell me you've finished the Lord's work."

"I think Providence is too busy to worry about me. I come hoping you can arrange for a brave soul to help me with mankind's simple work." Eli pulled his parka over his head and hung it above the potbelly stove.

Trader Paul blinked, then eyed Eli across the room. "What do you need, Mr. Bonnet? You'll find me brave enough to face any man's responsibilities."

"I want the mailman's sled and dogs back. I aim to tempt Jesse Peacock to escape once more. Transportation is the only thing that may get him out of that cabin."

Simon Paul's eyes blinked faster. "You should explain yourself, Mr. Bonnet. I'm not sure I understand your reasons for letting that awful sinner run again."

"I plan on replacing the sled's load. I'll hide under the canvas cover, and the moment he steps on the runners, he'll find my Colt Peacemaker pointed his way."

The trader spoke in dialect to the four Koyukon Indians standing with him. Then he listened to their muttered replies. Finally, with raised eyebrows, he turned back to Eli.

"Mr. Bonnet, we all wonder how you propose to keep your volunteer alive. What's to keep your sinner from shooting him the moment he comes up to that cabin?"

Eli reached inside the backpack he had carried along. He pulled out his spirit coat, unfolded it, and then pulled it over his head. Next he pulled his Colt out of his belt. Finally he answered, "Mr. Paul, please step outside. Bring an empty coffee can. Throw it as high as you can. I think I'll show you why Jesse Peacock won't live another day if he attempts to harm anyone."

The Indians broke into their odd pidgin, using the words "paleface, Colt, and shoot-em." Simon Paul spoke briefly to them once more, then reached behind his counter and grabbed an empty tin can. His eyes seemed brightened, and his lips curled at their corners. He walked from the room without glancing back.

Eli followed. The four Athabaskans trailed, in a row, close behind, still muttering back and forth. The instant the burly trader stepped out the door, he tossed the shiny vessel as high as he could, grunting with the strain. The can tumbled end over end through the air, then bounced higher from five quick explosions.

When the rapid gunfire faded, Simon Paul whistled, then spun around. "Mr. Bonnet, the Mighty One has blessed you. I've seen no man in Alaska shoot that well before. I'll mush that sled to the front of Lucifer's door if you wish."

"To the front of old Sasutna's cabin will do, Mr. Paul. Just back upriver is all I ask." Reloading his Peacemaker, Eli then felt the four Koyukon hunters touching his Sioux coat.

Two hours later Eli lay down on the bed of the sled and covered himself with its rough tarpaulin, leaving a peephole to see out from. Simon Paul stuffed burlap sacks here and there to smooth the load, then loosely tied the canvas cover. Next he mounted the runners, shouted at the dogs, and raced up the Yukon, his fox-tail cap flying straight behind.

In a few minutes the trader swung wide and pulled up to the porch of the squat cabin, shouting for the sled dogs to stop. He quickly threw down the snow hook, stomped it, and ducked behind the bulky sled, shielding himself the best he could.

Next he shouted, "Mr. Peacock, we've returned your outfit. We've reloaded your food and gear. Just get on downriver. Folks in town need this cabin back. We want you to go away. Now don't shoot me. I'm going back to Nulato. Don't shoot. We wish no harm to you anymore. Go with God, I say!"

Eli watched from his hiding place. The window glass and the door remained lifeless, completely empty. Then he heard the noises from Simon Paul's boots jogging away. Next the surroundings hushed to a fearful stillness, like an old graveyard. His heart thundered and his breathing roared under the sled's cover. Could it be that Peacock had fled downriver already, he wondered?

Suddenly Jesse's face filled the window, looking white and black from his whiskers and frostbite. His darting dark eyes glared through. His scarred nose pressed against the clear pane. The face stayed there for an hour. Until Eli began to think he would never come out.

At last the window turned black again. Then the door opened slowly, inch by inch. Peacock's eyes stared at the sled once more.

"I know you're trying to trick me. I know something is wrong!" A rifle barrel slid out and pointed at the sled.

Eli lay still, his Colt aimed back, cocked.

"Come out or I'll shoot." Jesse's head poked out farther.

Eli stopped breathing. His trigger finger tightened.

Just then the lead dog whined and jumped against the anchor, jerking the sled forward. Jesse instantly jumped out of the doorway, his eyes now rounded and darting back and forth again.

"Whoa, dogs! Easy now. Is there somebody back around the corner? Is that where he is?" Peacock pointed his rifle at the cabin's side.

Eli eased his knotted muscles. Now he knew Peacock would step closer. He sensed Jesse would relax his deep fear in a moment. Lie still and wait, he thought. Stay silent like the wild Indian. The enemy will soon look the other way.

Jesse Peacock sidestepped, with his back to the

wall of the cabin until he stood at the corner. He peeked, then peeked again. Slowly he returned to the door and stared at the sled once more. At last he leaned his rifle against the wall and reached inside the cabin with his one arm, pulling out his parka. Bending, he began to struggle with the long garment, tugging it over his head.

Eli flipped off the canvas cover and sat up. "If you reach for your rifle, Jesse, you'll do so with only one good leg."

The man he had marshaled for in Montana and Arizona fell onto his knees. The man he had chased so many bitter miles wept uncontrollably, wiping at his tears with his single hand. Eli stood silently, listening to the lonely cries.

CHAPTER SIXTEEN

Death

"I didn't do what you think, Eli." At last Jesse Peacock had calmed himself enough to speak.

Eli waited to reply. All through his many years of arresting killers he had learned not to listen to their pleas of innocence. All their mournful appeals had proven false in the end. No one ever freely confessed their guilt. Why would he think Jesse would behave any differently?

"Jesse, I've done my duty, and I've caught you. By your own words over a year ago you instructed me to let the courts decide. I plan on doing so."

"But I didn't do what you think I did. I only killed Twait when I found out he planned to kill me." Jesse began to cry again.

"Will you shut up, Jesse. Lord . . . the last thing in the world I want you to admit to me is the crime of murder. I saw the bones you left behind. You ate the flesh of man. I'm a Deputy U.S. Marshal. You know I'm duty-bound to repeat your words of confession to anyone who has the right to hear it."

Peacock sobbed louder, more pitifully. Eli stepped by him, picked up the rifle that Jesse had leaned against the cabin, and waved at Blueberry, still peering from behind the pile of logs upriver. Waiting for his young friend to walk across, Eli wished his uneasiness would go away. He had seen Jesse's crimes. Why feel sorry, he wondered?

When the Minnesotan reached the far side of the dog sled, he stopped. "I better not come closer. If I get near him, I'll kill him for killin' Fincher."

Instantly Peacock jerked upright. "But I didn't kill Fincher. Twait did it—not me. Then he threatened me. I had to go along or get shot. You must believe me. I'm telling the truth."

"You fed on Fincher like a hungry dog. I saw it for myself." Then Blueberry stared at Peacock with dark, frowning eyes.

Levering all the cartridges out of the rifle Jesse Peacock had carried, Eli faced the Minnesotan. "Blueberry, keep your head. We've worked hard and captured our man. The law will decide what to do next. Now help me get loaded. We've got to get back to Sleepy Lake as soon as possible. I know Hannah is waiting . . ."

They drove the dogs back to Nulato. Simon Paul locked Jesse Peacock in a storage room for the night, with a plate of food and a winter bedroll. Then he prepared a room for Eli and Blueberry. In an hour both men had thrown open the windows, letting in the cold air. They couldn't bear the warmth of the trading post.

When Eli looked into the room's mirror, he

drew back in fright. Somehow he had thought he would look the same as always. His blackened and bearded face frightened him. How could the Alaskan winters be so cruel, he wondered? How could he have been so weatherbeaten by just one winter?

At least he could look forward to better weather and longer days washed in bright sunlight. Already the midnight sun shone early in the morning and its golden sphere glowed till late evening. Now the daytime temperature warmed to ten below, sometimes to zero, instead of the deadly thirty and forty below Fahrenheit he had lived in all winter. Memories of the bitterness of the past months, the awful hoarfrost clinging to everything—the trees and brush, the dogs and sled, and every bit of exposed beard and clothing still shook shivers down his spine. He had endured the wintertime of the Montana Territory, but he had never before fought for his life against a cruel, slithering killer like the deep cold of Alaska. It frightened him more than any other enemy he had ever faced. The dangerous, creeping iciness had stalked him and Blueberry daily, without rest. No wonder Jesse Peacock had broken down under its strain. Only the strongest men could survive its deliberate pursuit.

The next morning they waved good-bye to Simon Paul and swung the mailman's dogs up the Yukon River in the gray light of dawn. Jesse Peacock, grim-faced, sat on top of the sled, now piled high with new supplies. Eli and Blueberry chased behind, taking turns riding the runners, driving the long team, and jogging to keep up. Settled snow, hardened back trails, and long reaches ruled the river's course as they shot toward the Tanana River once more. And the country slipped by, countless rolling hills, with thick trees all about, as wild and free as any land Eli had ever seen.

He had learned to love Alaska like no other, and even in the awful grip of wintertime. All the wilderness around seemed sacred, unspoiled by human ways. It lay free of man's endeavors and was untrampled by his busy feet. He rejoiced in its glory and worshiped its power. Perhaps, he thought, the brutal winters, the mighty mountains, and the foaming rivers will keep people away this time. Perhaps the last frontier will survive forever. Maybe the savage animals, large and small, can run loose, unafraid of the fatal aim of the buffalo hunter, the pioneer's breaking plow, and the fences of farmers and ranchers.

Up the bottom of Tanana and past the Indian fish camp they raced. Eli drove the dogs on and on, like the grayed veterans of Alaska, the wily messengers who mushed the U.S. mail. Then early April skies slipped over them—lengthy cold days, hard and blue, with crusty snow and waking life all around. Hunting hawks wheeled overhead and a few woodland birds sang to them every morning. In a month or so, they said, the snow would melt, the ice would thaw, and new grass would sprout. Springtime would surely break winter's hold. Sweet, green summer would soon follow.

They camped overnight at the mouth of the Kantishna River, resting for the struggle up the winding route toward Denali Mountain. Their hard pace slowed the next day. Now every mile had to be gained by breaking trail through new soft snow. First Eli led the way, then Blueberry took his turn, stepping one snowshoe ahead at a time, the dogs lined out close behind, whimpering under the load.

That night Blueberry cooked their supper, blinking and shying away because of wayward smoke. Eli squatted nearby, repairing the snowshoes with boiled babiche, then setting them by the fire to dry. Jesse Peacock lay across, on the other side, staring darkly into the leaping flames. And all their sled dogs' eyes glowed like red fireflies, back in the blackness whenever they looked toward the unsettled light.

Blueberry stirred his bubbling pot of beans. "Peacock ain't said a word for a week."

Eli glanced at Jesse. Blueberry's remark sounded strange. Its subject rested close by, within earshot.

"I've known Jesse for many years. He isn't the same. He's not well. I blame myself for letting him come along. I should have known better. Most men are not suited for this kind of country. Most men can't bear up under its loneliness, its hard ways."

"I've walked across this country for more than a year now. Come from Valdez, down the Kluntina

River, up the Copper River, crossed the mountains, and been up and down the Tanana and Yukon rivers a couple of times. I ain't gone crazy."

"But you were born to lonely lands. Jesse has always lived with people in populated places. Even Indians avoid living all alone for the most part. Perhaps the true craziness lies in you and me wishing to live by ourselves." Suddenly Eli felt Peacock's sour eyes search his own.

Blueberry dropped the lid on the blackened kettle he had stirred earlier, clanging its top. "Well, I wish he'd talk. It ain't natural for a man to just stare. He hardly even blinks."

"Take it easy, Blueberry. Jesse will speak when he feels ready. Most men I've arrested remained silent for long periods of time. What would you expect him to say? Besides, the court has the right to hear his answers, not us."

"You don't think he killed Fincher and Twait, do you?" The young Minnesotan's eyes searched Eli's also, joining Jesse's steady gaze.

Eli picked up a stick, poked the fire. "I don't believe he killed Fincher. I know he killed Twait, probably in self-defense. When we get him back as far as Fortymile, we'll let the miners decide. My guess is they will let him go. He's a veteran of the War Between the States and sick as well. Pioneers always seem to find the simple truth."

Silence fell over the camp. After supper Eli slipped into his bedroll, lying awake for an hour before he fell asleep. What, he wondered, had Jesse gone through back at the mouth of the Kan-

tishna River, so many weeks ago? Why had he
killed Ollie Twait later on? He then concluded
Twait must have caused the breakdown Jesse had
suffered. And it made sense Oliver Twait had
murdered Fincher. But had Jesse killed Ollie in
self-defense? He tossed and turned. Would he
ever know the truth?

In the morning east winds beat back and forth
and tumbled snowy clouds sideways over the river's frozen surface. Wind chill and low visibility
punished Eli as he busted trail for the dogs again,
pulling hard in their harnesses. The storm battered
everything with its frosty gales and hid all the
surroundings in spooky whiteness. Shorelines became lost to view, pressing Eli to one side or the
other side of the Kantishna to find his way
upriver. And when he looked back, it seemed
sooty shadows followed him, not Jesse Peacock,
the dogs, and Blueberry, pushing on the sled.

He didn't see the danger until he felt himself
plunge downward. He tried to jump away, but
his legs simply pushed his snowshoes deeper into
the black water. Instantly he realized he had
stepped onto bad ice, thinned by beavers, burrowed in the nearby house he'd missed seeing. He
had made the fatal mistake, the one that had killed
more woodsman than any other hazard of the
wintertime in Alaska. The sourdoughs across the
land had warned him repeatedly—never get wet.
Now, if he didn't stop sinking, his life would be
lost forever!

"Grab hold, Eli. Grab my hand. Stay still, so

you don't go down." A loud voice spoke above the wind.

Eli whipped his head around. Jesse Peacock lay on his stomach on the dangerous ice, close, his one arm stretched out. Then he saw Blueberry running with an ax clenched in his mittens. Next he saw the lead dog swing the team away. Then, slowly, the white mists blown by the awful storm fogged everything. Only the lonely hand lay in sight, its fingers beckoning.

"Jesse, get back. Get off the ice. It's breaking down." He watched in horror, as the foggy form of Peacock sank down.

The two of them thrashed around, Eli with both arms, Jesse with one, trying to stay afloat. At last Eli felt one of his snowshoes settle down on sunken branches, letting him stand upright, neck deep, padding with his hands to keep his balance on his perch. Then he watched Jesse sink down, float up, wildly flapping his arm. Finally Jesse found a shelf of ice and braced himself, holding his head above the dark water.

Eli heard screaming. "Grab the pole, Eli! Hang on. Grab tight. I'll pull you out." A wood pole floated across the water to him.

Instinctively he gripped the slim treetop in his sopping mittens. He peered ahead and saw Blueberry crouched a few paces away, pulling hard. Then he felt his body float up and skid across the snow like an odd water creature hooked for the kill. The weight of his soaked clothing and snowshoes fouled by the beaver's feed bed seemed enormous, but did not overburden the Minnesotan at all.

Then he heard Blueberry scream again. "Let go, I got to get Peacock!"

He released the pole's top and sat up. Then he watched as his friend shoved out the cut-off tree again, bumping Jesse Peacock's single hand. But the five pale fingers stayed stiff, clawing the thin ice.

"Peacock, grab the pole. I'll save you." Blueberry hollered as loudly as he could, then gently prodded Jesse's fingers once more, with the topmost part of the long pole.

The pink fingers straightened, then slipped off the white ice, sinking below the murky water. Next Jesse's face, ghostly and bearded, with hollow eyes and lips painted blue, appeared to drift just above the waterline. Then, slowly, the forlorn mask sank as well. Finally everything seemed peaceful. Only unequal bits of ice bobbed on the blackness of the pool, each circling on the moody roll of the river.

Blueberry began yelling in Eli's ear. "Get up. Get up and move. Help get dry wood. Eli, you'll be as dead as a box of rocks if you don't move."

Eli shook his head, then shook it again. He sensed Blueberry's panic. But his world appeared so tranquil just now. The awful burden of Jesse's guilt had slipped away. Hannah seemed nearby— smiling, warm, and loving. His surroundings looked sweet and safe, with dusky light shining all around, keeping off all evil. He felt the need to sleep. Why would he want to gather dry wood?

He heard Blueberry yell louder. "Eli, you're freezing to death. Wake up. Get up or you'll die." Then he felt someone beating on him, someone rubbing snow on his face.

His mind jumped back. Get on your feet, he thought. Get up and help with the fire. Move! Suddenly he realized he had only a few minutes to live. He rolled to his hands and knees and awkwardly stood up. Then he saw Blueberry sprint for the sled, and grab their can of emergency firestarter, sawdust soaked in kerosene. He threw some out and ignited it with a flashing match.

Walk. Break off dead branches. Walk—throw them down on the fire. March back for more firewood. He voiced the commands inside his brain. The movement seemed to wake him. But he could feel the scheming, deadly cold as it crept around. He felt so sleepy . . . if he could just sit down for a little while. If he could just cross over and rest on the other side . . .

"Eli, stay awake. Get over by the fire. Sit down. You got to start warmin' up."

He felt Blueberry pull him to the fire. Suddenly orange flames and hot smoky fumes seared his face, waking him from his deep daze. Opening his eyes wide, he sensed his head clearing. My God, he cried inside, Jesse Peacock is gone—and my life hangs by a thread. He reached for his belt knife, fumbled for it, and began cutting away his frozen clothing. He saw that his whole body lay encased in a circle of ice.

Then he wanted to speak; he felt compelled to join the living with his voice. "Blueberry, I've been wounded before. But this is the first time I ever wished for my own death. Now I know why the Indians and Eskimos leave their old ones outside in the cold. I sensed no pain ... only sleepiness. At least I know Jesse passed away in peace. Lord rest his soul. He's now food for the fishes!" Suddenly hard shivers shook his body.... But that told him he would live to see another day.

Blueberry knelt alongside. "Give me that knife. I save you from drownin' and freezin' to death—now you're tryin' to cut yourself to death."

The young man grabbed the knife and beat on Eli's parka with the haft, cracking the icy cloth and fur so he could pull it off. Next he cut the leather laces of Eli's winter boots, then removed them.

At last he shook his head, smiling a little. "Eli, you're lucky you can wear wool close to your skin. If you had cotton on, you'd be deader than a doornail. A lot of men can't stand wool. But if they get wet like you, there's no way to save them. Wool's the best for winter. You can get wet, but it'll still keep you alive."

Eli groaned, stood up, loosened his belt, and pushed down his heavy trousers. "I wonder how poor Jesse dressed?"

"Eli, I think Peacock could have saved himself. He still had strength left. It appeared to me he just didn't want to live anymore. He just gave up . . ."

Eli paused. Blueberry's statement made sense. Now that he could think more clearly, it did seen that Jesse had simply let himself slip off the ice. The shame of murder, cannibalism, and thievery had been too much for his old boss to endure, he supposed. Peacock had always been a man of pride, a man of prominence, and a friend of politicians across the Union. How could he have lived down there again? How could he have stayed in Alaska? Perhaps Jesse had chosen his only possible sanctuary. Who knew what thoughts crept around the hollows of the human mind? Maybe he had known honest men wouldn't judge him too harshly in his last place of rest.

"Blueberry, if that's true, I will always say Jesse died bravely. When I served as a young soldier, I watched soldiers charge the Union lines without any hope to live. Their choice was surely suicidal. But afterward those men were said to be courageous and honorable. I want to remember Jesse that same way."

Blueberry hung his head, then looked back up. "Eli, I had mostly forgiven what he did. And I truly tried to save him. I thought about what you'd said before . . . about the folks in Fortymile lettin' him go. I decided I better think about doing that myself. It don't do a fellow much good to stay mad all the time. I didn't want to act crazy like him."

"Blueberry, I saw you try to save Jesse. Feel no

fault whatsoever, you did your best. Now help thaw me out and let's mush for Sleepy Lake again. I've had this worry there's trouble there. And I'm ashamed I've let Doll Girl down for so long. The winter is mostly gone and I haven't found her mother like I promised to do. No matter how one looks at it, I'm three months late. It's bothersome for me to have been so careless with my word."

The young Minnesotan stared. Finally he threw the green boughs that he had gathered on the fire, torching a high blaze. Reckless volleys snapped as the sap of the spruce branches burned and filled the air with noise, smoke, and light. When the wildfire settled down, Blueberry spoke once more.

"Eli, if there's any fault to find, you have only to look at me. I'm the one who led you away. I'm the one who kept naggin' to get even with poor Jesse for what he'd done. Well, looks like I got my wish. But I ain't feelin' too good about it!"

Blueberry trudged away with darkened eyes and looked for more firewood.

They thawed and dried Eli's clothing, painstakingly softening the leather of his boots and parka with bear's grease to drive away the wetness. Blueberry pitched their tent and sheltered Eli inside, next to their little tin stove, healing from his dunking under the freezing water. All the following day he lay exhausted and sickened by the ordeal, only weakly able to help restore his clothing.

Indeed, wool had saved his life. Nonetheless, now it seemed like forever to dry each garment, without shrinking it to an unusable size. Finally, by suppertime on the second day, he felt strong once more. By morning, he thought, he would feel ready to break trail again. Then he heard wolves howling in the distant mountains. Could Hannah hear them, too, way over on Sleepy Lake, he wondered?

They struck their camp, loaded, and worked up the river again, mile after hard mile. At last they found the trail leading off the Kantishna River and across the low foothills guarding their destination. Then the skies cleared and Denali stood over them, sunlit white, with snowy plumes blowing off its crown. Eli wondered if man would ever climb the holy peak. Then he wondered if he should try someday. Maybe the boy back in Fort Yukon would go with him. Perhaps they could be the first men to gaze down on Alaska from its top. What a wonderful sight that must be, he mused.

Two days later they stopped the dogs in front of the little trapper's hut where he had pinned the letter for Hannah. When he peered inside, he saw someone had pulled down the message. His heart leaped. Tomorrow he would see Hannah for the first time in months. Lord, he thought, the joy of holding her, making love—he could hardly wait. When you loved someone so much, only their warmth, closeness, and humid breath on your cheek could fill the need, end your longing for their touching softness. He ran from the campsite and quickly led Blueberry and the dogs away.

In the sunset of the next day, under a copper sky, clouded with pink and purple, he spotted

Sleepy Lake from a faraway hillside. Red Shirt's cabin sat in the shadows of the trees edging the clearing, chopped into the timbered shore. Rising smoke floated straight up, then flattened into a lazy haze, about one hundred feet up. Lean dogs lay around the yard, tethered by their necks, and resting on their sides in front of small log shelters, drifted over by snow. And the Great Mountain stood above, rosy in the setting sun, its heavy eminence darkening all the little things below.

"I hope that's Hannah waiting down there . . ." Eli's voice waned into the silence of the coming night.

"You ain't seen her for a long time, have you? It's hard to be away from home . . . or the folks you've loved for so long. This beautiful sight makes me want to go back and see my mother in Minnesota. I get so lonely sometimes."

Eli lowered his binoculars and eyed Blueberry. The young man stood quietly, his head drooping down, looking exhausted from his long, hard winter. It seemed time for them to rest for a while. He walked to their sled, shouted for the dogs to get up, and called for Blueberry to come along. They would reach the cabin in an hour. Then he could cross over and rest on the other side. . . .

CHAPTER SEVENTEEN

Reunion

Eli watched the dogs around the distant cabin jump up on their feet. Then he listened to their howling, as he and Blueberry sledded the last mile of Sleepy Lake. His own dogs answered back and ran faster, eager to gain the shore and join their own kind. The team's joyful racket touched him inside. He felt at last like he had made it home as well.

Suddenly he saw the door of the cabin swing wide open. Then Noodles stepped out with his little Winchester held high, pointing dangerously. More startling, the little withered prospector stood alone, without Hannah and Doll Girl by his side. In a single instant his heart fell. Why had his old friend come outside by himself?

As soon as the dogs swung around in front, Noodles yelled, "You two stand easy. Tell me who you are and what you want."

Eli stood on the sled's runners, dumbstruck, numbed, forgetting even to throw out the sled's anchor. After a moment, he called, "Old man, it's me—Eli. Why can't you see who I am?"

Noodles lowered his rifle, aiming it away. He then turned and wept, covering his eyes with one hand.

Eli sprang from the sled and ran to his friend. He reached out and pulled on the old man's shoulder, facing him around. "Where's Hannah? Tell me quick."

"Eli, you don't look like yourself no more. You're all weatherbeaten and bearded. You look half dead. I didn't know who you was. Where you been? You been gone so long, I about gave up on you."

"Old man, where's Hannah?" Eli tried to peer into the cabin, but his eyes couldn't pierce the blackness just beyond the woodshed door.

"Hannah got hurt real bad. Doll Girl's run off and left us. I been waitin' so long for you to come back." The old man wept louder.

Eli shoved by and bolted through the doorway. Once inside the cabin, he stopped, blinked, and then saw Hannah lying on a bed in a corner. A lone candle's newly lit flame lighted her dark-eyed face.

"Hannah, what's happened to you?" He reached her side in three quick paces.

A curling smile tipped up the corners of her mouth. She held out her left hand, reaching for his hand. "Eli, you've finally come back. My goodness, you look worse than I look."

Eli leaned over and kissed her lips, then held his face against her, tears moistening his eyes. "Hannah, what has happened? I can't bear to think I've been gone so long, while you've been injured."

"Phew, Eli, you smell terrible." Hannah started to laugh, then moaned. "Don't make me laugh, my ribs are cracked on my right side, my right leg, too. I'm black and blue from head to foot. But I'll get better soon, now that you've come back." She smiled again.

"How did you get hurt so badly?" Eli straightened back up and wiped at his tears with his parka sleeves.

"I shot my first moose, but that brute nearly killed me instead. I had no idea those ugly beasts could be so dangerous and could run so fast."

Eli stared, rounding his eyes. "Why did you get so close? Why did the old man and Doll Girl let you hunt by yourself?"

"It's not their fault. We were coming back with the moose Noodles had shot earlier. Another huge bull attacked their sled and killed four dogs. I ran up to stop him." Her eyes grew humid and her lips trembled.

"Don't talk. You've always been so fearless. I can't imagine another person who would face over a thousand pounds of angry moose like you did. They're nearly as big as a buffalo and just as mean-tempered. Now we've got to figure out how to get you well."

"I feel better already, with you here. Eli, where have you been? You look awful. What's happened to you?"

"Jesse's dead. Two other men are gone. I nearly

starved to death. Thank Providence for my new friend, Billy House, 'else I would have drowned just days ago."

Hannah's face paled, then her dark eyes widened. "Jesse Peacock is dead. Eli, what's happened? We saw two skeletons when we came up the Tanana River. Oh Lord, what an awful sight that . . ." Her lips quivered again.

"You shush up and don't cry. It's best that Jesse's gone. He may have killed the two men you found. By his own admission, he ate one. He drowned himself in the Kantishna, trying to save me. But I believe it's for the best. His poor mind had sickened so much."

"Is that why you've been gone so long?"

Eli leaned over and kissed Hannah once more. "Yes, but I shouldn't have chased poor Jesse like I did. I could have waited for you at the mouth of the Tanana. I'll never forgive myself for what I've done. And the old man has told me Doll Girl is gone. That news breaks my heart even more. I've got to remember that I'm pledged to stay with you."

"Oh, Eli, you'll never change. And I suppose it would break my heart if you did. I've crossed most of North America for the love of following you. Remember, I'm the one who left San Francisco to start a new life. I just wish it didn't hurt so much at times." Her face writhed as she rolled to her left side. Then she added, "I dream of sleeping for one whole night on my side. A person never knows how awful it is to be forced to lie on your back for days on end, until you have lost that ability."

Eli reached out and helped Hannah roll sideways, grimacing himself because of her visible pain. "Tell me what's happened to Doll Girl."

"I'm worried sick about her. But then, in a way, I'm not. She's like one of the wild creatures that live all around this grand place. She helped Noodles care for me, until she knew I would get well. Then she ran away with old Wahnie. I know she's looking for her mother. Who can blame her?"

After sliding over a crude chair, Eli sat down by the bed and held her hand again. "My fault entirely. I should have waited and served my original purpose. If anything happens to that child . ."

"She's only a child in body—not in mind or spirit. And she knows more about her mother's kidnapping than she told last December. More than that, the old shaman back in Port Yukon knows some of her secrets."

Eli frowned his forehead and blinked his eyes. "Why do you say there's more to the mystery than we know?"

"We visited the medicine man in Fort Yukon who you talked about in the past. He stopped Doll Girl from telling Noodles and me something important." Then Hannah's eyes brightened. "He also told us you would come back, like the wolf. Now I see the old fool knew more than I believed back then."

"Indians tend to keep most of their knowledge to themselves. I don't think it's odd the old one would stop Doll Girl from telling us things about her past life. She said her father was a Koyukon medicine man. I'm sure she knows many secrets we would like to know."

"Do you believe the mountain called Denali is haunted—like all the Indians seem to think?"

Eli stood up and smiled, then shoved his chair aside. "Yes. Each time I see the mountain, I see its power. Now let's see your wounds—and how I can get them to heal faster."

Hannah groaned as she dropped onto her back again. After a pause, she began to open her night-gown. "Noodles said once he had a burro hurt worse. He said the poor thing fell to the bottom of a canyon. He claims he had that animal back up in the month. I hope he's done that well with me."

Breaking into laughter, Eli shook his head. "Hannah, I'm sure he's accomplished that and more. You lay still and let me look under his splints and wraps. You seem to move around quite well. I think you'll be up before long."

"The old goat makes me get up and hobble around on crutches now!"

Eli laughed louder. "I love you, Hannah. I love that old man, too. You'll never know how much I've missed you two." He wiped his eyes, which were wet with tears of happiness.

After examining Hannah's injuries and bringing Blueberry inside to meet her, he slipped from the cabin and found Noodles splitting kindling from a dry block of wood. The prospector, hunched over, swung his ax carefully, his face long and his eyes hollow.

"Old man, you've done miracles with Hannah. She seems to be healing like new."

"I love her like a daughter and blame myself for gettin' her hurt. No excuse for me not having my rifle ready. I been out in the wilderness before. All the critters up here are big and dangerous. None of it should've happened. It's all my fault, and I let you down." Tears dribbled down the old man's cheeks onto his white whiskers.

"Hannah told me she had run forward, shooting, trying to kill the beast. She said your sled had flipped over. Why would you blame yourself? I understand why you feel bad, but try to restore your spirit. Hannah and I want to see you happy."

"How can I feel happy? My little friend has run off, too. You don't know how much I love that girl! Now she's gone off alone in this land." The old man swung his head back and forth, his restive glances searching the great mountain standing overhead.

Eli gazed toward Denali as well. He never tired of watching its dark moodiness. One moment the mighty summit would be standing in plain view, its unequal cross lights shimmering, blinding his eyes. The next moment gray-rolling clouds would tumble down, casting murky light where the brightness had been just a moment before. Suddenly the whole great mountain would then vanish, making him wonder if, in fact, he had seen its beauty after all. Perhaps, his mind mused, it had been a midnight's dream. But his wondering gaze forever kept him searching, hoping to see more of its sunlit sides.

"Old man, that mountain tells me she's fine. And remember ... she's also part of this land. When her mother gave birth, she dropped her on this very ground, picked her up, and licked off the dirt, the spruce needles, and the leaves from her tiny body. You know how Indian women deliver their babies. How could a child begin life in this wilderness in a better way. She's as capable of surviving as any of the other young wild things that live here."

Noodles straightened and then shifted his full blue eyes to Eli's face. "By Jeez, you're right, Eli. I know those kind of things. When we goin' to go find her? You know she'll figure to tangle with that outlaw who took her ma."

Eli smiled, seeing his friend's brightened eyes and toothless smile again. "Old man, give me a few days to clean up and rest. Then I'll decide. Now tell me where you have Ironclaw tied. Hannah tells me he's a wise lead dog. It seems he was just a pup when I left Dawson City last winter. I find it hard to believe he's grown so much."

The old prospector grinned. "I don't tie him. He won't leave Hannah 'less she says. Every time he gets next to her, he's lickin' her busted leg. Did you know dog lickin' cures bad wounds faster?" His blues eyes then squinted.

"I learned that from the Sioux long ago. But I expect most folks would find that news disgusting, old man. You best keep that fact to yourself." Eli turned away and called his dog.

Noodles cackled. Then he called, "Eli, I ain't got much time on this earth. I ain't wastin' it on wonderin' what other folks think of me. Providence is the only thing I'm worried about now." The old man's cackles continued to echo around the clearing that circled the cabin.

Eli then whistled. Finally Ironclaw padded from the far side of the log cabin. The dog stopped, statuelike, and stared. He stood fully grown, his winter fur long and white. His face lay flattened and filled, his puppy features completely gone. Most noticible, his yellow eyes gleamed like a wolf's.

"Ironclaw, I see you're still angry I left you behind. Don't you understand it now seems best that I did—for Hannah's sake. Come here, my friend, and let's make up. I've a notion my life will soon depend on it."

The dog's tail slowly snaked back and forth. At last the dog trotted to him, eyes gleaming brighter.

"Good boy. I'm surprised you've grown so large and strong. The man I'm after will jump in fright when he sees the likes of you." Eli laughed and hugged his dog. Ironclaw answered by licking his face.

The next day the three men repaired the sleds and gear. Then Eli and Blueberry took turns shaving their beards and bathing for the first time in months. Finally Eli could endure looking at himself in the mirror. And Hannah's approving smile added to his redeemed spirit. His restless strength seemed to flood back.

He sent his two friends across the cabin's clearing to pitch a bachelor's camp for themselves. At last he and Hannah could sleep together. He had forgotten the comforts of a warm cabin and a soft bed. And, most of all, he had missed the joy of loving her.

They lay together, touching for hours. Hannah's injuries stopped their common passion . . . but not their sweet need for each other. Slowly, patiently, they used the intimacies of their past to help each other with new lovemaking.

Hannah curled on her side and Eli lay behind. Their bodies mixed inside each other, letting hardness and softness and hot minds reach for high moments. Then they found new ways to touch each other. They learned hands and lips could satisfy as well. And when they finished, they felt more love than ever. Finally they rested, staring, melting into each other eyes. They told about things only true lovers could confess, becoming one in their sharing of love.

Afterward Eli bathed Hannah, like a mother would bathe her child. He spent hours washing and rinsing her hair, legs, arms . . every part of her, until she lay clean and pink from the warm glow of rubbing. Then they hugged once more and slept, each of them finally feeling healed by the joy they felt from being united again.

Three days passed, with Noodles fussing more and more about his runaway friend. At last Eli felt he couldn't endure the old man's worries any longer. And Hannah said she felt the same misgivings, too. He began to search the border of the clearing around the cabin, looking for small footprints and other signs of human use.

Ironclaw led the way, sniffing rabbit and squirrel tracks as he trotted along. On the side of the cabin facing Denali, the young dog stopped and stared down an old path. Recent winds had drifted snow, like low waves lapping sidelong here and there, along the long trail snaking through the woods. The dog whimpered as he stood still, testing the cold air with his nose.

"So this is the way they went, my friend. The same direction Jesse and I walked from, after we'd lost our sled and dogs last winter."

Eli stepped forward, eyeing the bushy branches beside him. He found the end of one twig snapped and pointed southwest. Doll Girl has done this, he mused. She knows most men would miss seeing the sign. But she knows I'll read this tiny message. He turned around, whistled for Ironclaw, and marched back to the cabin.

Once inside he pulled off his parka, hung it up, and walked to Hannah, who was sitting on her bed. Noodles and Blueberry stood on the other side of the smoky room, in front of the stove, stirring stew meat and baking sourdough bread.

After kissing Hannah, Eli sat down next to her bedside and glanced at his two friends. "I'll start after Doll Girl in the morning."

Noodles swung away from his pot of bubbling

meat. "Eli, I want to go, too. Don't leave me behind. I know you mean to go alone."

Eli dreaded breaking the old man's heart. "Old man, You need to stay behind and guard Hannah. I will hunt for Doll Girl by myself. I'll take Ironclaw, my pack, snowshoes, and a rifle."

Blueberry turned around. "Then can I go? We been together all winter . . ."

"No. Both of you need to stay here and guard this cabin day and night. If I miss catching the man I'm after, I'm sure he'll head back here. I want Hannah protected at all times. The dogs will sound an alarm if anyone tries to sneak up."

Noodles' long face lifted; he squinted his eyes. "This place ain't suitable for a gunfight. There's no windows on the back and sides. Maybe we better cut holes, just in case. We can stuff 'em with rags to keep the cold out, till we need to see out."

Eli narrowed his own eyes, then leaned forward and pointed at the whiskered prospector. "Blueberry has little experience in these matters. You've fought Indians and outlaws all your life. Make no mistakes—'else you will see Blueberry and yourself shot down one by one."

The cabin fell silent. He felt Hannah touch his back with her fingers. He then watched his two friends trade sober glances before turning slowly back to their cooking. He stood up and held Hannah's hand for a moment. At last he leaned over and kissed her, straightened, and looked for his backpack.

PART IV

Spirits

CHAPTER EIGHTEEN

Secrets

"Wahnie, we have found Mother." Doll Girl ducked behind a knot of alders and high brown grass. She stared down into the valley, hazy with sleepy blue smoke.

She had learned about the odd ways of the white man in the past wintertime. It had taken the same passage of time to master the English language. Her newfound wisdom had led her to the hidden valley.

She had found out that the Yellow God was the mighty spirit that had called the white people north. They worshiped the golden gleaming pebbles her father had shown her several times in the past.

But she didn't understand their crazy lust. The soft stones weren't useful for ordinary living. She did recall her father melting handfuls into bullets, when she yet sucked on her mother's breasts. She could still see him placing the shiny balls on top his old muzzleloader, then pushing each one down with a long wooden stick to the black powder he had poured in first. But that appeared to be the only daily purpose for the gift from Denali.

During her stay in Dawson City, her adopted grandfather Noodles had shown her small sacks full of the gold pebbles he had dug up. He had also taken her into a tall building, with black iron bars across the windows and unfriendly men armed with rifles and pistols, and pointed out heavy bricks of the yellow metal.

But everyone just seemed to hide away their gold, like the silly red squirrels, gathering and storing more than they could ever eat. None of it made any sense to her. What did the white men intend to do with the Yellow God? They all had new rifles now, with much, much better bullets. Rifles and bullets that empowered hungry hunters to kill more than they could possibly eat in a year. She wondered if there was some piece of knowledge missing in her mind. Otherwise she would know the reasons for the white men's madness. She supposed a little way further in her life she would understand. Meanwhile she had begun to grasp why her father had told her the D'en'e Indians were the only sensible people on Mother Earth.

Nevertheless, thankfully, Grandfather Noodles' simple, honest heart had given her the strong intuition of where to find her mother. His constant pattering about prospecting, gold mining, old outlaws, and Eli Bonnet had slowly led her to believe the stranger who had kidnapped her mother had only wanted the Great One's gold. Somehow he had found out about her father's ancient secrets.

Then he must have forced her mother to lead him to the sacred valley.

Doll Girl watched her mother shuffle between a woodpile and the fire she was tending. The black-bearded stranger stepped out of the low dugout that sat beside the water that flowed along the valley's bottom, year-round. The young sled dogs he had stolen cowered and slunk to the ends of their chains. Her mother's head dropped—she moved off to the end of her chain as well. The worn iron links flashed sunlight up, like the sparkling hot spring, flowing nearby.

"Wahnie, the bad man has whipped Mother, like the young dogs. I'm afraid he will kill her soon. We must get her free." Then she listened to her old dog sigh.

Her father had shown her the holy place twice before. They had drunk the bubbling mineral water, filling their bellies full. Then they had bathed and splashed around, cleansing their souls with the sacred medicine of the Great One. Nibbling caribou and moose had wandered back and forth. Pecking ptarmigan had stood nearby. Hunting had been forbidden long ago, her father had explained. The green valley, the hot spring, and the magical peace were to be worshiped forever.

After their ceremonies her father had taken her to the far-distant cave where all the dead Athabaskan shamans stared out at Denali. More than a thousand human skulls sat on rocky ledges, piled altogether like white face masks, with hollow black eyes and toothy jaws gaping out. She had jumped back in silent horror when she had first seen the fateful secret of her father. Not even her mother had been shown the burial cave. Then her father had sworn her to deep silence. Only one other person knew the whereabouts of the skulls—the ancient medicine man back in Fort Yukon—and he would never tell. She had also given him her solemn pledge to carry their bones to the cave. A promise she now wondered how she would ever fulfill.

But her greatest problem stood across the valley—the black-bearded kidnapper. He seemed invincible. She had no weapons, other than Wahnie. She knew he would rip the bad man's throat wide open the instant he saw the chance. Yet she could see the stranger constantly kept his rifle by his side. He would shoot the moment he saw her dog.

She felt Eli Bonnet and Ironclaw would track her down and help her in a few days . . . if he had stayed alive through the long winter. His spirit coat had shown her his magical powers and useful courage. Nonetheless . . . had he been strong enough to survive the deep cold? What could she do to rescue her mother without him, she wondered?

Then low winds on her face reminded her to move away. The hard afternoon sun had swung down from its perpendicular place in the blue sky. Rising warm air now hid her and Wahnie's scent from the sled dogs below. But April's midnight sun always turned wide sweeps on the far horizon. Soon the air would cool and sink into the valley. The young dogs would smell her, bark, and warn the kidnapper. She rolled onto her hands and knees and crawled up the hillside, whispering to Wahnie to sneak behind her.

Once she had slipped over the topmost part of the high hill she had come up, she stood upright and walked down the other side. Springtime had thinned the snow on the sunlit sides of all the mountains around. On the north slopes and where the winter winds had drifted deep snow, the warmer weather had beaten the snow down like hard earth. She and Wahnie could walk around freely, except for places where the snow lay softened by the heat of midday.

Since babyhood, April had always been her favorite month. The days stayed forever blue. Sweet sunlight danced on the snow for endless hours, helped at night by the white moon. It made no difference when you wished to hunt, eat, sleep, or play ... the daytime waited for you. Darkness never covered the land.

When she had seen Hannah Twigg healing fine from her wounds, she had decided to search for her mother. She would not wait patiently any longer. She would simply hope that Eli Bonnet had lived, that he and Ironclaw would read her signs, and follow them across the steep mountains to the hidden valley. Regardless ... she would find out for herself if the spirits had whispered truthfully inside her head.

She smiled a little, recalling one of her father's

early lessons. It had permitted her to feed herself on the long march she had just finished.

Every autumn her father had carried sacks of dried Yukon River salmon to their home at Sleepy Lake. Red squirrels had always stolen some of the fat fish, hiding little piles inside hollow trees and in nests up in tree branches. At first she had chased off the squirrels. But her father had scolded her, explaining that they needed to share with their noisy friends. Then he had taught her the squirrels actually ate very little of the salmon. She should just watch carefully. She could steal back the fish whenever she needed some for herself.

Her father also had told her the D'en'e people could walk forever on just pockets full of the rich dried salmon. Everything their stomachs needed for long expeditions lay in their favorite food. And she had found it to be true. She and Wahnie had stayed strong. . . .

Finally she found the deep snowbank she had been looking for, on the far side of the hill. Kneeling, she began to dig with her hands, like the burrowing ground squirrel.

"We will dig a snow cave and rest, Wahnie. By morning I will have a plan . . ."

That night she huddled inside her little hollow with her dog. Snow caves were the best camps up in the cold mountains, she remembered. She watched the newly lit candle she had carried along. One little flame would keep her warm.

Then she worried about her mother. At last she fell asleep.

In the bright morning light she crawled from her cave. She now knew her plan. Denali's spirits would have to watch over the remaining part of her life.

"Wahnie, stay. Don't follow me. Stay away." She watched her dog sit down, his head low and eyes cloudy.

"You listen to me, you old dog. Don't follow. Go away."

She turned around and began to climb the high white slopes. She had promised herself never to cry again . . . but she couldn't hold back her tears any longer. Glistening teardrops ran down her cheeks. Muffled sobs ebbed around the hillside. She really had no plan—she simply wanted to hug her mother.

CHAPTER NINETEEN

Captivity

Doll Girl stopped when she crested the hill overlooking the valley. She knew the young dogs would instantly see her dark human shape on the skyline. All Mother Earth's creatures looked peculiarly conspicuous against the white snow and blue sky of the horizons. She had seen this for herself, while hunting caribou with her father. No one could mistake odd silhouettes on the tops of hills. No one would miss seeing her—even her poor mother.

She started down, stomping her heels into the hard snow of the hill, to keep her footing. The dog's noisy barking bounced up the valley's walls at once. Even so, she could hear her mother's hard wails above the sudden racket. In a single moment, she thought, her mother had seen the awful jeopardy in her coming into captivity.

Suddenly Doll Girl saw the stranger leap out of the dugout, his trouser suspenders flying up behind his rear end, and his rifle pointing up at her. She prayed to her mountain spirits and kept walking downhill.

At last the stranger lowered his rifle and walked forward. He swung his head back and forth, his wild gaze sweeping all the high snowfield around.

"Unbelievable. How did you get here? Who's back on the other side?" His mouth hung open on his bearded face—his eyes continued to shift around.

"I am alone. I came here to live with my mother." Doll Girl wiped her wet eyes on her parka sleeves.

The kidnapper's eyes stopped. "Where's that gray dog of yours?" He stared at her with the same sharp, black eyes she remembered from the past wintertime when he had first pushed his way inside the cabin on Sleepy Lake.

"He is dead—"

She wondered what had happened? She lay on the snow, blinking to clear her mind. Then she began to hear her mother's screaming and the dog's howling. Her head throbbed and one side of her face felt numb.

Then the bad man's voice growled again. "Don't you lie to me. Where's the dog and who's with you?" The stranger's eyes gleamed. Then he raised his right arm like a club.

She rolled to her hands and knees and crouched low. "Wahnie died last winter and I ate him." She glimpsed the arm strike down once more.

Her mother's voice, the hard blue sky, the early-morning sun resting near the distant white moun-

tains . . . She lay still and gathered her wits.
Slowly she remembered and then sat up.

Her mother's voice sobbed, "Daughter—daughter, why have you done this? My dreams have
been good until now! I saw you alive, among
other people, happy. Why did you ever come
here?"

"Where is he?" Doll Girl quickly shifted her
eyes, as afraid as she had been when she had seen
the grizzly bear for the first time.

"He is walking around the hilltops. He is
searching for Wahnie and your friends. Where are
they, daughter?" Her mother's hard crying carried on.

Doll Girl paused, then shook her head to clear
her thoughts. Finally she wrapped her arms
around her mother, crying too. "There is no one
with me. I sent Wahnie away. I learned how to
find you, but I could not see how to get you free.
When I saw you, I had to come down. You need
me to help you, until we can get away."

"Oh, daughter, I don't think we can ever get
free."

Then her mother held her as close as if she were
yet a baby. At last, after a few minutes, they
quieted themselves and dried their eyes.

Her mother touched her head, looking for cuts
and bruises. "Do you hurt inside? He struck you
so hard. The side of your face is puffed up by
your mouth." Her mother grabbed snow and held
handfuls against the swelling.

"I have a bad headache . . . but I think it will

go away soon. My parka hood protected my head a little, when he hit me. Did I pass out long?"

"Just a moment. I am so afraid you are hurt badly. Please, please do not make him angry anymore. He just wants your father's gold. But I have told him a thousand times I cannot help him. Your father never told me how to find the secret place."

"I can see he has not believed you. He has hit you many times, hasn't he, Mother? I can tell by your face. When he comes down, I will try to get him to listen to me. He cannot find any gold until summer . . . maybe not even then. Father told me how to find the Yellow God, but I don't understand his words. He told me I must first wait for the hummingbird. What is a hummingbird, Mother? I have never seen such a bird."

Her mother's face paled. "Daughter, the hummingbird is a tiny bird that flies to Denali Mountain when Athabaskan medicine men die. It comes only in the summertime. I have seen this little bird only once. When it flew here to tell your father to carry the last shaman to the secret cave up in the mountains. Now this bird will fly again. It will come to see you."

In an instant Doll Girl understood the prophecies her father had talked about so often. She had been too young to listen before, and she had not asked all the questions she should have asked. But now she grasped the awful legacy her father had left behind—the sacred petition she had to fulfill.

But, perhaps, she had made the fatal choice, when she had come down to join her mother.

How could she carry her father to his grave, and the ancient shaman in Fort Yukon as well, if the bearded stranger killed her? She turned her head and stared at the giant mountain standing overhead. Then she listened to the low thunder of the avalanches that always tumbled down its steep slopes. It seemed now that the Great One sounded more angry than ever. Had she stupidly displeased the mighty spirits, when she had decided her mother's life was as precious as her own? She knew the spirits never forgave people who violated the rules. Her father had warned her many times. Had she failed again?

Her mother's fearful voice wailed again. "Daughter, you cannot tell anyone about your father's secrets. If you show this man the place where your father found his gold, death will silence us forever. Denali will send us to an evil grave. Our tongues will be cut out and our eyes blinded. Our spirits will never fly again."

Doll Girl's mind raced through her mother's warnings. She would just have to pray for miracles.

"Mother, I don't know how, but Wahnie will come back to help us. He is like the wind now. You will feel him on your face, but your eyes cannot find him. He is the ghost of our land." Then she paused and watched the bearded stranger start tramping toward them, off the valley's east sidewall. At last she added, "Maybe there's a white man coming to help, too. The ancient one who lives in Fort Yukon told me this man is like the hunting wolf. And I have seen his magic coat. Yes . . . I think he will come."

Her mother stared at her. "Daughter, you are talking queer and frightening me, like your father. Is his spirit inside your head? Have you seen a vision?"

The two questions puzzled her. She didn't know what to say. Finally she answered, "I am an Indian. That's all I know."

Her mother's eyes widened, looking troubled.

A few minutes later the kidnapper stood over their heads again. "I don't see nobody. I can see for miles but there ain't nothin' to see. Maybe you didn't bring anybody along. But where's that dog? I ain't stupid."

"My dog is dead. My mother says you want gold. I know where the gold eagle lives on the mountain." Doll Girl then saw her mother's eyes turn even more fearful.

The stranger immediately squatted in front of her, with his black eyes beaming. "That's what your pa said about the gold. He said there's enough gold to fill a hundred sleds. Where is this place?"

Doll Girl saw the man's crazy weaknesses in his eyes—his mad wishes for the Yellow God— regardless of the costs. And he had confessed, in fact, that he had killed her father. Suddenly she wanted to kill him. Somehow she wanted to get revenge.

"I will take you there if you stop hurting my

mother. She has never seen this place. I am the only one who knows about my father's secrets."

She then watched the bearded man's eyes blink. He seemed suspicious . . . still uncertain.

"Little girl, what are you up to? If you're tryin' somethin' fancy, I'll kill your mother. Then I'll kill you. You better believe I'll do it."

"My father didn't care about the gold. I don't care about gold either. You can have it all."

Instantly the dark eyes quit blinking. The stranger tilted his head back and peeked down alongside the length of his nose. At last he grunted, "All right, start talking. Tell me more about the gold eagle. How do I get there?"

Doll Girl's heart pounded. Now her life and her mother's hung on the stranger's terror of Denali's creeping glaciers. Did he know about the awful dangers?

"At the end of this valley there is a pass leading up to the great mountain. At the top of the pass you will see a blue glacier on the other side. You must climb—"

"That's the glacier your pa pointed at. Ain't there another way to get up to that mountain? You fall in one of them crevasses, you're gone for good. I been lookin' up there already with my spyglasses."

Doll Girl purposely widened her eyes, focusing her steady gaze on the kidnapper's eyes while keeping the rest of her face plain. "I'm not afraid. My father showed me the secret path."

"How far up there? How long does it take to

walk to this gold eagle? And what about your pa talking about the hummingbird? Ain't no hummingbirds in Alaska I ever heard about. I told him that sounded like a lie. You better explain what he meant by tellin' me that tall tale."

She glanced at her mother's colorless face. "My father was the last medicine man of the Koyukon people. The hummingbird will come in the summertime, to fly around my head. Then I will know that it's time to carry his bones to his grave."

The stranger's eyes danced. "I knew it. I guessed I was on to somethin' big. I figured there was some truth in that tale. Hell's fire, I'm gonna get rich!"

Suddenly his eyes frowned again. "Now let's make the bargain clear. You say you got to bury your father. Well ... you can't unless you stay alive. If you show me the gold eagle on the mountain, you can bury him in hell for all I care. If you behave yourself from now on, I'll let you live ... your ma, too. Them's my promises, you understand?"

Doll Girl nodded her head. She kept her eyes steady and her face calm, but inside she felt the savage longing to kill the stranger. If she ever saw the chance, she would do as her father would have done, if he had lived long enough.

The stranger stood and turned away. Then Doll Girl listened to his fading footsteps while she eyed her mother sitting motionless nearby.

"Daughter, now I am more scared than ever. I

am also afraid of you. What have you become, since you left my side?"

"I feel Wahnie's eyes watching, and I hear my father's voice." She stood up as well and walked to the steaming springwater running just in front of her. She knelt down and drank. Her fears had somehow changed to the human need to find a way to destroy the black-bearded man. But, she wondered, why wasn't she afraid anymore? Suddenly she didn't feel like a small girl.

After an hour the kidnapper walked back with a heavy pack slung on his back, his rifle and snowshoes gripped in his hands. "You get away from your mother so I can cut her loose from the chains. Go get what you think you want to carry from the dugout. We're leaving here right quick, so don't dally around."

Doll Girl instantly forgot her wild killing passion. Cold anxiety crept inside her heart. Her mother appeared too sick to climb Denali Mountain. Somehow she had to leave her mother behind.

"My mother is weak and will slow us down. Leave her here. She will not run away. She can feed the dogs while we are gone."

"No." Then the stranger's eyes blackened. "Now do what I said, unless you want to get knocked flat again."

"Daughter—go. Do as he says. Get me a little food to carry along. Bring things for yourself— light things so you can stay strong." Her mother gave her a gentle shove.

Doll Girl walked slowly away, her head turned, eyeing her mother's right leg getting cut free of the same chains the stranger had used to leash the young dogs. Then she ducked into the dugout she and her father had slept in so long ago. The hollow room felt unholy now, dirty because of the white man who had spoiled the peacefulness of the place.

Nothing remained that could be used as a weapon. A careless pile of dried fish, canned goods, and pilot bread lay on the little table, against one wall. Stinky socks, shirts, and pants hung low on a thin rope, strung across the enclosure. She grabbed an old burlap bag and stuffed the sack with the lightest foodstuffs she could find. She and her mother would have to survive on dry food.

When she returned to her mother's side again, she found her bent over, rubbing her ankle where the chain links had chafed her skin raw.

At last her mother smiled. "We will take turns carrying your sack. Now don't worry about me, daughter, I will be strong. You walk ahead and lead the way."

Doll Girl glanced at the stranger. It seemed clear he had threatened her mother a few moments earlier. She pinched her lips together and looked at Denali Mountain. Whispering to her spirits and feeling sick to her stomach, she turned up the hidden valley. Glancing back, she saw her mother limping and the black-bearded man grinning as he strolled along in last place.

They walked up the rising, rolling bottom ground, toward the high pass at the far end of the valley. Doll Girl wandered a little, keeping clear of the alder patches blocking their way. She chose circling courses across the great reaches of deep snow and along the barren hillsides, melted brown by the sun. Her tracks zigzagged as she marched on and on, looking at her mother and the stranger over her shoulder from time to time.

She knew she and her mother weighed half as much as the kidnapper, with his lumpy pack strapped on his back. She knew, as well, that the sun grew hot at midday. Sooner or later the snow's crust would soften and they would begin to break through. And then the man following them would fall through the most. After a while he would strap on his snowshoes and find that hardship even worse. The sticky snow would drag down each of his steps, eventually exhausting him.

She prayed for a mistake on his part. Maybe he would fall through to his waist and get stuck, she thought. Then, perhaps, she and her mother could jump into a hollow, run, and leave him behind.

Suddenly the stranger yelled, "Get up on that dry hill and sit down! I ain't crazy enough to kill myself by sloggin' through this snow. We'll wait till it turns cold tonight."

Doll Girl's heart sank. The white man knew, she reflected, that people living south of the midnight sun rested during the day and traveled at night, when the snow lay hard, like ice. Everlasting light from the sun and moon left the nighttimes bright. They would have little trouble seeing where to walk as they climbed the pass.

That night they began marching uphill again, their steps crunching the snow in an odd rhythm as their unequal footfalls mixed together. Doll Girl purposely measured herself with short paces. Her mother matched her gait, hobbling on her sore ankle. The powerful stranger walked lazily behind, watching alertly whenever brush or trees or terrain might hide his captives from his rifle's aim.

After several hours the nighttime's murky light began to brighten with the stronger rays of the rising morning sun. Then at last they reached the top of the pass at the head of the hidden valley. Doll Girl stopped and peered down the falling mountainside beyond her feet. In plain view, at the bottom of the steepness, lay the jagged snowy face of the glacier they all had to scale. Tilting her head back, she looked up at the most distant point of the white gleaming snowfield. She could just see the hillside blue of the perpendicular parts of Denali Mountain, where the skulls of the shamans lay watching from their secret cave.

Suddenly the stranger's fit of fear shook her from her wondering gaze. His loud voice sounded awful in the muffled silence of the solemn mountain peaks standing all around.

"God—how we gonna climb up that? How do you know where to go?" Then the stranger's mouth withered to two quivering lips. His eyes squeezed to hollow holes.

Doll Girl stood quietly thinking. She had not seen the giant glacier after the snows of an entire winter. She had last walked its length in the summertime, when the ancient cairns had stood in plain view. Now everything lay blanketed in deep snow. She had no idea of where to go.

But one thing seemed clear. She needed to lead the man standing by her side across all the false lying levels of snow she could find. Then the dead shamans might drop him inside one of the hidden crevasses forever.

CHAPTER TWENTY

Calamity

Eli fell more and more under the spell of Denali, as he walked the rugged foothills bordering the great mountain's bottom. The weather charmed him as well. Warm and pleasant sunshine beamed every day—clear morning sunrises lit every night.

He watched restless wildlife with their shaggy winter coats scurry back and forth, searching for the secret places. He knew helpless babies would be born soon. The time had come for pregnant mothers to conceal themselves from all the cunning varmints. And the mating calls of the springtime birds filled the sunny skies.

His lonely pride soared. At last he walked alone once more in a primitive wilderness, unspoiled by the trampling feet of people. He saw why Red Shirt had hidden his family so far beyond the reach of others. The land lay like the Old West once had been—wild to the horizons, untamed in every way, ageless in its eminence. Finally his old way of life had come back to him. He felt like the hasty veteran on the dodging search again, happily tracking the lost trail.

Ironclaw led the way, somehow finding Doll Girl's faded footprints and Wahnie's scent on the grasses, bushes, and old hard snow. He wondered how his dog could smell the messages that had been left behind. How could his wily four-footed friend detect the direction of the tracks and the other signs he appeared to read? And where had his dog learned to communicate by eye contact? A moment's glance seemed plenty to send a command. Ironclaw then sensed his needs and obeyed every time.

He saw Ironclaw lift his nose and sniff the rising air off the lowlands, three days after they had departed Sleepy Lake. Had his dog scented Doll Girl and Wahnie or one of the grizzlies prowling in the distance? He had learned that the dangerous bears hibernated in winter dens dug out on the mountaintops. He had also seen two hunting bears slide downhill on their bellies, stalk, then kill moose with stunning swats of their front paws. If he and Ironclaw stumbled onto one lying on its kill, they would be instantly attacked. And his experiences had taught him that his borrowed Winchester wasn't powerful enough to stop an angry grizzly. He and his dog needed to stay vigilant and watch ahead.

He knelt on the snow and searched all around with his field glasses. Suddenly he saw an odd black shape pop up and move across a distant hilltop. He flattened himself and snaked behind gray rocks, poking through the snow nearby. Then he blew air through his pinched lips to call Ironclaw to his side. In a moment he saw the dark figure walk like a man and appear to glass the countryside, too.

Strong intuitions told him he had just discovered the man who had carried away Doll Girl's mother in the past winter. But where were the little Indian girl and her dog? He peered through his field glasses, trying to find some telltale signs of their whereabouts. Ironclaw had led him straight on, he thought. It made sense that she and her dog were squirreled away close by. His dog hadn't shown any uncertainty about the trail at all. Then awful fears began to build in his heart.

He judged that his hiding place was three miles away from the man on the hilltop. Using his glasses once more, he picked out the scattered hollows and hillsides to hide behind while he stole his way to the low mountain south of the wary stranger. When he reached the peak of the rough summit, everything would lie in plain view.

Beckoning to Ironclaw, he skidded downhill and stalked toward the mountain. Three or four hours would pass by, he mused, before he could possibly reach his destination. Regardless ... he would soon find out what had happened to Doll Girl and Wahnie, and why the stranger seemed so worried.

Up on the mountaintop his worst fears appeared true. Doll Girl, her mother, and the kidnapper stood together down below him, plainly ready to abandon camp. And, he fretted, the stranger must have shot Wahnie. Why else would the old gray dog desert the little girl? Thank God, he thought, they, at least, were leaving the other dogs behind. That would enable him to follow along without the risk of being scented on the fickle spring winds.

After half an hour he saw Doll Girl turn up the valley. Then her mother and the stranger trailed behind. Watching for several minutes, it became clear to him they planned to climb the high pass a few miles distant, and the white gleaming glacier beyond. Why would they want to do that, he wondered? What on earth could be worth the awful danger? As he swept the surface of the glacier with his field glasses, he noticed deep chasms all across the steep surface of the rough ice. Had Doll Girl gone mad?

He slipped down the mountain, stashed his pack and parka, and pulled on his spirit coat. It had been a long time since he had ambushed an outlaw. There seemed time to run ahead, select a hiding place, and set up for the capture of the kidnapper. Doll Girl had walked out of camp, favoring a slow pace that her crippled mother could sustain. He could easily outdistance all of them on his long legs.

He jogged along the far side of high country, running sidelong to the hidden valley. Every so often he peeked over the mountainside and glassed the little party, far below. His plan looked sensible.

Then he saw everyone resting in the middle of the day. Puzzled, he wondered why Doll Girl hadn't come up higher, like he had, where the snow remained frozen in the colder air. Slowly he understood; she wanted to keep the heavy man slogging, stumbling, exhausting himself. Clever, he thought. But what had possessed her to head up to one of Denali's deadly glaciers. Suddenly something Hannah had warned him about back at Sleepy Lake flashed in his mind. She had thought Doll Girl and the old wrinkled medicine man in Fort Yukon shared a secret. What could it be, he wondered?

"Ironclaw, it seems we have a peculiar mystery on our hands. Why do you suppose Doll Girl is headed for Denali? And what has happened to your friend Wahnie?"

His dog looked at him with his yellow eyes, fidgeted, then sighed.

Eli glassed ahead, examined the mountains and chose his path across the topmost parts. A rough climb, he thought. Then he would have to scramble down a long chute, falling behind a high black outcropping, beside the glacier. From there, he saw, the kidnapper would have to eventually pass within rifle range. And when he did, he would be walking in the wide open.

"Come on, Ironclaw. I see where we'll set our trap."

He fought his way up the far side of the mountaintops, slipping, falling, climbing, sliding down, climbing higher again. From time to time he peered backward with his field glasses to settle in his mind that Doll Girl, her mother, and the stranger still trudged along the same frightful course. Finally he saw all three standing side-by-side, stopped at the summit of the pass above the glacier's jagged front. Now he had to keep from killing himself as he skidded his way down to his hiding place. And from freezing to death while he waited. He regretted leaving his parka behind. Although, he thought, the extra clumpy weight would have tired him even more.

Three hours later he sat in place, soaking up the sun. The outcropping seemed perfect for the ambush. The black rock pinnacle stood fifty feet above the surface of the snow and ice, offering him an ideal shooting platform, with an open view for several hundred paces. And it had turned out to be fairly cozy in the bright sun. In addition no one could see him until he stood up. Best of all, if he ducked down the kidnapper couldn't hit him with rifle fire.

"Ironclaw, we're inside a fortress fit for a king. Our man will find himself in deep trouble if he tries to run. Now if he stays as far behind Doll Girl and her mother as I think he will, we'll have him at our mercy."

He surveyed his position once more, smiled, and fished several strips of smoked meat out of his pockets that Noodles had given him. He tossed half of the meat to his dog, then chewed the other strips himself. Good food, he thought! His old friend had always shown an uncommon talent for cooking outdoors. Then he wished Hannah and the prospector weren't so far away. He would have his prisoner soon.

Ironclaw roused him with a low growl. He sat up and peeked out between two rocks. Suddenly he saw Doll Girl walk over a small rise on the glacier's uneven top. Next he saw her mother hobbling close behind. Both were tapping the snow with long sticks. Testing for thickness, he thought. But where was the kidnapper? Then he saw the heavyset man following in their footsteps, in the distance.

Perfect, he thought! He signaled Ironclaw to stay down. In ten minutes the man would walk just below. No one could possibly see him first. He would have the man well within rifle range and fixed in his gun sight in a moment. Even if the man tried to run, he had plenty of time to knock him down with a well-placed shot.

He waited. Doll Girl, and then her mother, tramped by, both drumming with their sticks. At last the kidnapper shuffled along. Was it the Cannibal—the killer he and Jesse Peacock had chased for so long? He couldn't tell. The man's parka hood hid his features. No difference. He jumped up, pointing his rifle.

"Stand still or—"

The man instantly fired his own rifle. Bits of rock sprayed Eli as he ducked. Then he peeked out. The man had turned back and had begun racing downhill. The last echo of the gun blast bounced across the glacier. He had plenty of time. He stood up, aimed, and touched the trigger.

Suddenly he heard low thunder—an uncommon grumble on the mountain above him—high up. He spun around and looked. My God, he thought, the kidnapper's rifle fire has knocked an avalanche down! He spun again. Where were Doll Girl and her mother? Then he saw the two of them standing still, staring up as well. Even in the distance, he saw their frightened faces, heard their hard screams above the echoing blast and the roaring river of snow tumbling down toward them. He glanced at the fleeing stranger. The man appeared to be running faster.

Then the images changed, moving in odd, slow views of fatal pictures in his brain. He crouched, grabbed Ironclaw, and watched. Now Doll Girl and her mother were dashing uphill. The man had disappeared in a white rolling cloud of snow. Then snowy breakers and flying gray debris came crashing down. The whole mountainside plowed across the glacier, smashing everything in front.

At last the booming, battering tide calmed to dead wintry bleakness. A muffled silence settled down. The sun cast murky light in the blue misty air.

"Ironclaw, find." Eli scrambled down the rock pinnacle, as fast as he could, pointing to the last place he had seen Doll Girl and her mother.

When he reached the surface of the avalanche, he leaped across the high piles of dirty snow. Ironclaw bounded ahead, weaving back and forth, his nose low.

"Search, Ironclaw, over there." He tried to judge the direction and distance from the rocks.

Then his dog began to cry wildly and dig with his front paws. Eli knelt down and began digging himself with his bare hands. As he broke loose lumpy blocks of packed snow, he flung each aside. He knew his dog had smelled something. Finally he found a patch of brown leather. Clawing more snow away, he grabbed two fistfuls of parka and pulled hard. Doll Girl's little body jerked out of the bottom of the deep hole. She looked crushed—dead.

He jumped out of the hole, cradling Doll Girl in his arms and and cleaning her face. Pulling off her parka, he lifted her other garments, and held her chest against his ear. Strong heartbeat—but her breathing had been squashed away. He quickly blew air into her mouth. Then he remembered . . .

"Ironclaw, find her mother, search." He swung his arm in a circle. His dog began to trot around again, sniffing.

He blew air into Doll Girl's mouth again. Hanging her body over his knee, he pressed down harder. Then he hit her back with the flat of his hand. The little girl sobbed. He repeated his false respiration again, praying to every saint, spirit, and charm stitched on his magic coat. Then he saw, finally, his luck had saved her life.

Laying Doll Girl on the snow, he watched her breathing and sobs strengthen. Then he saw her eyelids flick up, letting him glimpse the black pupils inside.

"Ironclaw, find her mother. Come on, find her." Then he felt his heart fall. His dog looked unsettled, unable to pick up any scent whatsoever.

He picked up Doll Girl, found a snowbank to sit on, and rocked her in his arms, like a tiny child. She cried louder and louder, then seemed conscious of her surroundings.

"I'm sorry, little girl. I blame myself. If I'd stayed back, thought of a different way, this would not have happened. I'll never forgive myself for my own stupidity."

He sat holding Doll Girl, crying, too. He knew her mother lay dead. She had been swept into a crevice, buried under twenty feet of snow and muck, and killed forever by his own carelessness. All the years of living around the mountains had meant little in the end. He had forgotten the awful springtime hazards that were waiting up on the steep slopes. Denali had warned him as well. He had sat in his hiding place and listened to the rumbling of snowslides in the distance. What had he been thinking? Had he really believed the stranger would just stand there with his hands held high? The only glimmer of satisfaction was that the man had been killed also. Denali had dealt out the fatal penalty for the abduction of innocent people.

Still hugging Doll Girl, he wandered back and forth, trailing his dog. He hoped for a miracle; he searched for any sign of life. Nothing but long rows of gray snowpack lay around. He walked for hours on end. Then, at last, the midnight sun drifted down and threw lonely dawn light across the mountains. He had to walk away. Doll Girl lay shivering in his arms, stone quiet. But her black eyes yet blinked back her tears. They both knew the time had come to leave.

He walked down the glacier, following Iron-claw. His dog would lead him off the ice safely. Once he had climbed the high pass ahead, the remaining miles to the dugout lay downhill, an easy hike for him. Perhaps, later on he thought, Doll Girl would feel strong enough to walk. Hopefully, by tomorrow, she would speak again. Maybe they could share the sorrow they felt. Then each could begin to heal.

"See!" Doll Girl's cry startled him. Her skinny arm shot straight out.

Footprints. He stepped ahead and stared. Boot tracks stretched ahead, down the glacier, across the new white surface, scattered by the rolling clouds of snow thrown up by the avalanche. Somehow the kidnapper had lived.

"Doll Girl, get on my back. Ride piggyback, if you know what I mean. I've got to get back to Sleepy Lake as fast as I can."

"It is no use. He will take the dogs and sled. We cannot catch him. Denali will decide."

He stared into Doll Girl's black eyes. He had never felt so helpless before.

CHAPTER TWENTY-ONE

Murder

"Them's sandhill cranes!" Noodles pointed straight up at the brown birds gliding lower and lower in lazy turns. The long-legged birds called back and forth in lonely shrills, echoing like old rusty hinges.

Blueberry shaded his eyes from the midnight sun with his right hand. "I wonder if they're good to eat. I'm pretty tired of moose meat and beans. Sure would be nice to cook somethin' different for a change."

Noodles grinned with his toothless gums. "By Jeez, I used to eat 'em back in the Dakota Territory, when I was a kid like you. They're delicious. You cook 'em like turkey. I could make soup for myself, if we got one."

"Maybe I should go hunt some down. I could do it in half a day." The Minnesotan peered at the distant marshy grasses across Sleepy Lake, where the cranes were landing after they finished their spirals.

Noodles scowled, shoved his hands in his pants' pockets, and stared at his feet. "Nope, we can't let Eli down. We promised we'd stand guard day and night. I ain't breakin' my word, no matter how hungry I get."

Blueberry dropped his head, too. "I forgot. I sure hope he gets back before them big birds fly off. One of them would feed me for two days!" He then turned back toward the cabin.

"There'll still be birds around by then. This Alaska has more birds than I ever see'd before. Did you see them white swans flying around this morning. I bet their wings must be ten feet across. I recollect they're called trumpeters. Beautiful things, they are—"

"I used to watch them back home when I was a kid. They mostly got shot off by folks. Then there wasn't no swans anymore."

Noodles bounded after Blueberry. "Sonny, you ain't see'd nothin' till you see'd millions of buffalos shot down. The Dakota prairies was black with them critters when I was your age. Herds so big it took days to ride through 'em. Now there ain't none. It's sure hard to believe they're gone."

"Why do you suppose folks was so foolish to kill them all? It don't make sense."

"Sure it does, sonny. It was the politicians that wanted 'em dead. The boys in Washington wanted the West for themselves. Back in the sixties the Dakota and Montana country belonged to the Injuns. All there was down below was the Sioux, Blackfoot, Crow, and Injuns like that. And there was a few folks like me—prospectors, traders, and trappers. None of us shot any more buf-

falo than we needed for food. But buffalo and
Injuns don't give the government no power or
money. So the politicians sent the army, railroads,
and all the farm folks they could find who was
willin' to plow up and fence off the land. Right
quick the buffalo got shot off and the Injuns
locked up on reservations."

Blueberry spun on his heels and sat down on a
patch of dry grass, with his back propped against
the sunny side of the cabin. Then he stared down
the lake at the cranes again. "I don't feel like
killin' them big birds no more. At least the politicians ain't goin' to come up here, it ain't possible
to farm."

Noodles peered off toward Denali Mountain,
shading his eyes like Blueberry had before.
"Sonny, you wait and see! Soon as them politicians hear how beautiful this Alaska is, they'll
want to control it, too. And someday they'll figure
out how to make money off that great mountain
as well. You mark my words. Washington ain't
never goin' to let nothin' stay free."

Blueberry looked up at Noodles with muddled
eyes. Finally he said, "It'll be a long while yet
before the politicians come this far. I've walked
across lots of Alaska. There ain't hardly any people for them to worry about. Why would they
bother comin' up here?"

The prospector began to cackle slyly and his old
blue eyes beamed. "Gold, sonny, gold. There's lots
of gold here! I can smell it. And as soon as the

boys in Washington smell it, they'll come up here, too."

Suddenly Hannah stepped out of the cabin's door, hobbling with a willow cane. "You two gossiping about gold again. Go cut some firewood, you seem to have too much idle time on your hands."

"By Jeez, we got enough firewood ricked up for two years already. Besides, Eli said to stand guard over you." Noodles sat down beside Blueberry and leaned on the cabin's log wall as well. Then, after a long pause, he asked, "Hannah, how long before he gets back with Doll Girl and her ma? How long do you think?"

Hannah walked over to the two men and sat nearby, murmuring a little about her soreness as she settled down. "I don't know but it shouldn't be long. I miss him, too."

She rested her back against the wall, then stretched her legs straight out. Her injuries had nearly healed. The strong sunshine, warm air, and the calls of the springtime birds had lifted her spirits and restored her strength. Each day she sat in the same place, soaking up the sun, gazing at the mountains, using Noodles' long spyglass to glass the top of Denali.

She wished Eli hadn't had to leave. This would be the perfect place, she thought, to spend the summer with him. Simply lie back, make love, and explore the mountains and rivers a bit, perhaps even prospect for gold like Noodles always wanted to do. Was there a more beautiful home than this, she wondered?

Most of the winter's snowfall had melted. The shady woods, high country, and rugged mountains had blankets of snow yet, but all the lowlands lay barren. And when she limped around the cabin, tiny green plants stuck up by her feet. The hot sun had thawed the ice along the shores of Sleepy Lake, leaving the shallows wide open for all the waterfowl. The offshore ice, over the deeper water, had turned milky white, with black patches scattered here and there. Now, when the nighttime wind blew, loud, booming noises woke her. She sensed the thick ice would break up soon, leaving the lake clear of its hard surface.

The magical change of Alaska had amazed her. Only a few days back the land had seemed forbidden, shrouded forever in evil snows. Then, suddenly, clear and fine weather had come along. Relentless sunshine, like hard afternoon sunlight, had begun to stream down.

First the dark evergreens shook off their winter coats of white. Then all the sunny hillsides melted free of snow. Lastly the lowlands turned into damp marshy places, colored blue, where the meltwater flowed.

Then screaming gulls and honking geese and squawking ducks filled the skies. A muffled silence had gripped Alaska all winter. But, instantly, like flying phantoms, flocks of birds wheeled overhead. Spring had sprung, she thought, with a moment's notice.

Suddenly a sharp slapping sound surprised her. She glanced at Noodles.

"By Jeez, the skeeters are here already. How can them bugs survive when there's still snow and ice around. A fellow would think it'd be too early."

Hannah smiled. "There's not many mosquitos yet. Wait till summertime."

The old prospector grinned. "They won't bother me so much then. I plan on movin' too fast for them to catch me." Then he laughed, filling the yard with his happy cackles.

"What are you planning now?" Hannah cocked one eyebrow and squinted at Noodles with her other eye.

"Me and Blueberry figure on finding him a rich gold mine. Once we get back to Dawson City, we'll buy a good grubstake and head out. Maybe come back down to this country. Has to be gold around here close, I can smell it." Noodles' voice cackled once more.

"What are you going to do with the gold mine you have on Chickaloon Hill? It's one of the richest around."

"Maybe sell it. I don't need to sluice out any more gold. I'd rather go prospectin' with Blueberry. He needs to learn the ways of a wily old varmint like me. Anyways, I ain't waitin' for Providence to come get me, I'm goin' to keep on runnin' ahead."

Hannah laughed. She had known Noodles for more than a year. His unconquerable spirit set a useful example for everyone. He would die digging in the dirt, she mused, forever following the dream of every man on earth. Was there a better way to pass away, she wondered? He had led a pious, honest, happy, and ambitious life. What more could a person strive for till the very end?

"Noodles, come inside and help with supper. Blueberry can stand watch while we cook something special. I heard his wish for something more tasty than meat and beans. Perhaps you and I can whip up a cake." She rolled to her hands and knees and stood up, pushing with her cane on the ground for leverage. Then she turned and walked back inside the cabin.

After their meal they sat gazing through the cabin windows, sipping coffee. Sunlight still bathed the outdoors, even though evening shadows had cooled the air. The blackness of nighttime had vanished several weeks before. They could read or write without the glow of lamps, even at midnight. And the constant sunshine had energized them, possessing their minds and bodies with a subtle frenzy. Somehow the Alaskan springtime had enlivened them, as much as the migrating birds.

Noodles set his coffee mug on the table. "Blueberry, why don't you take first watch tonight? Let Hannah and me rest early. I can't never sleep much anyways. 'Bout three in the morning I'll come change places with you."

"Do you want me to hide out like before? So nobody can see me watchin' the cabin."

"It's the best way. And don't forget your Winchester or dare go to sleep. You might die if you do. This chore is 'bout like watchin' for Injuns in the Old West. By Jeez, them devils could be on top you before a fellow know'd they was there."

Hannah set her cup down as well. "Can't I help watch? I don't need sleep any more than the two of you."

The old prospector grimaced. "Now, Hannah, don't start peckin' at me. You heard me promise Eli that I'd keep you inside at night. Don't ask me to break my word."

"I know ... but it's so frustrating to feel trapped, when I'm well enough to help."

"You been helpin' plenty by cookin' and cleanin' up after us. Now quit fussin' and let's get some sleep."

While the two men waited outside Hannah changed to her nightgown and crawled into bed. Then Noodles stepped back indoors, threw his bedroll on the floor, and instantly fell asleep. His ragged snuffles drifted around the room as he slumbered, dead to the world.

Hannah lay awake, worrying about Eli and Doll Girl. Then she listened to the low peeps and the patter of tiny feet as mice scurried back and forth, searching for crumbs. At first she had been afraid of the little creatures, but then she had found them harmless and impossible to keep out. The dirt floor and nooks and crannies of the log cabin let the mice live free and easy. She then dreamed they were close by, wiggling their whiskered noses, watching her with their beady black eyes.

Suddenly she woke up. The muffled voice called again, on the other side of the cabin's door. And all the sled dogs were barking. What's wrong, she wondered? Next she heard Noodles jump up. She rolled on her side, so she could see across the room.

Blueberry's voice cried once more, "Noodles, Noodles, somethin' is wrong. The yard is full of dogs, six or eight of 'em are runnin' round."

The old prospector peeked out the door of the cabin, poking his head into the woodshed entryway. "What you talkin' about? Did our dogs get loose?"

"No, no, they're strange ones. It looks like somebody's dogs got loose and run away. They come to our place."

"By Jeez, come in here and let me look. Open those holes we cut in the walls and keep an eye out." Then the old man brushed by Blueberry, after the Minnesotan had stepped into the cabin.

Hannah watched Blueberry lean his rifle in the corner of the cabin nearest the door, run along the walls, and yank rags out of the small gun ports he and Noodles had chopped through the logs. She jumped out of bed, slipped on her moccasins, and buttoned a long wool shirt over her nightgown. Then she heard odd noises—human sounds above the dog's racket—stirred with thumps, like heavy stones hitting the ground. She hurried across the room and peered out the front window, looking for Noodles.

"Blueberry, something is wrong—. I heard noises, did you—?"

"Something—! But the dogs are barkin' so loud— I don't see nothing yet. Wasn't very loud! Can't you see the old man? All I see is those darn dogs runnin' round."

Hannah ran to her right and peeked out one of the portholes. Noodles lay facedown on the ground, with two strange sled dogs standing over him, sniffing his body.

"Blueberry—I see him. He's lying on the ground by the woodpiles. Two dogs are over—!"

"Let me see." Blueberry jumped across the cabin, leaned over, and stared out.

"Hannah ... I think the old fool has just fell down. Tripped over one of those dogs that's jumpin' round. They sure got our dogs makin' a fuss. I'm goin' out."

"You be careful ... I'm not sure ..."

"I got my Winchester. Don't worry 'bout me. We can't leave Noodles just lay out there. And I don't see any blood on him or nothin' anyways." The Minnesotan reached for his rifle, ducked through the low door of the cabin, then walked through the woodshed and outside the door.

Suddenly Hannah heard an awful scream, then another. She at once recognized Blueberry's shrieks. The young Minnesotan wailed again, but then his cry faded to one last hoarser sob. Next she listened to more muffled blows, like someone punching a soft sack. Lastly all the dogs howled in awful calls.

Jumping, she grabbed a butcher knife and backed against her bed. Both doors of the cabin stood wide open. The hard light hurt her eyes. She blinked, trying to mend them to the brightness.

Nothing . . . then footsteps. Suddenly the woodshed's doorway darkened. The man stood still, his black eyes beaming and both arms dangling down. A long knife hung from his right hand. His fingers and the bloody blade they held dripped red drops on the ground.

"Hannah, you remember me? You got away last year, but you won't get away this time."

"I'll shoot if you come in." She stared at the Cannibal in silent horror, not believing the killer could be standing just outside.

"You ain't got no gun, woman. I can see you just got a knife. What do you think you goin' to do with that?" The Cannibal walked through the woodshed, ducked into the cabin, and then stopped. "Well, come on, go ahead an' try to kill me."

Hannah stood still. Her mind seemed so clear, but her arms and legs felt sickened with sudden fits of palsy. Her mind raced through various last things. Perhaps she could stab him once, live for yet another minute. Then her eyes focused on the killer's eyes. Eli had described the eyes of wild predators. He had said their savage eyes twinkled just before they murdered their helpless prey. She could clearly see the Cannibal's passion for killing, his love of murder. His black eyes seared her soul.

Once before the Cannibal had tried to kill her.

Eli had captured him in the Yukon Territory, during their long journey to the gold fields in the Klondike, over a year ago. By accident she had been left alone with him in a boat, floating helplessly down the Yukon River. He had killed Eli's last dog, Sorrowful. Then he had threatened to kill her and rape her dead body. She had escaped within an inch of death, only to be lost in the Yukon wilderness all alone. At last she had saved herself by sheer stubbornness.

But now she stood trapped inside four thick walls. At last her lips quivered, "All I can do is wait to die. I know you will kill me. But I'll try to hurt you as much as I can. Perhaps I can cripple you . . ."

The Cannibal's smile and eyes dropped a little. He stepped forward and stopped again. "I'm gonna kill you like I promised a year back. And then I'll do what I said I'd do afterward."

Hannah felt herself grow sick to her stomach. She felt the sour vomit coming up. Then, strangely, she wondered why the dogs had stopped their howling. Instantly the whole world seemed wrapped in fearful stillness. What had darkened the doorway this time?

She looked past the Cannibal. Then she saw old Wahnie standing soundlessly, his eyes burning like the Cannibal's had the instant before. She screamed as loudly as she could, partly from fright, partly because she didn't want to watch the fight that she knew would surely come.

Shocked, the Cannibal glanced backward, lowering his hands a little. Wahnie hurtled into the cabin in a flash of gray. He seized the hand that held the knife and then whipped himself around, flipping the Cannibal off his feet and the knife across the room. Before the killer could roll to his hands and knees, Wahnie ripped his throat open, splashing blood on the floor. Then the old dog leaped again and clamped the Cannibal's neck in his fangs, biting down hard.

Hannah watched the killer and Doll Girl's dog tumble around the dirt floor of the cabin, knocking over the table, all the chairs, even the stove kitty-corner. Mad snarls filled the room—choking human sounds as well. Her own screams screeched over and over. All the sled dogs outside howled once more, wailing their yowls louder than before.

At last the Cannibal lay on his back, his corpse jerking back and forth in its death dance. Wahnie stood above him, still throttling his throat, his furry face running with blood. Hannah clapped her mouth shut, balled her fists against her lips, and stared in silent horror again. Then the dogs outside stopped yowling, as fast as they had started. Finally the old dog sighed, opened his fangs, and looked around at her. Slowly he turned and skulked back out both doors, disappearing.

She slipped outdoors herself. Blueberry lay by the front of the cabin. She instantly saw he had been brutally stabbed to death. His body stretched lengthwise along the log wall of the cabin, like a queer, bloody bundle. Seeing Noodles lying dead-like as well, she limped to his side as fast as her sore leg would let her hurry. Falling to her knees, she then burst into uncontrollable tears, never feeling more helpless, frightened, and ill in her life.

"Wake up, old man, wake up!" she bawled. "Noodles, please wake up. Please don't be dead. I need you so much. Please come back to me."

The fearful stillness crept around the cabin once more, only broken by Hannah's sobbing. Then a wolf howled far off in the distance.

CHAPTER TWENTY-TWO

Redemption

Sometimes Eli carried Doll Girl on his back, telling her to hold on tight as he jogged ahead. Sometimes he made her run alongside as he hiked the high country. But he kept on day after day, refusing to rest for more than a few hours at a time. He often wondered about his great hurry. He knew he couldn't catch up with the stranger and the dogs.

He found tracks where the stranger and his sled had bogged down on muddy ground and thawing snow. Nevertheless, he judged the dogs were outrunning him two miles to one. Sliding a sled across soil or grass appeared much less difficult than a man slogging along on foot. And the kidnapper had stayed up on the highlands most of the way as well, on the harder snow and in the colder air. Clearly the man had learned about springtime travel in Alaska.

Thank the Lord for Doll Girl's dried salmon strips, he thought. She had carried plenty in her pockets. The fish had saved them, kept them reasonably fit, and Ironclaw strong as well. But the fishy food had nearly gotten them killed.

One day, while they lay sleeping in the sun, an awful racket had awoken them. They had found Ironclaw standing face-to-face with a grizzly bear.

The hungry grizzly had smelled the salmon on the spring breezes. Odorous, the scent had lured in the monster. Then, the instant the bear discovered that two-legged creatures carried the food, he had roared and popped his teeth. Next he had prowled back and forth, stomping his feet. But he'd acted a little wary of Ironclaw, who had raged back just as loudly. Eli remembered worrying about whether to shoot, yell, or move off while his dog struggled to keep the bear at bay. Meanwhile Doll Girl had simply stood by, acting indifferent about the danger.

"Mr. Bonnet, don't be afraid. Your dog will chase him away."

Eli recalled his astonishment at the little girl's fearlessness. It now seemed she had known more about bears and dogs than he, or, at least, had watched her old dog Wahnie drive off one in the past.

Doll Girl's revelation had come true. Ironclaw had attacked the bear, running in wild circles, forcing the bear to swing round and round. Whenever the grizzly had tired or become careless, his dog dashed in and bit him. The bear's fury had grown louder and louder, finally sending him after Ironclaw on the dead run. But his dog had simply darted away, easily outrunning the bear's best speed. At last the grizzly had given up and lumbered off, searching for less frustrating food.

Watching the bear amble away in the distance, he had stood dumbfounded beside Doll Girl. He hadn't expected to see his dog attack an Alaskan bear all by himself. He had begun to admire Iron-claw more and more. The young wolf dog had become a mighty weapon, or the strong medicine that the old shaman had prophesied back in Fort Yukon.

Afterward he'd run on, with Doll Girl on his back, trying to reach Sleepy Lake as soon as possible. His belly had felt unwell with worry all along. Would Noodles, Blueberry, and the sled dogs tethered around the cabin spot the stranger first, he had wondered? Or would the stranger find a way to confuse everyone, permitting him to sneak up without anyone knowing? He had begun to wish he'd just shot the man on sight. He had learned about outlaws long ago. Compassion simply jeopardized more innocent people. Now Doll Girl's mother lay dead, and Hannah, Noodles, and Blueberry sat in harm's way. How could he have been so stupid, he asked himself over and over.

At last he stopped on a hillside overlooking Sleepy Lake. He saw that the lake had busted open, with only remnants of white ice bordering a far shoreline. Peering through his binoculars, he glassed all around the cabin. All the dogs lay in the sun nearby. There were more than he remembered. Not one wisp of smoke spewed from the chimney pipe. The woodshed door leading into the cabin hung wide open. Someone had thrown canvas tarp from the sled over something near the front of the cabin.

Then he saw the stranger's dog sled about a mile from the cabin, hidden among the trees.

"Doll Girl, I need to run the rest of the way with Ironclaw—sneak up on the cabin for a look. Can you hide until I call you?"

The Indian girl blinked her black eyes. "I can hide forever. I know many places."

"I'll come find you when I'm done—listen for my voice!" Without glancing back, he turned, whistling between his teeth for Ironclaw.

As he jogged downhill, he opened the lever of his Winchester and peeked inside the chamber. Yes, a round sat inside the barrel. He set the rifle's hammer back down on half-cock. When he neared the cabin, he mused, he would walk cautiously and sneak through the woods. He knew the dogs would smell him, hear him crunching over the old dry leaves left by the last autumn. But he would kill the stranger the instant he saw him. No mercy anymore, he reflected. The awful winter had taught him that he lived in a world full of wrong-doers. The time had come to stop their crimes.

When he sensed he had gotten within a mile of the cabin, he crept forward, step by step. At last he saw the shine of the skyline through the trees. The cabin sat just ahead. He slowed even more and motioned for Ironclaw to stay alert.

His dog gazed peevishly at him and then trotted ahead without glancing back, looking unconcerned. In a single instant the other dogs broke into long howls, warning about the danger. He sprinted to a spruce tree and peered at the cabin and then watched his dog stop in front of the open door, bark, and wag his tail.

Finally Hannah stepped outside, looking haggard, with tears pouring down her cheeks. When she saw him step out from behind the spruce tree, she ran straight to him, hitching along on her sore leg.

"My Lord, Hannah, what's happened? Where's Noodles and Blueberry? I've prayed for you for days! Thank God you're alive!"

Hannah sobbed, "Eli, Blueberry is dead. Wahnie has killed the Cannibal. You need to come see Noodles. He's been hit on the head."

Eli threw down his rifle and scooped up Hannah in his arms. With her clutching onto his neck, he ran to the cabin and ducked inside. The old prospector lay on the floor, covered by a blanket. His face looked as white as his whispers. Setting Hannah down, he quickly knelt beside Noodles.

"Old man, can you hear me? I'm here now. Come on, talk to me."

Noodles opened his eyelids a little. "By Jeez, Eli, Hannah and I worried so much 'bout you and Doll Girl bein' dead. Did you find my little friend and bring her ma back home?"

"Doll Girl's fine, but we've lost her mother. Listen, old man, we need to talk about you. How bad are you hurt? How do you feel?"

The old prospector sighed. "I got hit awful hard with somethin' . . ."

Hannah wiped her eyes with the back of her hands and knelt down by Eli. "I found a block of firewood beside him. The Cannibal must have hit him with it. I'm so thankful Wahnie killed that man. But I never want to see such an ugly horror again." She began to cry once more.

Eli reached across and hugged her close. "Listen . . . both of you need to get well. We all need to heal. Old man, go back to sleep for a while. Doll Girl is a little ways off, hiding. I'll go find her. She feels worse than we do . . . and for good reasons. Let's try to help her."

Noodles sighed again and closed his eyes. "You go get her, Eli. That'll make me happy, to look at her pretty face."

Eli stood and pulled up Hannah alongside. "Come on, let's let him sleep. I think he'll feel better soon."

After he had walked back out of the cabin, he glanced at the sled trap spread on the ground. Black bugs buzzed back and forth, and he smelled dead bodies.

"Hannah, is that Blueberry . . . or the Cannibal?"

"I left Blueberry where he lay. I used the dogs to pull the Cannibal out . . . then cleaned up the cabin the best I could. I should have buried them . . ."

"You've done too much as it is—besides the ground is still frozen. I'm worried about your leg and ribs. Are you sure you haven't hurt yourself again?"

"No, and now that I know that Doll Girl and you are safe, I feel ten times better. That seemed the worst, not knowing whether you and her were dead or alive. I was so afraid the Cannibal had killed ..." Her tears streamed down her face again.

Eli held her, gently rocking her in his arms. "Hannah, try to calm yourself. Let's go find Doll Girl. She needs us." Then he called for Ironclaw and tramped back into the woods, holding on to her hand.

They found Doll Girl by yelling at the top of their lungs. Eli wondered how she had hidden herself so well. The more time he spent around the dark-eyed girl, the more puzzled he felt about her mysterious ways of living in Alaska. She acted like a little phantom sometimes, or some kind of mountain spirit herself. Whatever, he wished he knew more about her.

As soon as Hannah saw Doll Girl, she squeezed the Indian girl in her arms and sobbed, "Wahnie saved me. He killed the man who kidnapped your mother. But where did he go?"

Doll Girl's face fell. "He is ashamed that he killed a human. He will run with the wolves for a while."

Eli blinked and wondered about the girl once more. Why was she such a riddle? Apparently the death of her parents had changed her forever. She wasn't an ordinary child anymore, regardless of her size. And then he began to sense surprises yet to come.

After they had returned to the cabin he loaded the corpses of the Cannibal and Blueberry in the birch-bark canoe he had found stored in the woods. Then he paddled across Sleepy Lake and threw out the Cannibal, leaving him on a rocky beach, out of sight of the cabin. Let the wild animals destroy him, he mused. In a few days no one would ever know that the killer had existed. The foxes, bears, and wolverines could carry his carcass away and leave no trace of him. Denali's spirits would surely laugh and sing while the devilish feast took place.

Next he paddled to a high bluff towering above the lake. He carried Blueberry up, laid him down, and stacked dry wood all around his remains. Then, after igniting the funeral fire, he watched the black smoke blow away. The long winter had tired him. The loss of life had wearied him more.

Then the wind switched and started blowing toward the mountains. The best place for Billy House, he thought. Let him go there.

He stood beside the fire till the following day, adding wood, poking at the leaping flames, and stirring the dying gray embers. At last just ashes lay on the ground.

He raised a crude wooden cross, then gazed at the site where Blueberry had lain for the last time. The ever-present perils of life had taken another friend. Life seemed like the uncertain gleams and shadows cast by the sun. Who knew the random reasons men were selected for their death? When would his own end come? He walked back down the steep hillside, boarded his canoe, and pushed off for the cabin. The sun felt warm on his face. He knew the time had come to move on.

Days, weeks passed. Noodles mended. Doll Girl sulked. Summertime flowed down the Alaskan Range and over the adjacent lowlands, just as quickly as the spring had sprung before. Eli watched Hannah renew herself also, fully recovering her smile and strength. Then, finally, he realized they had to leave, even though Sleepy Lake seemed to him an eternal and enchanted place.

He found Doll Girl sitting by Sleepy Lake, skipping flat stones on top of its calmness. She had spoken very little in the last few days.

"Doll Girl, we need to leave. Wahnie isn't coming back. Your parents are gone forever. Come with Hannah, Noodles, and me. We love you like our own daughter."

"Wahnie will come back. Then he and I will find my father. You should go. I want live alone."

Eli sighed. He had expected as much. He sat down nearby and threw a stone himself and watched it hop across the water. Finally he asked, "Did your father want you to become a medicine woman someday? Is that one of your secrets?"

Doll Girl gazed across the lake. "He is waiting for me now. I must take him to Denali. He cannot sleep until I do."

He pitched one more stone and then stood up. Turning back to the cabin, he asked, "Will you come find us when you're done? Will you remember how much we need you?"

The Indian girl nodded her head and flipped another rock. Eli walked away, hanging his head, thinking of ways to tell Hannah and Noodles that they must let Doll Girl stay behind. He knew Hannah would cry and that the old prospector would argue half the night.

But he would stand against them. His Sioux coat seemed part of it. Red Shirt deserved his destiny, not an afterlife that had been cursed by others. He stepped into the cabin, and saw Hannah and Noodles waiting for him.

In the morning he and Noodles loaded the canoe for the journey back to Dawson City. They had stored most of the food in the cache and left a few of the best dogs for Doll Girl. She stood close by, watching. Her face appeared brighter than the day before.

At last they paddled off, Hannah waving again and again while she cried. Eli wondered if he would ever see the little girl again. Then he felt the loneliness of the land settle down. Had he chosen wisely, he wondered again?

The summer's heat had flooded the Kantishna River with the meltwater off the glaciers on the mountains behind them. They shot down the river's course, fighting the wild currents and portaging by the white water too rough to risk their lives against. Ironclaw followed along the shores, leading the rest of the dogs downriver. Later they paddled along the peaceful parts, enjoying the busy beavers, fishing otters, and newborn ducks swimming after their mothers.

"By Jeez, Eli, you suppose we'll ever come back this way? Maybe visit the place where you burnt up Blueberry. I'd sure like to prospect for gold around that country sometime—find a gold mine and name it after him."

"The way you wander around, old man, I'd worry if you didn't meander back someday. But, for now, we need to get back down to the Yukon River as fast as we can. We've got to return the dogs I borrowed last winter. We need to catch the first boat steaming for Dawson City. Our mines will be open. We should bag the gold we've discovered already."

Hannah frowned and narrowed her eyes. "Eli, we're getting married—on the boat, in Fort Yukon, at the first church I see. You promised—"

Eli laughed. Suddenly he felt happy once more. The hard winter had passed, and he sensed Doll Girl would be fine. He then answered, "I did, indeed. Pick up your paddle and help. It's time to keep my word." He turned and called to Ironclaw, hurrying him and the other dogs along the shoreline.

The river swept their canoe by the little island hiding the Tanana River. Gathering speed, they then floated out of sight of the dogs. But, he thought, Ironclaw would follow him forever. He knew his wolf dog would reappear at the shore of the Yukon River, without even the loss of one of the other dogs.

They fell silent as they paddled by the places that the fateful winter had etched in their memories. They saw all the deaths, cannibalism, starvation, and awful cold again—and every time Hannah's eyes grew humid, and Noodles' lips pinched together.

Nonetheless, Eli loved the Alaskan wilderness more than ever. The Old West had been wonderful. But this last frontier seemed timeless. For as long as he breathed, he hoped it would last. And, he prayed, for as long as frontiersmen roamed the earth, they would keep it whole. He couldn't bear to see another wilderness being cut down, plowed under, and fenced off, like down in the Union. And he couldn't bear to see the Indians lose their heritage once more. Let them hunt and fish forever, he thought. Let them live in their ancient ways, if they choose to live that way. Then he thought of Doll Girl. . . .

When Noodles finally spied the Yukon River's waters ahead, he hollered, "By Jeez, would you look at that. There's hundreds of boats passin' by."

They paddled into the middle of the channel and hailed over one of the boats to their side. Eli studied the two men on board. Could it be, he wondered? Then he heard the old prospector speak again.

"Where you fellows off to? Where you goin' in such a all-fired hurry? By Jeez, you look loaded heavy."

One of the men aboard grinned and then answered, "Where you been, old-timer? Haven't you heard? Richest gold strike ever made up in Nome.

The beaches along the ocean are covered with gold. All the cricks are running rich. Dawson's done for—been abandoned. I never made much there, anyhows. Once I get up north, I'll get rich there."

Eli saw his old friend's face lift and his eyes beam. Then he remembered Noodles telling him once about joining the last great gold stampede, seeing one more herd of buffalo before he died. . . .

"Old man, why don't you go? We'll sell your mine and bank your money when we get back to Dawson City. Go on . . . we'll come visit you someday."

The old man's eyes darkened a little, his mouth fell. "Can't you two come? You been like family to me. I want to go real bad, but I don't want to lose you two." Then his eyes wetted.

"No, we've got to be off the other way. But you shouldn't miss this chance—" Suddenly he sensed his own tears.

The stampeder in the boat added his voice. "Come on, old-timer, you're holdin' us up. Get on board. You look like you been around. We don't know much about prospectin' for gold. We sure could use the help."

"By Jeez, I'll go. Hold on—let me get my stuff. I don't mind partnerin' up with you two fellows."

A few minutes later Eli saw Noodles disappear around a bend in the Yukon River. He then heard Ironclaw barking close by, from the riverbank. He swung the canoe around and pointed the bow at the shoreline his dog stood on. Hannah turned, peering downriver.

"Eli, why did you let him go? You love him as much as if he was your father. It doesn't make sense . . . unless you plan on following—"

He didn't answer. He thought his tears would tell the truth. But it had been worth the loss, to see the old man happy again.

CHAPTER TWENTY-THREE

Good-bye

Fields of fireweed painted the land, where snow-slides had ripped out the alders, berry bushes, and runty spruce that had grown on the mountainsides. More pale red flowers covered the land, wherever wildfire had destroyed the dry leafage in past years. Alaska had become a mosaic of deep colors. Green trees, pink flowers, white mountains, blue skies, and tawny tundra lay in every direction.

Doll Girl sat quietly every day, watching the summer creep along in its rhythm of colors. July's hues now spread across the country. Soon August's dark shades would take over. The reds and browns and yellows would abound thereafter, she mused. Then winter white would fall once more. She knew Denali's spirits only let mere mortals see her land's beauty for just a little while. She recalled her father saying that unbelievers would corrupt the great wilderness, if the Alaskan summers ever became long and pleasant.

Then one afternoon she heard an animal sound as she sat on the shore of Sleepy Lake. The lonely sob cried again. She slowly turned her head.

"Wahnie, I knew you'd come back. I've waited and waited so long for you." She jumped to her feet and ran to her dog, hugging her neck.

"Old dog, I thought you would hide until the bad man had forgotten about you. I knew you'd wait till he set his rifle down. I'm happy you killed him forever. My father and mother thank you, too."

Wahnie licked her face and whined once more. Next he trotted back to the cabin and lay down, sighing as he settled against the bottom logs.

Doll Girl ran after him. "You rest now. I will feed you. Tomorrow you will feel stronger."

The following day they wandered side by side through the wildflowers, searching. At last she found the tiny bird—the first hummingbird she had ever seen. The little pearly bird flitted from blossom to blossom, sitting motionless in the air, whenever it chose to sip nectar with its long beak. Her father had been right, she thought, there was such a creature.

Then she wondered how he had known the bird would fly to Alaska on the first summer after his death. There seemed to be so much wisdom for her to remember. Now only she and the ancient shaman in Fort Yukon knew the holy secrets of the Athabaskans. Soon she would be the only person to carry on the old ways of her people.

She and Wahnie walked behind the iridescent bird as it flew along, seemingly waiting patiently for them. Then she recognized the little lake just ahead. Her parents had always harvested beavers from its waters. This must be the place where the stranger had killed her father, she thought. His bones must rest nearby.

Suddenly the hummingbird vanished, flashing away in the blink of her eye. Then the surroundings seemed peaceful, with just a few lazy birds whistling their songs. The sweetness of the fireweed blossoms, spruce and birch buds, and ripe blueberries scented the air. She stood still, smelling the wild fragrances. She realized the time had come to fulfill the promises she had made to her father.

"Wahnie, find Father! Come on, gather his bones. The wolves have tried to hide him from me, but they can't fool you. You can smell where they buried his bones."

The old dog began to hunt, his nose low, sniffing the ground. She hurriedly tramped to a gravelly esker, kindled a small fire, and sat in the smoke, brushing the no-see-ums away. Within minutes after settling herself, Wahnie trotted back, carrying a human bone in his mouth.

"Wahnie, you've found Father! Bring him here . . ."

Then she cried. The loss of her parents seemed too much to bear any longer. She wished with all her heart she could somehow slip back in time. Her happiness had been stolen so quickly . . . and she wondered how she could continue with her life all alone.

By the next day Wahnie had recovered most of her father's skeleton. She cried again when her dog came back with his skull, gnawed clean by the scavengers, and bleached white by the sun. The time had come to leave for the great mountain, she thought. The secret cave lay waiting.

She pulled off her summer dress, knotted the top of the garment to fashion a loose sack, and bundled her father's bones inside. Then she heaved the heavy bag over her shoulder and marched back to Sleepy Lake, stark naked, with Wahnie leading the way. She stubbornly ignored all the mosquitos, black flies, and no-see-ums that stung her. Her greater misery prevented her body from feeling the little bites of the bugs.

That evening she measured her height against the notches her mother had previously cut every year on the cabin's doorpost. She stood there, staring, astonished. The last mark lay level with her eyes. How could she have grown so tall in one year, she wondered? She wished her parents could see her now. Then she remembered they had been watching her every day.

The next morning she closed the cabin and headed for Denali Mountain, still clutching her sack of bones. Wahnie led the way again, his back saddled with the supplies for their long journey. They would be gone many days, she reflected. By the time they returned to Sleepy Lake, the land would be all red and yellow from autumn's long frosty shadows.

She tramped along, unafraid. Her old dog would protect her. All the bears and wolves and wolverines looked fat and lazy in any case. They had eaten their fill of moose and caribou calves, mountain marmots, fish, and berries. It would be wintertime once more before they would grow hungry. She only had to avoid mother bears and their bumbling cubs. She knew the short-tempered sows would attack her and Wahnie in an instant.

At last she stood above the hidden valley, where her mother had been held captive in the past winter. The hollow seemed tranquil, misty green in the late sunlight, with cow moose wading in the hot spring, peacefully feeding on weeds. Wahnie stood by her side, stonelike, looking down as well.

"Old dog, we'll stay here for a while. We'll clean this place until no sign of the white man can be found."

She worked two days, sweeping the dugout, searching for trash, burning piles of refuse. Then she buried the ashes, removing the last traces of inhabitation by anyone.

"Wahnie, only Mr. Bonnet knows where this valley is, and he'll never tell. You and I will keep this place for ourselves. If I grow old like you, maybe then I'll tell someone. But for now this place is ours. And I know you'll always keep my secrets."

Then she smiled for the first time in months. But she wondered why. Her silliness about her dog never betraying her secrets seemed childish. And she felt so much older and wiser. Perhaps finding herself several inches taller had something to do with her unexpected cheer. Whatever the reason, she felt renewed, stronger, and ready for the rest of the journey. Only one more task remained, she thought.

She washed herself and her father's bones in the hot spring water. They had always bathed together when they had visited the hidden valley. Now the ceremonial bath seemed even more essential. The water, soil, air, and sun were gifts from the holy spirits. An Indian could reach out and touch his soul at any time. He could clutch his beginning in one hand, and he could see his end beside his feet. From dust to dust, her father had said repeatedly. Now the time had come to take him home.

As the sun settled toward the skyline she climbed the long hills to the pass sitting above the foot of the glacier. She stretched her long legs for every inch of ground, loving every moment of being tall and skinny. And she smiled at her gray dog as he eyed her new pace. Finally she could keep up and carry just as much as he. When she reached the face of the ancient ice she hurried behind a hillside and hid from the hard winds gusting off the glacier.

In the morning the sun would rise and the winds would subside, she thought. And she needed the best possible light. She had to find the little rock cairns the old shamans had set up long ago. Without those manlike markers, she knew she would fall to her death in one of the many crevasses, hidden beneath the snow and ice.

When she located each marker by mindfully fol-

lowing her father's lessons, she repaired the ones
that had been knocked down by snowslides or
earthquakes. Each had been built from flat stones
of several different sizes. Two slabs set side by
side as the feet, a stack of stones for the legs, one
or two larger rocks for the body and arms, then
one round rock on top for the head. From the
distance they looked just like miniature men. Up
close they told her secrets that only the eldest Athabaskans remembered. Somehow most of her people had forgotten their messages. She often
wondered why they had been so foolish.

At last she reached the mountainside where the
cave lay hidden. She rested and stared up at the
cliff that shielded the cavern's mouth. Ravens
soared overhead, climbing, diving, and winging
over as they played on the rising wind. My ancestors, she thought, forever watching over my land.
Nothing ever escapes their beady eyes.

She ducked into a dark hole beneath huge boulders the size of her cabin back on Sleepy Lake.
Just inside the cavity, she looked up. Sunshine
streamed down through a small hole. She climbed,
grunting and pulling the sack of bones behind,
then she watched as Wahnie worked for his footing as well. Finally they stepped out into a narrow
notch cracked open behind the cliff face, leading
higher like stairways to the sky. Five hundred feet
later she reached the top.

She stopped and faced Denali Mountain. The
burial tomb sat wide open on her right hand,
clearly exposed to the sunlight. She slowly swung

her head and stared at all the human skulls staring out at her.

"Wahnie, this place makes me so confused. How could my people have lived around this mountain for so long? Only the shamans get to come here. There are so many."

Her dog stood soundlessly, his tail pointed straight back. His yellow eyes seemed to study the rows of skulls neatly stacked on the rocky ledges running along the back of the cave. Piles of other human bones lay down on the floor. The persistent chill of the icy glacier had preserved everything. The earliest medicine men who had migrated to Alaska were first in line. Then all the others rested alongside, in the order of the generations that had passed away afterward.

She crept forward, opened her sack, and set her father's skull in its proper place. Next she knelt and heaped his body's bones on the floor near all the other skeletons. Then she stood up and stared again. Her resting place lay on her left, close by. But she was unafraid. She knew the rules of life.

She stepped away and sat in the sun, dangling her legs over the edge of the cliff, with the burial cave just behind her. Wahnie hunkered by her side, sitting quietly on his haunches, staring off, too, across the great blue glacier. Denali Mountain sat in front of them, thundering, rumbling, seemingly telling of its imminence and immortality.

"Old dog, look. From here we can see where my mother rests. And there's Sleepy Lake, and all our land, way off, for as far as our eyes can see."

Then she sat silently and waited. She waited two days, shivering, huddling with Wahnie under blankets and nibbling on the dried salmon she had stolen back from the squirrels. At last she heard the thunder-boom.

A hanging glacier on the great mountain's slope broke away, across from her. Water and white ice, finally rotted loose by the sun, burst off the gray rock. Large and small pieces tumbled down, leaving the mountainside barren where the small glacier had hung before.

"Wahnie, there's the golden eagle my father told me about. That's the secret no one has seen but me."

An outcropping of milky white quartz laced with gold stood against the mountain. A yellow beak and two eyes and two legs glistened in the sun on the birdlike monument. Wings and feathers seemed highlighted as well. Brown stone composed the rest of the formation.

She and Wahnie sat together for a long time, watching the meltwater seep off the remnants of the glacier still hanging above the sacred eagle. Icicles froze, one after another, until the statue became veiled, covered once more by the eternal ice.

Finally she stood up and looked back at her father's skull, pausing for a moment. The cave seemed less forbidding now.

"Come on, old dog, let's go find our friends."

We invite you to preview a thrilling
new novel of adventure and peril
on the Alaskan frontier:

Whispers of the Wind by Tom Hron
coming soon from Signet Books

Withered old prospectors yet sit beside the Bering Sea
and watch the sidelong surf roll ashore. They still gaze
steadily at the waves and wonder about the gold.
"Where is the mother lode?" they cry against the icy
winds. "Did the glittering dust come up from the eddy-
ing depths of the ocean? Did the shiny nuggets wash
down from the distant mountains standing across the
tundra plain?" Finally they creep away, seeing the dark
waters will never tell.

Men have explored the seacoast near Nome, Alaska,
for a century, searching for the gold that founded the
last great boomtown of the Old West. No one has ever
solved the riddle. To this day weather-beaten miners
sluice out nuggets and dust from the beaches, creeks,
and tundra. "Where did all the treasure come from?
Who will find the true source? Why has the secret
lasted so long?" they ask.

The Alaskan gold rush began when three lucky
Swedes, Jafet Lindeberg, John Bryneson, and Eric Lind-
blom, paddled up the Snake River on the west coast of
the last frontier in the autumn of 1898. Suddenly they
found sweet bits of the bounty America had promised
them. They panned out a handful of coarse gold and
staked their claims. Anvil Creek, Dry Creek, Glacier

Creek, Rock Creek, and Snow Gulch would become the richest ground ever discovered. Three poor, hollow-cheeked immigrants who could not tell a placer mine from a plowed field had struck it rich. Soon the world would hear of their good fortune.

By the summer of 1899 three thousand men had massed at the mouth of the Snake River. Tents and shacks covered the tundra, just above the damp sandy shore of the stormy ocean. Fifteen hundred mining claims lay filed—not enough to go around.

Claim jumping broke out, gunfire echoed, and the U.S. Army struggled to keep the peace. Yet more stampeders poured in, from the Yukon, Kobuk, Kotzebue, and Council country, older mining districts to the east and north. Suddenly the wildest, most dangerous town of all had burst upon the nation.

Then men and women who had always followed the frontiers across the Old West began to journey north. Somehow they sensed that Nome, Alaska, would be the last boomtown forever.

These middle-aged adventurers had watched the western frontier vanish before their eyes. Buffalo bones lay everywhere and most Indians lived on reservations. Worst of all, the magical land they had loved so much, when they had been young and free, sat fenced and plowed. It seemed time, they said, to wander a little way further. One more hurrah might lessen the painful long-ings for days gone by. They solemnly hurried north to Nome.

Wyatt Earp landed in the new boomtown in 1899, looking paunchy and aged with his walrus mustache. He was beyond doubt the most celebrated stampeder of all. But he refused to prospect or mine for gold. His life's work had been gunfighting, gambling, and overseeing barrooms. He promptly built the Dexter Saloon and carried on with his old occupations.

Nome's population reached twenty thousand in the summer of 1900, then fell to a few thousand by winter. Suddenly the gold rush was over. Few men had made any money—Washington politicians had seen to that unjust end. All the best mines had been stolen by corruption reaching as high as President William McKinley. Later McKinley lay assassinated, perhaps the fate he had earned for himself. But he and a few crony congressmen had ended the freedoms of frontier life for all time. The opportunity for daring men to make their fortunes by self-reliance, independence, and bravery had been everlastingly ruined.

This story is dedicated to those men and women who refused to grow old back then. God bless Wyatt Earp, Bat Masterson, Calamity Jane, and all the others. They lived life with passion and courage—the stuff of Alaska's legends.

* * *

Old Noodles peered back and forth, then pawed his white whiskers with one hand. Suddenly he dropped to the bottom of the boat, hunkered down, and peeked over the starboard side.

The tall man in the back of the boat heaved on his long pole and forced the flat-bottomed craft against the river's waves. When he turned toward the bow for his next push backward, he paused for an instant and frowned.

"What you doin' down there, old-timer, you sick or somethin'?"

"Ain't no birds singin' and all the itty-bitty critters have hid away. Some kind of varmint is about." The little wizened prospector warily eyed the nearest riverbank. He then scanned the open tundra beyond the shore. Low bushes lay here and there, pucker brush, an odd idiom used by sourdoughs for the leafage of the barren land.

The boat rocked ahead again. The man turned a second time, planted his pole, and pushed once more, quicker this time. His eyes surveyed the wilderness as well.

At last he answered, "I don't see nothin' noplace. You been worryin' ever since we left our claim. You know we had to float down to Nome for grub. I think Harley is just fine. Takes a powerful trick to fool him. He'd fight a brown bear barehanded to keep that gold mine we got. There's a million dollars of nuggets for us to sluice out."

"By Jeez, I don't care 'bout the million, I'm worried for our lives. I ain't never see'd so much claim jumpin' since Deadwood, back in the Dakota days. You best get down till we figure what's wrong."

"Just keep an eye out and your rifle ready. I can see a country mile in every direction. We gotta get back upriver. If there's genuine trouble, Harley will need our help."

The old prospector reached for his Winchester, ratcheted the lever, and set the hammer at half cock. Then he settled his back along the bow boards and searched the horizon further with his pale blue eyes. Why had he sensed danger? Had old age and loneliness spooked him, he wondered?

He had journeyed north to Nome, the wild new boomtown on the Bering Sea, in the past summer. Now autumn hung over the coast. Reds and yellows and browns smudged the foliage everywhere, colors spread by the first frosts of fall. Soon hard storms would slant across the land, leaving only the strongest and tallest standing against the snow. Then he would hear the hunting wolves howl in the endless wintertime, long echoes he had come to fear. The calls meant some poor creature had been ripped apart while still alive. His mind's eye could see the bloody murder of the moose or caribou unlucky enough to have been cornered by the cunning packs. All life had become precious to him now, perhaps an uncommon denial of his own impermanence. He was past seventy and his end seemed near.

The man poling the boat broke the muffled silence of the shorelines once more. "You look scar't—never saw you so scar't before. Maybe you should calm yourself some."

Noodles looked up, widening his faded eyes. "Sure wish Eli was here. Never felt scar't of much when he traveled with me. Maybe I should've gone back to Dawson with him and Hannah. I didn't need to find more gold anyways. Don't have time enough left in life to spend what I got panned out already."

"Old-timer, me and Harley would never've found the gold claim we staked in a hundred years without you. We'll take care of you as good as Eli Bonnet. We owe you and won't forget."

The prospector swung his fearful gaze to the low mountains to the east, standing between him and his distant friends. How far was home, he wondered—more than two thousand miles? He needed to sail from Nome, across North Sound of the Bering Sea to Saint Michael, then up the Yukon River the entire length of the Alaskan Territory to Dawson City. He knew of no more distant point in North America.

In 1897 Eli Bonnet, Hannah Twigg, and he had trekked north to the Klondike gold fields, in the Yukon Territory of Canada. Bonnet and he had come from Arizona; Hannah had journeyed from California. The following year they had chased down the Yukon River on dogsleds, then up the Tanana and Kantishna rivers to Denali Mountain, the highest peak they had ever seen. Finally the murderer they had pursued for so long had been killed himself, by a wolf-dog belonging to a little Indian girl named Doll Girl.

He had grown to love the child as much as his own granddaughter, and he planned to leave her everything. Eli and Hannah had already banked more gold than they could ever spend in a single lifetime. And he had no living family. Someday soon, he mused, Doll Girl would be richer than the bankers and lawyers he had hated so much throughout his long life. They were the ones, along with the paunchy politicians, who had ruined the Old West. They all were the ones who forever financed the farmers and loggers and merchants, the pioneers who inevitably cut down the trees, plowed the earth, and overpopulated the prairies. Lord, how he hated progress, the ubiquitous and unholy coffin-march of man.

Suddenly his partner pitched headlong into the boat's bottom. Next he heard scattered shots echo in the distance. He instantly cowered below the cover of the sideboards and listened to the bullets strike inches away. Thank the Lord for thick lumber, he thought. He appeared safe for a while. Finally he felt the river sweep the boat downstream, turning the vessel round and round. Please God, he prayed, let me float back onto the ocean. They can't kill me there.

Then his wounded friend stared up at him, with black rounding eyes. "Noodles, I'm goin' to die, ain't I? I been gut-shot bad." The man screamed afterward, wild shrieks which shook the autumn air.

"Stay quiet! We'll get help for you somehow. Let me get the laudanum we bought. It'll ease the pain." Noodles snaked along the boat's floor slats to a pile of crates and cans. He began to pry off the tops of the wooden boxes with his skinning knife.

"Old man, laudanum ain't goin' to do no good. I got a blown-up belly. Oh, God, it hurts!"

After crawling back, Noodles shoved a brown bottle against the man's mouth. "Drink, I tell you. It'll numb you up so you don't hurt so bad."

The man sucked on the thick liquid, crying while he swallowed. At last he fell silent and stared straight up with sunken eyes, his body quivering with sudden fits of palsy.

Noodles cocked his rifle, slipped the barrel over the side, and fired blindly. Then he quickly peeked above the sideboards, searching for the men who had ambushed them. He glimpsed two dark silhouettes diving for the pucker brush alongside the river.

The boat spun faster on the unsettled waters of the river. Seawater must be nearby, he thought. Thank God the tide seems to be running out. Otherwise they might lie beached, fair game for the men who wanted to kill them.

He peeked out again. Instantly wood flew up within inches of his eyes. Dropping down, he rubbed his face and prayed for his eyesight. Cheechako, he cursed to himself. You have been shot at by Indians and outlaws for fifty years, yet you behave like a freckled boy. He needed to stay calm and recall the many battles he had won in the past. Just because he was old did not mean he needed to give up without a fight. The time had come to let wisdom work, rather than fear.

Opening his eyes, he found his vision cloudy, with starry sparks floating around. He sensed no pain—but the terror of blindness frightened him more than the gunfire had before. Now God appeared to be wholly against him. What on earth could he do, he wondered?

Don't give up, he thought. Fire a few shots over the side. Keep the killers down until he and his wounded friend had safely run out to sea. Suddenly saltwater, smelling like musky weeds, teased his nose. The boat pitched higher on rolling waves. They must be hitting the surf. Soon they would float beyond rifle range. He found his Winchester with his hands, held it high, guessed where levelness might be, and pulled the trigger. Levering, he fired again and again, until the hammer simply clicked.

Afterward he lay flat on his stomach and searched for the laudanum. Now his head ached deep inside, and his ears pounded from the blasts of the rifle. He sipped on the bottle once and turned over to rest. The rocking boat began to soothe him; the heavy surf sounded distant and peaceful.

Hours later screams woke him. His partner's pushing, hitting, and craziness shot him to full consciousness. He still couldn't see—but shifting gleams and shadows let him fight off his friend. He knew the solution of opium in alcohol had worn away and agony was driving the poor man mad.

He kicked with his feet. "By Jeez, quit hittin' and lay back. Leave me be. I can't help you if'n you hurt me!"

"Noodles, I'm dying of pain. God, make it go away. Give me more medicine so I can sleep. Where are we anyways?"

"I don't know. The last time we got shot at I got blinded by the bullet. We must have floated out on the ocean." Noodles rolled onto his knees and began to feel for the laudanum. Then he wondered what his partner might do after the bottle had run dry. His own injury seemed less important now, weighed against his friend's wound. And perhaps his eyesight would return in a day or two. He could see sooty shadows already.

He found the laudanum, crawled back, and fed his partner. Then he shook the bottle and listened. Soft, sloppy sounds crept into his ear—nearly empty, he mused. What about next time? How would his friend endure the agony later on?

"Noodles, you got to kill me. I know the laudanum is about gone. There's a little left if you want it. Best you shoot me while I feel fine. Be the kindest thing." Then the man quietly wept.

"I can't do that. By Jeez, what a sin to ask of a friend. And help might be close. Maybe if'n you can help me find more shells for my Winchester I could fire three shots. Folks might be floatin' nearby!"

"Crawl over here and help me sit up. You can't see but I can see good. I'll bet there ain't nothin' or nobody in sight. The way the boat is bobbin' I think we're clean out to sea."

Noodles paused. He did need to know their position. At last he answered, "I'll come over and sit you up for a second. But I ain't killin' you. That's against my beliefs for sure."

"Come sit me up—let me look."

One minute later Noodles lowered his partner back to the bottom of the boat. The man had begun to weep once more.

"Old man, I told you. We look to be about a hundred miles out in the ocean. There's no hope for me and darn little for you. You got to kill me. I can smell my rotten belly already. Don't let me lay here dyin' for days. It ain't sensible."

"I can't kill you. You're my friend and Providence will be my wish when I die. Ain't goin' to get there if'n I blow off your head. That's a mighty bad sin."

His friend's voice shrilled higher. "You'd kill your dog or horse if they was wounded like me. Why can't you kill me? Don't you love me as much as some dumb critter?"

The old prospector began to weep as well. His friend

had spoken the truth. He had spent untold years crossing wild frontiers. He would have put any animal out of its misery by now, without hesitation. Didn't humans deserve the same kindness?

At last he answered, "I love you, but that don't mean I can kill you. Horses and dogs is different. They're God's helpless critters and deserve man's respect. Lettin' one roll 'round in pain is wrongful. You know the Lord's laws as well as I do. Why you askin' me to commit mortal sin? You know my soul would run to Lucifer if I did such an awful thing."

"Why would it?—that don't make no sense. Besides you can't leave me lay, it ain't right. At least you got to help kill me."

Noodles shook his head, but without the certainty of the moment before. Careful judgment of the sin of suicide crept around inside his brain. Was that the lesser evil? Should he keep his firearm away from his friend?

Finally he said, "I can't do that neither. It's wrong. Don't ask me to help. You should hang on ... the Lord always provides. You watch, help will come along soon."

"Noodles, you're a mean old man. Even if someone was to come along, they couldn't save me now. There ain't no doctors for a thousand miles. They couldn't put new guts in me anyways. . . . We're out in the middle of an ocean and there's wilderness all around. I'm done for and you are too." Then the wounded man laughed, loosing a wild cackle that covered the sounds of the sea battering the boat.

Then Noodles saw shadows and glimmers, something moving. He sat straight, listened. Suddenly he heard the splash from his partner jumping overboard. Finally the fateful sounds of the rolling waves slipped by the boat again. He sensed he had failed his friend. He wondered how long it had taken him to drown.

Don't miss Tom Hron's first novel of Alaska!

**THE GREAT GOLD RUSH TO
THE ALASKAN FRONTIER**

They came from an Old West no longer wild and free—lured by tales of a fabulous gold strike in Alaska. They found a land of majestic beauty, but one more brutal than hell. Some found wealth beyond their wildest dreams, but most suffered death and despair. Prospectors and adventuresses, gamblers and swindlers, merchants and mavericks, the pride of past frontiers and the scum of the nation stampeded north to find their destiny.

With this rush of brawling, lusting, striving humanity, walked Eli Bonnet, a legendary lawman who dealt out justice with his gun . . . and Hannah Twigg, a woman who dared death for love and everything for freedom. A magnificent saga filled with all the pain and glory of the Yukon's golden days. . . .

WHISPERS OF THE RIVER